The Other Side of Brett McKay

Red Adept Publishing
Unlocking New Worlds

The Other Side of Elsewhere
Red Adept Publishing, LLC
104 Bugenfield Court
Garner, NC 27529
http://RedAdeptPublishing.com/

Copyright © 2018 by Brett McKay. All rights reserved.

First Print Edition: August 2018

Cover Art by Streetlight Graphics

No part of this book may be reproduced, scanned, or distributed in any printed or electronic form without permission. Please do not participate in or encourage piracy of copyrighted materials in violation of the author's rights. Thank you for respecting the hard work of this author.

This is a work of fiction. Names, characters, places, and incidents either are the product of the author's imagination or are used fictitiously, and any resemblance to locales, events, business establishments, or actual persons—living or dead—is entirely coincidental.

This book is dedicated to the friends I grew up with in Riverton. We had some great adventures, and I wish my departure from you had gone differently.

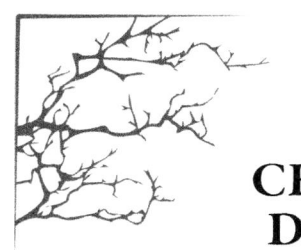

CHAPTER ONE
Dead Man's Hill

I stared down the steep slope of Dead Man's Hill, gripping the handlebars of my BMX bike until my knuckles turned white. At the bottom of the hill was a bump in the dirt, a natural ramp kids used to jump over the small creek. I'd never attempted the treacherous hill before. My two buddies, Gary Mass and Jax Goodman, were egging me on—they had dared me to go down. Jax and Gary hadn't tried the hill, either, which gave them more incentive to coax me into it.

I was twelve years old, and I'd just finished sixth grade. It was the summer of 1982, and I was transitioning into my teen years. We lived in a small rural town called Riverton, the first place in a long time I could call my home. For most of my life, my family had moved every year. It'd almost become a joke. But we'd been in Riverton, Utah, for three years, and I felt settled. I had good friends, I liked my teachers at school, and the whole town was my playground.

My friends and I were daredevils. We rode our dirt bikes everywhere—and so often that our butts were practically glued to the seats. We didn't go anywhere, short of dinner, without those bikes, and we never wore helmets.

My favorite spot was the Moguls, rolling dirt hills where developers had prepped to build new homes but stopped for lack of money. My older brothers, who were skiers, called them moguls, and the name had stuck. We would hit them hard and fast, catch good air, and fly over jumps.

On occasion, we crossed the field behind my house to Dead Man's Hill. I didn't know who'd named it, but the title was appropriate. The daunting slope at the end of the field was tall, fierce, and filled with stories of broken bones and wrecked bikes. The hill called to us, saying, "Yeah, go ahead and ride me. See if you make it out alive!"

On the other side of Dead Man's Hill, another trail led downward, curved at the bottom, and went back up, but it was much tamer than Dead Man's Hill. We always rode down the opposite side first, to get up our nerve. Then at the crest of Dead Man's Hill, we froze.

"Just do it. It's not that scary," Gary shouted. It was easy for him to say that since his bike wasn't sitting on the edge. "Just go down and turn before you hit the jump."

"Yeah, you don't have to do the jump. Not at first." Jax's nasally voice had a distinct croak, as if he plugged his nose while he talked.

Gary smiled. "Just do it. Get it over with. You've been up there for an hour."

It hadn't been an hour. Ten minutes, tops. My nose itched from the scent of sage brush in the hot air.

The steep hill didn't look too bad from a distance, but on the edge, it was terrifying. The hill went straight down.

"I just don't want to wreck my bike," I lied, trying to pretend my nerves weren't getting the best of me.

"Come ooon," Jax groaned. "We gotta get home for dinner. My mom's gonna be pissed."

I took a deep breath and flew down the hill. The pedals spun out of control, so I had to lift my feet off them. The bike bumped and jerked from left to right, but I held it steady, my heart in my throat, my bladder ready to explode. I couldn't breathe.

The jump came at me fast. I had a choice to make: stay on course and jump the tiny creek at the bottom or turn my wheels and try to stop. If I turned, I would have no choice but to crash, but a controlled skid would be enough to prevent damage to me and my bike.

I wanted to stop, but I was frozen in position. Feet still out at my sides, I hit the jump and shot off into the air. Heart still in my throat, I hit the ground on the other side of the creek, and my bike bounced and threatened to fall, but I held the handlebars straight, planted my feet on the pedals, and skidded to a perfect stop. Completely unscathed, I looked back at the conquered hill, and my two friends jumped up and down, howling.

"All right, guys!" I hollered. "Now it's your turn!"

They looked at each other hesitantly, and I thought for sure they were about to turn away, but to my surprise, Jax approached the hill and drove his bike over the edge. His bike bumped and flailed so much that I thought he would go flying, and I wondered if that was what I'd looked like—eyes bulged with fear and a face so white, it would glow in the dark.

"Oh, shiiit!" Jax hit the jump at an angle and flew off the side of it. His front tire hit the ground, and he toppled over the handlebars. So as not to lose face, Jax hopped up and kicked the bike. "Stupid piece of shit!" Swear words made Jax feel tough. Our parents would have killed us if they'd heard our mouths, but when I was alone with my friends, we cursed from time to time.

Gary pushed his glasses up on the bridge of his nose and sailed down the hill. We watched him bump left to right along the rough terrain. When his front tire hit a rock and popped his butt off the seat, I was afraid he would wreck, but he gained control and skidded to a stop before the jump. Relief and excitement hit me, and we high-fived each other.

We headed back to our houses for dinner, but because we couldn't carry our bikes over the chain-link fence that separated my house from the field, we had to cross the field to get to Beck Street. At the north corner of the field, east of Beck Street, stood Farmer Joe's giant red barn. We didn't know his real name, so we called him Farmer Joe. He was a mean, wiry old man who scowled all the time and always shouted at us for trespassing.

"Better hurry past Farmer Joe's!" Jax yelled. "I just saw him! I think he's got his shotgun!"

Farmer Joe was known for shooting at kids who crossed his property and stopped to mess with his cows or hang out to smoke in his barn. He filled the shotgun shells with rock salt. It wouldn't wound them, but it certainly hurt like hell.

The previous summer, a group of teenagers had snuck into his barn at night and left a cigarette burning. A stack of hay bales thirty feet high had caught on fire quickly. The local fire department hadn't been able to save the barn. It burned down to a black skeleton in minutes. The insurance had kicked in and built him a new one, and Farmer Joe had started carrying the shotgun full of salt pellets.

Stories floated around about how Johnny Gray had taken his girlfriend to Farmer Joe's barn to mess around, and Farmer Joe shot Johnny's right butt cheek full of salt. I didn't know Johnny well because he was an older kid in high school, but he did go to our church, and he had walked with a heavy limp for two weeks. That was enough evidence to solidify the story for me.

So we took the rough trail through the field of tall grass and weeds, riding over bumps and around large boulders until we hit Beck Street. The trail led us past an old abandoned house. With its steep-gabled roof, it stood alone, weathered and cracked by years of neglect. As the sun set, it glowed crimson through the scattered clouds along the horizon, silhouetting the steep roof.

I stopped in the middle of Beck Street and looked at the old house.

"Hey, what're you doing?" Gary screeched to a halt, and so did Jax.

Instead of answering, I stared, mesmerized by the gray two-story home. We called it the Crooked House because it *was* crooked. The southern portion of its foundation had sunk into the soft, swampy earth several years ago, and that was why developers hadn't built any more houses around it, or so everyone said. The house conjured stories and speculation in the neighborhood, especially among the kids. Some said it was haunted by ghosts. Others said murders had happened inside, and a few said it was the devil's home. The claims made for good campfire yarns, but I didn't know what was true and what was not. I *did* know that looking at the house made my skin crawl, but it didn't stop me from riding my bike toward it.

"Ret, where're you going? Stop!" Gary's voice went higher.

"I gotta eat! I can't be late," Jax complained but followed me anyway, along with Gary.

I stopped twenty feet from the house and stared at it. Its tall, narrow face looked down on me, mocking me much worse than Dead Man's Hill ever did. The yard was a forest of dead weeds, rocks, and one blackened, deceased walnut tree dangling its branches toward the house. The sidewalk leading up to the front porch steps was cracked and buckled, and all the windows had been knocked out from years of kids throwing stones. In those empty spaces, raggedy drapes blew in and out with the soft breeze.

"This place gives me the creeps," Gary muttered.

"Yeah, what gives, man?" Jax brought out his tough bravado voice, like he did whenever he was scared.

"Well..." I turned to them. "We've never seen inside. If we can beat Dead Man's Hill, we can do this too."

"Do what?" Gary asked.

"A sleepover inside."

"Are you crazy?" Jax exclaimed. "People have died in that house!"

"I guess if you're too chickenshit..."

"Chickenshit? I'm not being chickenshit! *You're* being stupid shit!"

"Other kids have done it," I said.

"Yeah, older kids. Doesn't mean they're smart."

"I'm with Jax on this one," Gary said.

So was I, in all honesty. My body trembled just being so close. A dark energy radiated from the house, and it shook me. "I'm just kiddin', guys. I wouldn't step one foot into that house if you paid me."

Gary and Jax each took a deep breath of relief. If I had forced it—if *any* of us had forced it—we would have done it because not one of us could let the others upstage us.

"Come on, guys." Gary turned his bike around. "I got macaroni and cheese waiting for me at home."

"Well, you wouldn't want to miss out on that," I teased, and we rode off without a second glance back.

WHEN I WALKED INTO my house, I smelled my mom's cooking and heard the sizzle and pop of the ground beef in the skillet. A portion of Mom's blond hair fell out of place and bounced up and down as she hammered at the beef with a spatula, breaking it up into small pieces, and steam rose from the rice cooking in a pot on the stove. She was making my favorite, rice casserole.

Forehead glistening with sweat, she raised her heavy ringed eyes and managed to crack a smile despite her exhaustion. It was a nice attempt to mask the stress overwhelming her.

"Hi, Mom."

"Hi, sweetie. How was your day?"

"Long and boring. We spent most of the day trying to find something to do. But then we went to Dead Man's Hill, and guess what?"

"What?"

I started to answer, but she cut me off by yelling to my brother, who was in another room somewhere. "Jeff! Can you get in here and slice the cheese like I asked?"

She left the skillet of beef and turned her attention to the rice, and I waited to see if she was still in conversation with me, but I could tell her mind was on a thousand other things.

When I walked out of the kitchen, my mom called out to me, "Ret, you were telling me something. About Dead Man's Hill?"

"Yeah, it was nothing."

"No, tell me," she said. "I want to hear."

I turned back, excited to tell my news. "Jax, Gary, and I rode up to Dead Man's, and I took my bike down it. I even jumped the creek." Pride and excitement rose in me.

"You're kidding." Her mouth dropped, and her eyebrows furrowed. "That's dangerous! You could have been hurt—or killed!"

I prepared myself for a scolding, but instead, my mom grinned.

"But, that was pretty brave. I've seen some of the tricks you do, and you continue to amaze me. I certainly couldn't do it." She winked at me, and it filled me with encouragement. "I just want you to be careful."

"I will."

I entered our family room, where my oldest brother, Tadd, was kicked back in our comfy chair, watching TV, and my younger brother, Scott, was on the floor, playing with a set of Star Wars toys. We'd both wanted *The Empire Strikes Back* toys, so we'd agreed to each ask for different items at Christmas and then share whatever we got.

"I just started," Scott told me. "Do you want to play?"

I hesitated because I wondered if I was too old to play with toys. After all, I *was* in junior high. "Maybe later," I said.

"Hey, Ret!" Tadd barked without turning from the TV. "Get me a glass of water."

I sighed, shrugged, and headed back for the kitchen. *Get your own drink of water,* I thought to myself. Of course, I would never say such a thing because I didn't want to get punched. Since turning seventeen, he'd acted like the king of the castle, always ordering everyone around. Everyone but Mom, of course.

Rolling her eyes, Mom wiped sweat from her forehead with the back of her hand. "It'd be nice to get some help in here, boys. I've only been working all day!"

"I'm here now," Jeff said, appearing in the doorway. "I'll get the cheese."

Jeff was my other older brother between myself and Tadd.

"I'll be back in to help you, Mom. I gotta get Tadd his water," I said.

"Tadd can get his own damn water," she spat, and I agreed.

My dad wasn't around much because he worked two jobs. He worked for the state during the day, inspecting pumps at gas stations, and at night, he worked as a butcher at the grocery store. My mom worked a full-time job as a bookkeeper and still had to take care of us when she got home.

My mom was everything. Sometimes she had to be both mom and dad. She was a mom when I was hurt or got sick. She was a dad when I needed help through my growing stages or needed advice on asking girls out. She was also my best friend when I needed someone to talk to. She worked hard and always kept food on the table, got us to church, and made sure we stayed on top of our schoolwork.

Of course, there we were, letting her make dinner for us after working all day, but once she pointed that out to us in no uncertain terms, we jumped in to help.

Scott and I set the table while Tadd and Jeff finished cooking the biscuits and green beans. Once she finally sat down to eat, her shoulders relaxed, and she breathed a sigh of relief.

She smiled at us. "Thank you, boys."

CHAPTER TWO
The Black Widows

The next morning, Jax and Gary came over about ten thirty, and we sat down in my living room and spent nearly an hour pondering how to fill the boring day. Our color TV only had three channels, and we weren't rich enough to own a VCR or video game console like Atari, so anything we did to pass the time involved an outdoor activity.

"You know what we should do?" I had what I thought was a brilliant idea.

"What?" Gary rolled his eyes and yawned.

"We need to start our own gang."

My parents had recently taken me to see the Clint Eastwood movie *Any Which Way You Can*, a sequel to *Every Which Way but Loose*, and it had become one of my favorites. It had lots of action and laugh-out-loud funny moments, especially all of the parts that included a bumbling biker gang called the Black Widows.

"Do you guys have a white T-shirt?"

Gary and Jax nodded.

"Go home and get your T-shirts, and we're going to make our own biker gang."

They came back within the hour, rumpled white T-shirts in hand. Jax's had yellowed with age, and Gary's had a shoe store logo in the top right.

"It's all I could find." Gary shrugged.

We used black and red markers to draw a black widow with a red hourglass on its back and write the words *Black Widows* above them on each of our shirts.

"I brought my dad's leather jacket!" Jax put it on over his new T-shirt. It was a classier style of jacket, like the one my grandpa wore, and it completely drowned him.

"That's not exactly a biker jacket," Gary said, and it wasn't.

"No big deal. I'll just roll up the sleeves."

"What should we do now?" Gary asked.

We all exchanged silent glances. It was one o'clock in the afternoon. The skies were clear blue, and the temperature had risen to the mid-eighties. We couldn't have asked for a better day.

"Let's finish building the Millennium Falcon," Jax suggested, and I sighed.

"All we have done is the boarding ramp," Gary said.

"Yeah, but it's an awesome boarding ramp."

"Jax, we don't have any more wood to build the rest of it. Plus, you always get to be Han Solo and make me Chewbacca."

"You *are* a good Chewbacca." Gary chuckled with a sly grin.

"Easy for you to say. You get to be Luke Skywalker."

"We could build a fort over at the Moguls," Jax said.

"What's with you and all the building? Last time, we spent three days building that thing, and then it fell apart," Gary said.

"Let's ride to the Moguls and practice our tricks," I said, and Gary nodded agreement.

Jax merely surrendered to the idea with a shrug of his shoulders.

We'd just stepped outside in the hot sun to get on our bikes when Devin, who was two years younger than us, rode up to my house on his bike. Fretful panic was written all over Devin's wide-eyed face.

"Guys, guys!" He jumped off his bike and let it fall to the ground as he ran over to us.

"What do you want, pipsqueak?" Gary called out to him, but Devin ignored his comment and turned to me.

"He took my bike pads! He stole them, took 'em right out from under me. I saw him. I was just washing my bike and—" Devin gestured with his hands madly.

I interrupted him to stop his words from coming at me like a speedball. "Easy, buddy, I can't understand a word. Someone stole your bike pads?"

"It was Fernando."

Fernando? I asked myself. He'd been my friend at one time, but we'd stopped hanging out together about a year ago. He was a decent guy, but we didn't have much in common.

"I just got brand-new pads for my bike," Devin continued. "They were sitting on my driveway while I washed my bike. I wanted it cleaned before I put the pads on. Then Fernando showed up and started making fun of me."

I thought of how long I'd scrimped and saved for my own pads. Sure, they were just decorative tubing that made the bike look classier and tougher, but they were like gold to us.

"Yeah, he was swearing and calling me names and things." Devin scowled.

"And that was it. I went to turn the hose off and get a towel to dry off my bike, and when I came back, Fernando was gone, and so were my bike pads. They're worth a lot of money, and my mom's gonna kill me. I know he took 'em. He was the only one that could've."

For a split second, I saw several holes in his story and things that needed more explanation. I knew Fernando, and he wasn't that kind of guy... at least he hadn't been when we were friends. Fernando came over to yell at him? He must have done something to start it. As my dad always said, it took two to tango. But I was a twelve-year-old kid with my new gang. We were suddenly being idolized by a younger kid who needed our protection, and our bravado took over. I'd heard enough to believe Devin and his story.

"Tell you what, Devin. We'll get those pads back for you. This is a job for the Black Widows."

Devin looked at me quizzically.

"You want to be part of our gang?" I asked him.

Jax opened the flaps of his jacket to show his T-shirt beneath, and Gary turned his back to him so he could see the spider and words written on his back.

"Cool!" Devin exclaimed. "Yeah, I want to be in your gang."

"All right, let's go! We'll make your T-shirt later."

I jumped on my bike, feeling tough and taller than my four feet and ten inches. We were heroes riding off to save the day for a victim younger and weaker than us. We rode side by side, our line of bikes stretched the width of the road. If we'd been in a movie, music would build behind us to add intensity. We were cowboys marching down the main street of town, shoulder to shoulder.

There was strength in numbers, and we felt it as we rode up to the front of Fernando's home. He was outside, watering their trees in the flowerbeds with a hose, and I realized I didn't have a plan. I had nothing.

Devin started yelling, the tension rose, and I went with it.

"Where are my bike pads, Fernando?" Devin shouted, braver now that we stood next to him.

"How should I know?" Fernando frowned and shrugged while holding the hose ready at his side.

"You stole 'em. After I washed my bike, you took them."

"No, I didn't!" He gestured wildly with his free hand.

"Don't mess with the Black Widows!" Jax said.

"Who's the Black Widows?" Fernando asked.

"We are." Chin held high, chest puffed out, I stared him down.

Why are you glaring at me? Fernando's face seemed to say. *What are you doing here?*

Gary turned his back to Fernando, so he could see the spider and the lettering to prove who we were.

"You're a gang?" He cocked his head to the side with an unbelieving sneer.

"That's right, and we're here to get Pat's bike pads back!" Jax said. "Where are they?"

"I don't have them." Fernando's voice cracked, and his body shook.

"Just give them back, Fernando. Don't make us have to come get them!" I said.

"You guys better get outta here!" Fernando warned.

"Or what?" Jax demanded.

Gary hung back and stayed silent throughout the entire conversation.

"I'm going to call the cops!"

"Oooh," Jax mocked.

Devin jumped off his bike and marched across the lawn toward Fernando. Fernando turned, hose in hand, and sprayed Devin. The nozzle blasted Devin with a powerful burst of water, and he turned and ran back to his bike.

Fernando targeted all of us with the hose, swiping the nozzle back and forth. "I'm going to call the cops!"

Gary had to take his glasses off and wipe them clean. Then we rode our bikes out of the range of the shooting water and circled back and forth.

"Did you take the bike pads?" I demanded of Fernando.

"I told you I didn't!"

"Yes, you did!" Devin shouted.

I motioned for him to calm down then turned to Fernando again. "Let's see your bike then."

"No! You get outta here, or I'll call the cops!"

He shot water at me, and I kicked my bike forward out of the way.

"Just let us see for ourselves. If your bike doesn't have his pads on it, then we'll leave you alone!"

"No! Get outta here!" His voice cracked, and I noticed his hands shaking. "I'm calling the cops!"

I was upset. I had come up with a brilliant solution, but he wouldn't let us see his bike, and that made me wonder what he had to hide.

Jax inched closer, and Fernando saw him. A jet of water hit Jax square in the chest, turning him back.

"Look, Fernando, we gotta go eat lunch. When we're done with lunch, we're coming back, and you better be ready to show us your bike, or give us Devin's bike pads!" I said.

"Or what?"

"We'll beat you up." My own words shocked me. I've never said those words to anyone. I saw the hurt in his eyes. *Why?*

I turned and led my gang away. Everyone headed to their own houses for lunch, and we planned to meet back up in an hour. Stepping inside my house, I felt the swamp cooler moisten my heated body.

I made a bologna sandwich and sat down to eat it in front of the TV, where Scott was watching cartoons. I told him the story of our gang, Fernando, and the stolen bike pads. He couldn't believe it.

Shortly after I finished my sandwich and chips, a knock banged on our front door. I walked to the door and opened it. Standing on the front step was the last person I expected to see.

Pressed pants, leather utility belt, gun holstered on the hip, and a sheriff's badge on his breast, the tall man looked down at me. "You Ret McCoy?"

"Y-yes," I stammered. *Oh, my hell. He actually called the cops!*

"Is your mom or dad home?"

Scott stared from the couch, jaw dropped and eyes wide.

I shook my head. "No."

"Can you step outside, please? I need to have a word with you."

Me? In trouble with the law? It was too incredible. If the cop had come and asked for Tadd or Jeff, that would have been no surprise, but *me*?

I walked outside and saw his police car parked at the curb. Several of our neighbors were standing on their front lawns to get a look. Mrs. Crawford from across the street walked out in her blue robe, which dragged on the ground. Tadd and Jeff had a reputation of getting into trouble, and I could hear the neighbors now. "It's those McCoy boys again. What did they do now?"

Sheriff Orrin Packard looked down at me. He was broad shouldered, with black hair cut short and clean, a square jaw, and ice-blue eyes. He looked tough, like he wasn't going to take any bullshit, so I shouldn't even try.

"Tell me what happened," he demanded.

I answered like any idiot would. "About what?"

He stabbed me with a look, and I spilled it. "My friend, Devin, had his bike pads stolen, and we went to get them back. That's all."

"Devin Mullins?"

I nodded agreement.

"He *knows* they were stolen?"

"H-he thinks so."

"And he saw who stole them?"

"No, he just... I don't know."

"What do you think he should have done if he thought they were stolen?"

I shrugged while looking at the ground in shame.

He hooked a thumb at his chest then at his car.

"Called the cops?" I asked.

"Called the cops! Brilliant idea! Maybe he could have talked to his parents first. Think that would be smart?"

I nodded.

"Fernando Gonzales said you and some other boys showed up at his house and threatened him."

A lead weight dropped in my stomach.

"He said you were going to beat him up."

I looked at the ground shamefully.

"Look at me, son."

I moved my eyes back up.

"What do you call your gang?"

"The Black Widows," I said, my voice barely a whisper.

"Turn around."

I did.

He looked at the design on my shirt and shook his head in disappointment. "Do you know what happens in a gang?"

I shook my head.

"Nothing good *ever* comes from a gang. You start getting into lots of trouble. Stealing, fighting, drugs, and alcohol. What do you think your parents would say?"

I gulped, imagining a scolding from my parents.

"There was how many of you?"

"Four."

"Four of you? And how many Fernandos?"

"J-just one."

"Do you think that's fair?"

I shook my head again.

"I went to visit him. He's shaking like a wet dog and crying. He is frightened that you and your gang are coming back to hurt him. Is that what you want to do?"

"No."

Sheriff Packard looked up at the sky then looked down the street in the direction of Fernando's home.

"I came to arrest you."

Hairs all over my body stood up straight.

"You're in some real trouble here," he said, laying it on thick.

I know now he had no intention of arresting me. He was putting the fear in me.

"I got a scared boy with no friends and a gang who wants to hurt him."

"No, I don't want to hurt him. I really don't."

"What should I do? What do you think you should do?"

I shoved my hands into my pockets and looked down the street toward his house like that would give me my answer. "I'll leave him alone. We won't bother him anymore." I looked back at Packard. "I promise. I'm sorry."

"You're sorry? Who else might you think needs to hear that?"

"He does." I nodded in his direction.

Sheriff Packard nodded. "That's right. You need to go down there and apologize to him. After that, you need to get rid of those T-shirts. No more Black Widows. Don't let me hear that your gang is riding the streets anymore. I'll be watching."

I nodded. "Are you going to talk to my mom and dad?"

Nothing frightened me more than my parents finding out.

Sheriff Packard paused, then he looked directly into my eyes. "I think it will be all right this time. I won't tell them, but you have to promise me no more Black Widows. And you have to go and tell Fernando you're sorry."

Bottom lip trembling, I said, "Yes. I will."

"He could use a friend." Packard's eyes grew softer, and a warm smile crept up. "Summer's too short not to have friends."

Sheriff Packard was wrong. The summer was too long without friends. I had spent those summers before, right after moving to a new town. They were long, boring, and hot.

The sheriff placed a pair of dark sunglasses on his face and looked around. Most of the neighbors had gone back inside once they'd realized no one was getting cuffed or dragged away. It was just a young boy learning a tough lesson. Only Mrs. Crawford lingered outside, pretending to water her lawn with a hose. She wasn't fooling anyone, though. She was the gossip queen of the neighborhood. Anyone who wanted to know what was going on with a certain somebody just had to go to Mrs. Crawford, and she would know about it. Well, at least she knew the rumors and half-truths.

"Be good, Ret." Sheriff Packard marched to his car.

"You too," I called after him, sounding like an idiot again. "I mean, have a good day!"

I turned back to my house and saw the drapes in our front room window ruffle. Scott had been spying the whole time. I couldn't blame him.

I DIDN'T CALL GARY, Jax, or Devin. They could do their own thing. I was doing mine.

As I rode my bike down the street to Fernando's house, I saw Sheriff Packard driving away, and Fernando sat on his front steps, head down.

I parked my bike on the sidewalk, slowly dismounted, and kicked the kickstand.

"Hey, Fernando," I called out with a friendly tone.

He barely glanced up and didn't say a word.

"Sorry about everything." I stood ten feet away, feeling awkward. "I just got carried away. You know Devin... so much drama."

Still silence. I waited for a response or a look... anything. I was about to turn away when he finally lifted his head and spoke.

"I thought we were friends," he said.

I wanted to cry. I felt like crap. "Well... yeah. Of course we are. I mean, we don't hang out anymore, but that doesn't mean we aren't friends."

"Why did you do that?"

"I don't know. Honestly, I don't. I'm stupid." I shook my head, frustrated. I had no answers for him or myself.

"I would never steal anything," he said.

"I know." I shrugged. "I know."

The look in his eyes said he was telling the truth. A million other things could have happened to Devin's bike pads. Several times, I'd accused my brother of stealing my toys, only to find out later I had misplaced them myself. I was sure Devin's bike pads were the same.

We shared an awkward moment of silence. The right thing to do was invite him to ride bikes with me and my friends, but I didn't want to. I wasn't that close to him, and I didn't know how he would fit in. I approached him and poked my hand out.

"Friends?" I asked.

He took my hand and shook it. "Friends."

"You know, you can come play with us. We're just going to ride our bikes over at the Moguls and mess around." I did it anyway. I'd invited him, but he didn't seem interested.

"Nah, I gotta do some chores around the house, and I told my sister I'd play with her."

"Okay. Well, if you change your mind, you know where we're at."

He nodded. We said goodbyes, and I mounted my steed and rode away. I'd done the right thing, and it felt good. I'd grown up some, I thought. Looking at the situation through Fernando's eyes, I knew I never wanted to hurt anyone again. I wouldn't want to be treated that way, and no one else did, either. I was glad Sheriff Packard had come to my house and scared the shit out of me. Sometimes, a kid needs it.

CHAPTER THREE
The Dare

It was another hot, sunny day, around a hundred and fifty degrees or something, and we had nothing to do. I told my buddies about my run-in with the law and Sheriff Packard, who hadn't visited Jax or Gary. They couldn't believe it, but I saw relief in their eyes that the police hadn't paid them a visit.

I felt like an outlaw. Not that I was proud of what I did to Fernando. If I could have taken it back, I would have, but having a reputation for being a bad boy, a renegade who ran a gang, was tantalizing. A squeaky-clean kid like myself needed a dark side, and that day, I'd had one for a small moment.

One day. That was how long the Black Widows had lasted—that was how bad we were. I hadn't thrown away my T-shirt like Packard had told me to. Instead, I'd folded it up and stashed it at the bottom of my drawer. *Who knows when my secret powers may be called into action again?*

The sun moved closer to the center of the sky. Our day was slipping away. Jax and Gary looked at me for an idea of what to do.

"Let's go to the Moguls," I suggested.

"Nah, we always go there," Jax whined.

"I do need to brush up on my bike tricks," Gary said.

"Exactly! That's what we need to do! We can put on a show and charge people money to watch it."

Finally looking interested, Jax said, "How much should we charge?"

"Like a buck or something."

"We can make some money." Gary got excited.

"I'll make a sign," I said.

We rode to the Moguls and practiced for our show. The jump at the bottom of the second hill, which was a smaller version of Dead Man's Hill, gave us the most air and the opportunity for a good trick.

We stepped out into the neighborhood where the streets crossed and held up our sign. It read Bike Show 2:00 pm $1. Three cars passed by in twenty minutes, and even with our hollering and spastic gestures, we couldn't get anyone to look our way, let alone stop for the show. An hour later, and in our moment of despair, Devin and two of his friends showed up.

"Devin!"

We practically attacked him.

"You gotta come see our show!" I said.

"Yeah, it's about to start!" Gary said.

"What show?" he asked.

"We're doing a show. It's pretty cool. You get to see all of our stunts and tricks for a dollar."

"A dollar?" he exclaimed. "I don't have a dollar."

"Fifty cents then," Gary said.

"I don't have that, either. Come on." He nodded to his friends, who started to turn away and ride in the other direction.

"Wait!" I stopped them. "How much *do* you have?"

"A quarter. Maybe."

"Okay. A quarter then. This time," Gary said.

"I'm not going to waste my quarter on that."

I rolled my eyes. "Come on, Devin. You're missing the best show."

We didn't win him over.

"Okay..." I dug deep for my last-ditch effort. "You can come see our show for free. Just this first one."

"Yeah, it'll be our practice show," Gary said.

Devin still wasn't excited, but after much nagging, we got him and his friends to watch our pitiful show.

Jax went first. He started at the far end of the Moguls and bounced up and down in the distance as he hit each bump and hill, wailing like a madman. Then he crested the final hill and soared down it. He jumped and landed with a lackluster finish, to a bored audience.

Gary went next, with the same results. Then it was my turn. I had to impress them and finish the show strong. I bounced through the Moguls like the rest of them had, feeling powerful like Evel Knievel, then I came to the last hill.

"This is it!" I announced. "The moment you've all been waiting for!"

Devin yawned.

I drove my bike down the hill and hit the jump. High in the air, I lifted one hand and twisted my bike for show, but I had hit the jump at the wrong angle. The twist sent me and my bike in the wrong direction. When I came down, I saw nothing but brown wooden planks. My bike hit the fence, and I tumbled over the handlebars.

As I got up and dusted myself off, I heard Devin and his friends cackling with unsuppressed laughter.

"You were right!" Devin giggled. "That was the moment I was waiting for!"

"Well, I aim to please one way or another," I said sheepishly and picked up my bike. Fortunately, my bike wasn't damaged.

"What's going on?" A different voice, deeper, spoke out, and I turned. Matt Griffin and his friend, Wes, approached. They were two years older than us and, therefore, much cooler.

"Hey, Matt," I said, walking over to them. They weren't on bikes. Too cool for that. "We were just putting on a show."

Devin and his friends started to ride away, and Jax and Gary chased after them.

"Hey what about our money?" Jax hollered. "That was at least worth a quarter!"

"I heard about your gang." Matt gave me a sly grin.

"Yeah, we're pretty tough, all right."

"The sheriff really came to your house?" Wes asked.

"Yes." My face went red. "He told me not to run the gang anymore." They both laughed.

"Oh my hell! First, a gang, and then this?" Matt gestured to the Moguls. "A circus show?"

"It's not a circus show." Jax walked over, coming to my defense. "We're doing bike tricks and stunts. Dangerous ones."

"Dangerous," Wes mocked. "What did you do? Hit your nose?"

"Huh?" Jax asked, perplexed.

"Why do you sound like that?" Wes pinched his nostrils, causing his next words to come out nasally. "Like your nose is plugged up."

"Shut up," Jax mumbled.

I should have defended Jax. They were mean and rude. But they were older kids, and I didn't want to start anything.

Matt was a semi friend of mine. When I'd first moved to Riverton, Matt and I had hung out together for a while, and sometimes, I'd hung out with both Matt and Wes. But there was enough of an age difference that Matt and Wes had grown tired of me and left me behind to pursue different interests.

I always had the underlying feeling that if Jax and I weren't friends, things would be different. Wes and Matt didn't like Jax, and they made no effort to hide that fact. They made fun of him, and because I was with him, I wasn't included anymore.

"You guys are pretty pathetic," Matt said.

"You guys are." Jax had balls.

"We are?" Wes puffed his chest out in attack mode. "You calling us pussies?" Wes stepped within inches of Jax's face, his fists clenched.

"No, no one's saying that." Gary stepped in. "Right, Jax?"

Jax, clearly frightened, nodded. "Yeah, I'm not saying that."

"Easy, Wes," Matt said, trying to cool him down.

"You guys are the pussies!" Wes said as he backed away from Jax.

"Hey!" I said but added nothing more.

"Wes is right." Matt nodded. Mischief stirred in his eyes. "I don't know if there's anything these guys can do to keep from being pussies."

"No. They were born that way," Wes concluded.

"Bullshit!" Jax said.

"Oooh, such a big boy because he can swear." Wes gestured with his hands, pretending they were shaking with fear.

"No. Maybe there is something they can do..." Matt said.

"What?" Gary asked, sounding afraid of the answer.

"No, it's too dangerous, and these guys would never do that."

Matt had put out the bait, and we snapped on it like hungry trout.

"What? What's too dangerous?" I asked.

"Nothing's too dangerous for us!" Jax said.

"Well..." Gary didn't seem so sure.

"We've done it, and our older brothers did it." Matt hooked a thumb at Wes. "But, it's so scary, I'm not sure you guys are up for it." He gave Wes a crazy look. "No, no, you are too young. You should at least be fourteen before doing something like this."

"Just spit it out," I said.

"The Crooked House." Matt put out the words that silenced the air.

Even Wes shut up. We stared at each other in awkward silence, waiting for Matt to elaborate.

"You gotta spend one night in that house."

Wes laughed way too loudly for something that clearly was not funny.

"In that house? Why?" I asked.

"You don't want to stay pussies, do ya?" Matt said.

"Yeah, but on the second floor," Wes added. "No sleeping by the front door so you can run out like little babies."

"You're cra—" Jax said, but I cut him off.

"Okay. One night. You're on." I turned to my gang. "Nothing to it."

JAX AND GARY WERE PISSED at me. They didn't say it, but they didn't have to. We left the area silently and slowly. Heat rose in my face and arms from too much sun exposure. I hadn't put on sunblock, and I was going to look like a lobster the next day. So were my friends. I saw it shade their faces.

We couldn't back out now. I'd made a promise. I put it out there, so we had witnesses, and if we chickened out, the whole neighborhood would know about it.

I told my parents I was sleeping over at Jax's, and both Jax and Gary told their parents they were sleeping at mine. Nothing would go wrong unless our parents called to check on us, then the jig would be up. I had a backup story just in case. I would play stupid and say we changed our minds at the last minute and stayed at someone else's house, along with "Sorry. I didn't think you'd have a problem with that."

It wouldn't keep us from getting into trouble, but getting caught sleeping in the creepy, abandoned house on Beck Street would be a ton worse.

It wasn't just the kids who feared the house; the parents were scared of it too. They never talked about it. One time over dinner, I'd asked my parents what they knew about the house and its history. They'd glanced at each other with a look of hidden truth but didn't want to share it. They wanted to protect their children, so they'd answered, "We don't know anything about that house other than it's a money pit. Once it started to sink, the people moved out. That's all."

The house stood before us at the end of Beck Street, tall, brooding, and alone. The structure was narrow, but the sharp gable and extended roof beyond it gave it the illusion of being taller than it was, and the roof was barely holding on to the last few shingles.

Over the years, weather had warped the wooden planks of the exterior, and what little paint was left had turned pale. The rest of the house was gray, except for the south side, which had been scorched black by flames. How the structure had survived a fire, no one would ever know—and that only fueled the ghost stories saying that evil intervention had saved the home.

A brick chimney, also scorched black, scaled the entire height of the house on the south side. The covered porch stretched halfway across the house, covering the front door and then some. The decorative carvings in the railing and the surrounding columns were unique, and like the rest of the home, at one point, the woodwork had been beautiful and exemplified wealth. Since then, it had deflated, darkened by neglect and a violent past, stuck in the middle of weeds.

The walnut tree stood nearly forty feet tall, its trunk nearly as thick as two men. The leafless branches seemed to claw at the house and anyone who got near it. The bark was riddled with damage from long winters, hot summers, borers, and carpenter ants that had killed the tree off from the inside. Many branches were broken, and the tree's lost arms were scattered across the ground.

Nothing in the vicinity of this house was alive, and even more perplexingly, the weeds, although tall and overbearing, were also dead. Weeds were the devil's garden. Nothing stopped them from growing, and normally, when they died, strong winds blew them away. Not the weeds around the Crooked House, though. Not a single one was green; the devil wouldn't allow anything green near the house, including weeds. Although yellow and dead, they stood strong like hay stocks and outlasted strong winds and punishing weather.

We sat on our bikes several feet from the house, pillows and sleeping bags scrunched under our arms.

"Are you sure about this?" Gary asked me.

I heard the fear crack his voice and knew I had to reassure him. "It's nothing. Really. It's all just ghost stories to scare kids. And we're not kids, are we?"

"Hell no," Jax said defiantly.

"We're sorta kids," Gary said. "Not even teens yet."

"Then it's time we become men." Though it was corny, the line boosted my courage, and I hoped it did the same for them. "Let's pretend it's just an ordinary house. We'll tell jokes, talk about the girls we like, things to do this summer. The key is to keep talking. Did you guys bring some snacks?"

"I brought some licorice," Gary said.

"Perfect. I brought a bag of nuts and a couple of sodas."

I pedaled my bike toward the house, and the others followed. The sun slid down the sky toward its hiding place for the night, its bleeding colors painting the clouds. We needed to settle into the house before the sun was gone. That would make the transition easier, or so I thought.

"I like that new girl, Suzy. She's the one in Mrs. Benson's class," Jax said.

"There ya go," I said, pushing as much cheerfulness into my voice as I could. "She's pretty cute."

"Not my type," Gary chimed in. "She's a little too tall. I like Chloe."

"Chloe's the one with the really long hair? She's cute too. She's quiet, but she's pretty."

"Who do you like?" Jax asked me.

I didn't have a girl picked out, but I felt like I needed to say someone's name since they both had.

"Sammy. The blonde in Mrs. Jenson's class."

We made it to the house, dismounted our steeds, and parked them. Without thought, I walked up the creaking steps to the porch. Immediately, the porch tilted to the south.

The door stood open slightly. *Was it open before?* My mind played tricks on me. *Did the house open its mouth to let us in?* Wary of opening the door, I pushed it open all the way, like ripping off a Band-Aid.

My friends tensed up behind me. The air inside was thick with dust, and the sunset struck the windows on the west to illuminate the floating dust particles. The musty odor wafted over me, like the smell of an old shirt that I hadn't worn in years and just pulled from the bottom of the dresser drawer.

I stepped inside. The wooden planks beneath my feet creaked, warped from age and moisture. To my right was the parlor, with fancy old furniture, a couple of lamps, and a desk. They were all gray with dust and cobwebs, but some of the red on the velvet couch showed through.

An archway on my left led into the living room with a fireplace, a couch, two chairs, and two more lamps. The others followed me through the room, stepping around the furniture. My legs and hands trembled, and I tried to force away my anxiety. The fireplace was ornate, from another age, like a living creature staring back at me, ready to pounce. I gave it a wide berth as I continued on through the archway, which led to the dining room. It consisted of the usual stuff: a long table, chairs and a heavy, lavish china cabinet. No dust covers. Nothing out of place. Everything was where it should be, ready to welcome new guests.

My stomach churned. I turned to the other guys, whose faces were white. They both looked sick.

"Let's not do this," Jax said. The strong-talking warrior had gone weak. "I don't have a good feeling."

"Me, either," Gary said.

The warped wooden floors let out a screech, causing us all to jump. Gary and Jax scuttled to the front door.

I ran after them and stopped them on the front porch. "Hey, we can't quit now."

Jax looked at the ground shamefully. Gary turned to look past me and cocked his head quizzically.

"What's that?" Gary asked. I turned to follow his gaze, and Matt Griffin's house caught my eye. The front porch had a perfect view of the houses that lined the border of the field. The raised porch on the back of Matt's house gave it a direct line of sight into the abandoned hell hole we stood in. I knew Matt's family owned a pair of binoculars because he'd brought them on campouts with the Boy Scouts before, and I suspected Matt and Wes would be spying on us. I saw a glint of light, and I knew it had to be them, standing on the porch, watching us.

"Shit." I pointed to Matt's house. "They're watching us."

"Bastards," Jax said.

"They're gonna watch us all night," I said.

"Well... maybe that's good," Gary said, and we turned to him.

"Good? What do you mean good?"

"I mean," Gary said, "if anything happens to us, then they'll know. They'll tell our parents or the cops or something to help us." He shrugged. "Maybe the ghosts won't come out 'cause those guys are watchin'."

His logic didn't make sense, but we were desperate enough to cling on to any hope, no matter how ridiculous.

Jax turned in the direction of Matt's house and flipped the bird.

"What're you doing?" Gary asked.

Jax shrugged. "Just in case."

"What if they decide to come kick the crap out of us now?"

"I dare 'em to."

WE JOURNEYED FARTHER into the dark domain. We took it slow, inspecting every square inch of the place—except for the basement. There were limits to our bravery.

The staircase was in the foyer, set into the wall of the front room. In usual Victorian-mansion style, there were fourteen steps, narrow and steep. At the top was a large landing that branched off into short halls to the left and right. They led to the bedrooms. We took the right hall first. The walls were lined with faded patches where pictures used to hang, and the wallpaper peeled back like skin after a sunburn.

Graffiti in red and black paint, most of which were crude images, marked up the walls, and kids had written curse words and phone numbers in permanent markers. The bedroom walls were faded and dingy, outlined with years of soot and dark grime, and holes and cracks revealed the house's wooden frame.

The floors groaned when we walked, and because of its sinking foundation, the house tipped to the south. My head and stomach spun with sickness after a while, but I couldn't be sure if my equilibrium was off or if the anxious terror of what might appear behind the next corner was causing my nausea.

We returned to the landing and took the left hall, which led to the bedroom that faced our neighborhood. We felt safer if every now and again, we could look out the window and know that Matt and Wes were watching us. None of us would ever tell *them* that in a million years.

"A million and one, maybe." Gary chuckled.

We all laughed, and I felt the mood lighten.

The hardwood floor was covered in small rocks, dirt, and broken glass. A broom, dusty and filthy but clearly purchased recently, leaned against the wall, and the swirled traces in the dirt on the floor made it clear other kids had brought the broom to clear space to sit or camp. There were also numerous cigarette butts, squashed soda pop cans, beer cans, and candy wrappers. It was sad to see people had left such a mess without care, but on the other hand, it gave me solace to know people had been there before and survived.

We swept an area clear and sat in a circle so we could watch each other's backs. I immediately took the side by the window so I could face the bedroom's door. Jax sat with his back to the entrance, surprising both me and Gary. I'm not sure Jax realized it himself, but we weren't going to tell him.

Jax and I had brought flashlights, but Gary had brought a lantern, which was much brighter and steadier than our flashlights. *Oh, thank heavens for Gary!*

The house made its sounds, just like mine did. My mom said it was just the house settling, but sometimes, I thought it wasn't. The squeaks and creaks were slow and had the rhythm of walking. Our parents always told us that was all in our minds. But I was never really sure. Still, as we told jokes and laughed, time went on, and I looked up at the door less and less often.

Jax pulled out a deck of cards, and we immediately started to play a number of games, including our favorite, called "BS." The lantern hummed as it burned its kerosene. I looked at the front door frequently to make sure no one stood in its frame, that no creature or ghost watched us. The window was broken, every last shard knocked out of the pane. The open window made for a quick escape if we needed it, and it led to the top of the porch roof.

The hour got late, close to two thirty in the morning. My eyes felt heavy, and Gary's were bloodshot. Finally, we crashed from the sugar and soda rushes.

We felt safe enough to sleep. There'd been no ghosts or peculiar sounds, and we protected each other. We kept the lantern on low and tucked ourselves into our sleeping bags for the night.

I stared at the door to make sure neither a ghost or an axe murderer entered, and after a moment, I closed my eyes. I snapped them open every so often to inspect the room, but as more time passed in silence, my body relaxed, and I finally fell asleep.

Bam! Bam! Bam!

The noise shook me awake like I'd been dreaming of falling off a cliff and woke up just before hitting the dirt. My eyes went to the door. Nothing. Then they darted to the closet, window, and walls around us. Nothing. The house was silent again for a moment, and I looked at the others, my heart pounding. Gary's face was green, like he was ready to vomit. Jax's eyes were wide, and his bottom lip quivered.

"What the hell was that?" Jax whispered.

I shrugged.

"Is someone coming in?" Gary asked, but no one had an answer.

Bam! Bam! Bam! It came from downstairs, sounding like a hammer against wood.

"Kitchen," I mouthed. It was my best guess.

Then the footsteps from someone's heels followed. *Clack, clack, clack, clack.* It was definitely coming from the kitchen. One set of footsteps. Someone was walking back and forth, and the floor creaked in its usual spots.

We couldn't move. I was too afraid to make a sound. There was silence again, then more footsteps.

They stopped.

"Henry!" a woman's voice called out from downstairs. The voice belonged to an older woman, maybe in her seventies, and the shrill voice drove spikes of hair up my arms, back, and the nape of my neck.

Bam! Bam! Bam! I imagined a mallet tenderizing meat.

"Henry!" She was louder, more irritated. Her patience wore out. She marched quickly out of the kitchen. *Clack, clack, clack!* The footsteps stalked down the hall then up the stairs.

No! Up the stairs? She's coming for us!

"Oh shit," Gary hissed.

Jax's face turned white. He jumped to my side and scrunched into me, and Gary quickly followed suit. We sat trembling with our backs against the windowsill. The air from outside blew against my back.

She reached the landing, and I saw movement beyond the door.

"Henry!" with more anger and frustration than before.

She burst into our room and stopped.

Tall and thin, she wore a black dress that covered her from neck to wrists. The bodice angled in at the waist, then the skirt flared out and draped down to her ankles. Her black hair with gray streaks was pulled into a bun so tight that it stretched the skin of her face taut. Her mouth was wrinkled, lips pursed. I saw every detail as if she were a living, breathing person. Yet I could see right through her. She was an image of her real self somehow transmitted beyond the veil for our viewing.

Her sharp eyes darted back and forth between us, registering us for the first time. Her brow wrinkled, and her lips pulled back in a snarl. "Dirty boys," she cursed with disgust.

She appeared ready to hurt someone, and we didn't wait to find out for sure. In unison, we grabbed our sleeping bags, pillows, whatever we could, and jumped to our feet. Gary and Jax practically pushed me through the window in their haste to escape. My pillow got caught on a nail and fell back into the room.

"Dirty boys!"

I hit the roof of the porch, and my friends came right after. We wasted no time before leaping from the roof and the short distance to the ground. We mounted our bikes and tore out of there.

I did look back. I had to, long enough to catch a glimpse of the woman standing in the window. White face glowing in the dark, she watched us ride away.

CHAPTER FOUR
Water Weenies

The next morning, I told my mom I'd come home because it got too cold for us to sleep outside at Jax's house. I didn't get much sleep. I kept staring at my bedroom door, fearing the lady dressed in black would be standing there, staring at me.

I had to rest my head on my arms because I'd lost my pillow. It was back at the house with the ghost. She had it. Maybe she would walk into my bedroom one night, holding it in the crook of her arm.

"Dirty boys..."

Sitting at the kitchen table in a stupor, I dipped my spoon in the cereal bowl and raised it to my mouth, but milk spilled over the sides.

Scott zombie-walked into the kitchen, curly hair standing out all over his head after a long sleep. He poured Cocoa Puffs and milk into a bowl and sat down across from me.

"Didn't you sleep over at Jax's house?" he mumbled.

I paused, debating whether to tell him the truth or not. I wasn't in the mood to. "Yeah, in his backyard, but it got too cold, and everyone went home."

He nodded and kept eating his cereal.

I MET JAX AND GARY at Dead Man's Hill. Other kids were there, including my brother, Scott, and his best friend, Daryl.

We were quiet, sharing glances reflecting our trauma. The sun was high and hot, without a single cloud to provide coverage. Summer allergies tickled my nose and eyes, tempting me to scratch. To avoid roasting on our steel bikes, we moved into the shade of a tree on the backside of Dead Man's.

"I didn't get any sleep last night," Jax exclaimed, and it was clear by his bloodshot eyes.

"Do you think we should tell somebody? Like our parents?" Gary asked.

I looked around to be sure no one heard us and kept my voice low. "Tell them what? That we lied and spent the night in an abandoned house and saw a ghost? For one, they wouldn't believe it, and two, they'd punish us for lying."

"No way. I ain't tellin' my parents," Jax said.

"It's not like there's anything they can do. It's a ghost. We'll stay away and never go back."

Gary nodded, but I saw hesitation in his eyes.

We'd been through a traumatic event together, and past experience said our parents could help us deal with that, but I didn't agree. Not in this case.

"Man, it is freakin' hot!" I said. "What should we do?"

My two friends mumbled incoherently. They didn't have a clue, either.

Scott and Daryl rode down the hill and skidded to a stop in front of us. Daryl Griffin was Matt's younger brother, and his personality was in exact contrast to Matt's. He was one of those boys who always held a friendly smile, no judgement in his eyes, and a face that glowed.

"What're you guys doin'?" he asked.

"Not much," I answered.

Daryl and Scott glanced at each other.

"Tell 'em," Scott said to Daryl.

"Guys wanna have a water fight?"

"A water fight?"

"Yeah. It's going to be the biggest water fight ever! Everybody's gonna be in on it. My brothers and their friends. Pat's going to get his friends—just everybody."

"Matt's going to be there too?"

"Yeah," Scott said. "And Tadd and Jeff."

"Wow," I said. It was rare we got included in something our older brothers did. I always wanted to be a part of their world, and this was a no-brainer.

"I don't have a water gun," Gary said.

I had some cheap plastic pistols, nothing fancy.

"My brother lost mine." Jax scowled.

"You don't need one." Excitement burst from Daryl again. "We're making water weenies!"

"Water weenies?" Jax asked perplexed. "What's that?"

"You guys each have a quarter?"

"We can get one." I nodded.

"You have to go down to Pederson's Drug Store and buy a length of surgical tubing, find a writing pen at home, and then I'll show you how to make one."

"A bunch of us are going right now. Do you wanna go?" Scott asked.

It was just what we needed to get our minds off the horror of the previous night.

We parked our bikes at Gary's house and walked along Redwood Road toward the city center. Our parents didn't allow us to ride our bikes along the busy road because there wasn't a sidewalk or bike path along that stretch of road. Walking was just as dangerous as riding, but we obeyed our parents because we didn't mind the walk. It was at least a mile up and back.

Daryl, Scott, Devin, and his two friends, Ralph and John, came with us. We all strode into the drug store and marched to the pharmacy in the back. Sheriff Packard's police car was out front. He was talking to a clerk when we walked in, but he didn't see me. I preferred it that way.

"What can I help you boys with?" The burly lady behind the tall counter was always grouchy, tight-faced, and scowling, and it reflected in the tone of her voice. "Let me guess. You want surgical tubing."

"How did you know?" I was surprised.

"A bunch a you was in earlier."

She took out the long, skinny latex tubes and cut off lengths of it for each of us while she mumbled under her breath, "I don't know what it is you boys do with this stuff, and I don't wanna know."

We paid our money, and while I perused the racks of candy, I heard the heels of boots click against the tile floor, and they got louder... and closer. I turned to face Sheriff Packard, who stopped a foot short of me, glowering.

"What are you up to, Mr. McCoy?" He looked at each of us frozen in our spots and silent like convicts on probation. My run-in with the law was no secret.

"Nothin'," I said. "Just buying stuff."

"Stuff?" He looked at the tubing clenched in my fist. "Whatcha got there?"

"It's surgical tubing." The pharmacy lady ratted us out from behind the counter.

"Surgical tubing?" He chuckled. "What do you guys need surgical tubing for?"

My mind was blank, my mouth dry, and I couldn't think of anything to say.

"Water weenies," Daryl belted out, grinning from ear to ear. "We make water weenies out of 'em."

"What the hell's a water weenie?"

"It's like a... homemade water gun. We're gonna have a water fight."

"Oh, okay." He turned his eyes back to me. "You staying out of trouble? No more gangs?"

"No, sir. I mean, yes. Well... no gangs."

"You sure? You guys look like you're fixin' to cause trouble." For the first time, I saw a smile behind his serious expression and realized he was messing with us. "All right..." He gave me a friendly wink. "Don't let me hear otherwise."

Seeing our cue to bail, we scurried from Pederson's and headed for home.

Once we hit our neighborhood, on the final stretch before we turned to get to my house, I saw her long strawberry-blond hair. She was around my age, and although I couldn't make out all her features from where I stood, I knew she was cute.

She sat next to Morgan Anderson on the front porch of the Andersons' home. We all knew Morgan. She was nice enough, with brown hair, glasses, and a mouth like a motorboat. From what I could tell, she was doing all the talking, as usual, and the new girl stayed silent and gave courteous nods.

"Who is she?" I asked my friends.

"I don't know," Jax said.

"I do," Devin said. "She just moved in a couple of days ago."

"What's her name?"

"I don't know. My parents went over and talked to them for about an hour. They made me come out and introduce myself."

"Then how can you not know her name?"

He shrugged his shoulders. "Can't remember, I guess."

We stood across the street and three houses west. Both girls looked our way, and I turned immediately, acting like I didn't see them. That'll do the trick.

"Go talk to her, Romeo." Gary smirked.

"You go talk to her."

"Are you serious? I've never talked to a girl on purpose."

"Come on. We got a water fight waiting for us." Scott urged us on before turning to walk away. We followed.

I kept my head down as we passed the girls, pressing my peripheral vision to the max to see her. I wanted her to look back. It was hard to tell, but I'm sure they looked at least twice. I stole another glance before we were out of range. I had to. In that second, I imprinted her image in my brain.

We finally arrived at my house, and my older brothers were there. They had their water weenies made, and they helped me make mine.

Jeff sat down with me. "Here." He took my piece of tubing. "You tie a knot at one end. You gotta make it a good knot so it will hold the water."

For the most part, my brothers and I went our own ways and hung out with our own friends, but occasionally, we spent moments like this, and I secretly cherished them.

Jeff picked up my ink pen and unscrewed the top from its bottom half. "You take the pen apart." He abandoned the bottom half of the pen and all the insides, including the spring, and held up the tip of the pen. "You only need this half. You push it into the other end."

Then I saw it. The top half of the pen became the nozzle for the water weenie.

"When you're ready, untie the knot and fill it with water, but you gotta keep your thumb on the nozzle so the water doesn't get out. Then when it's full, tie the knot again, and you're good to go."

He helped me fill it. The water weenie expanded to the size of an actual weenie dog and was about as heavy. I kept my thumb on the nozzle, turned so I wouldn't hit anyone, and tested it out. The water shot out of the nozzle. The stream arced and flew a good ten feet. I was impressed.

A ton of kids gathered at my house, people from all over the neighborhood, including some we saw as enemies or bullies. I didn't see Fernando, and I didn't want him to be left out. So Gary and I ran to his house and knocked on his door. No one answered, the drapes were closed, and we didn't see any vehicles.

We had turned to walk away when the door creaked open slightly and Fernando peered through the crack.

"Hey, Fernando. How're you doin'?" I asked.

"Good. You guys?"

"We're good," Gary said.

"We're having a large water fight. The whole neighborhood is in on it. Wanna come?"

"No, thanks." He shook his head. "I gotta help pack. We're moving this weekend."

"You're moving?" Gary asked.

Fernando nodded.

"Where? Why?" I asked.

Fernando shrugged. He appeared withdrawn and somewhat sad. An awkward silence followed, but I didn't know what to say. Finally, I managed, "Well, I'm sorry to see you go. Good luck in your new place."

"Yeah, best of luck," Gary threw in.

"Thanks. See ya." Fernando closed the door.

As we sauntered away, Gary and I shared a quizzical look.

"We better hurry and get back," I said.

Gary agreed, and we bolted into a run back to my house.

Tadd, Jeff, Daryl's older brothers, and some of their friends showed. Eight older kids and twenty-two younger kids ranging from my age down filled my yard.

"All right gather 'round!" Tadd stepped out and commanded the group. We all turned to listen. "We're going to separate into teams."

"I call captain!" Devin shouted, and then other kids started to repeat it.

"No, no, no. We're not picking captains. We're going to make this easy. It's us against you."

"You mean the older kids against the younger ones?" I said.

"That's not fair!" Jax protested.

"Yes, it is. There's like thirty of you rug rats, and only eight of us. We're outnumbered."

"All right." I liked challenges, and I felt confident about our team. "Let's do it."

Then they revealed a hidden weapon. Tadd's best friend, Sonny, stepped out from the crowd, carrying a water weenie the size of a giant boa constrictor wrapped around his neck. It was at least four times the size of ours, and he wore a cheese-eating grin.

"Go!" he called out and shot his fire hose at us. We ran from the stream, then everyone was spraying their water weenies.

Water flew everywhere. Nothing was off-limits. I got shot in the eyes and face several times, and the water fight expanded into the neighbors' yards.

We scattered like frightened mice without a game plan and hid where we could behind cars, houses, and trees. We snuck from spot to spot, inching closer to the enemy. Sometimes, we got them, and sometimes, they jumped out of nowhere and surprised us.

I saw the new girl and Morgan at the end of the street, next to a tree, watching the great water fight and laughing. I puffed out my chest, ran some cool sneak-attack moves to impress the girls, and acted silly at times to get a laugh. It'd worked, I was sure.

The water fight was epic. It went on for hours and escalated to water balloons. Parents who were home helped fill up balloons, and we carried them back to our stations in big plastic tubs and wheelbarrows. Water bombs filled the air, but most missed their targets. Some of the older kids were talented enough to catch them without breaking them and throw them back at us.

It all ended when the big kids brought out the garden hoses with spray nozzles attached. We couldn't get close to them when they had a weapon of that magnitude. It was cheating, and I reminded them several times the rest of the night.

The water fight accomplished our goal: we didn't think about the Crooked House or the ghost all day. At least I know I didn't... until I went to bed and rolled onto my side facing the door. It was cracked open. Footsteps squeaked down the hall. It was normal, but now it reminded me of that night. *Is it her?* I wondered, trying not to picture the ghost in the black dress peering in through the crack, her eyes wild, clutching my pillow.

I switched images in my head to the new girl and felt dreamy. I pictured us talking and laughing while she tossed her hair from side to side in slow motion like girls in the movies. It was a better picture to have in my head than thoughts of the ghost.

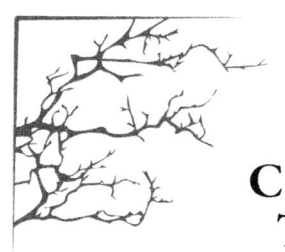

CHAPTER FIVE
The New Guest

Matt Griffin knocked on my door the next morning. It was just him, no Wes. The sun blared in and blinded me when I opened the door.

"Hey, Ret. You doing anything?"

"No."

"Do you wanna hang out?"

Hang out? He'd graduated to asking people to hang out, while I was still using the childish line "Do you wanna play?" *How cool is that?*

"Yeah. Sure."

Matt nodded, looking around awkwardly at the pictures on our wall, as if he didn't know what to say next. I didn't either for that matter. Talking with Gary or Jax was easy, but the last conversation I'd had with Matt, he was picking on me and my friends.

"What do you wanna do?" he finally asked me.

"I don't know." I shrugged. "The Colemans got a new trampoline. Said we could use it."

"Oh yeah. I saw them putting it in. It's one of those buried-in-the-ground trampolines."

"Yeah. It's pretty cool."

"Let's do it."

Matt was fourteen, so I felt pretty special because he'd come to ask me to hang out, but when I realized Wes was gone for the day, it was clear I was second-string. That didn't matter, though. We still had fun. The Colemans were good to let us play on their trampoline as long as their son, Chad, jumped with us. He was a year younger than me, and occasionally, we crossed paths. He'd fought on my team during the Great Water Fight.

Chad was full of energy, couldn't sit still, and didn't listen well. He asked tons of dumb questions and became annoying quickly. That was why people didn't play with him for long, but he'd become more popular once his parents bought the trampoline.

After we spent an hour jumping and trying out new tricks, Chad's mother called him in for lunch. She said we could keep playing while he ate, and his absense gave us a nice break.

We sat along the edge of the trampoline to catch our breaths and talked.

"I can't believe you guys did it," Matt said out of the blue.

"What? The Crooked House?" I said, trying to sound nonchalant.

"Yeah! I can't believe you stayed the night. That place is so haunted."

"Well, actually... we cut out about three in the morning."

"I know. We saw you guys tear out of there. We'd dozed off, but we heard Jax screaming. I can't believe he didn't wake up the whole neighborhood."

We laughed. "Yeah, he's not the most quiet person."

"You still did it, though."

"Not like you guys. We didn't stay the whole night."

"Well..." He looked down at the ground shamefully. "I might have stretched the truth a little."

"What do you mean?"

"I've never stayed the night in that creepy old place. I've barely stepped foot in it during the day, and no one else has slept the night, either, as far as I know. No one's dumb enough."

I raised my hand. "I am."

We chuckled.

I felt really proud. I couldn't wait to tell my friends. We'd done what no one else had.

"You oughta sleep over tonight. Do you think you can?"

"Yeah. My parents are pretty cool. I'm sure they will let me."

It was a Saturday night, and I could sleep over as long as I came straight home in the morning and got ready in time to go to church. The same went for Matt. His family went to the same church as mine.

We had a Boy Scout meeting that afternoon before our sleepover. Todd Harrison was our Scoutmaster, and Matt and I went over to his house together. As we approached his house, Todd and his wife were in the front yard with a group of boys, a mess of camping gear sprawled across the grass around them. Gary was among them, and he smiled, but the expression dissapeared as soon as he noticed Matt alongside me.

I knew what he must be thinking. *Why are you hanging out with him? He's the one who bullied us into sleeping over at the haunted house.*

"Where's Jax?" I asked Gary.

Without looking at me, he shrugged. "I don't know."

Gary walked away and began talking to Billy, who had just turned twelve and graduated from Webelos to Boy Scouts.

"All right, boys," Todd Harrison called to us, but everyone continued with their own chatter.

Todd was a tall, slender man with a black crew cut. He was always sharp and clean, except for an occasional scruff on his face. He stood straight, in full Scout uniform, and everything he did was orderly, like a soldier. He was a military man.

"Boys! Attention!"

"Yes, drill sergeant!" we all answered, laughing. We turned and stood in our imitation of military attention.

A smile crept up Todd's face. "At ease, soldiers. All right now, we're gonna prepare for our Scout camp tonight," his deep, Southern drawl rolled out. "I wanna see if you boys can set up yer tents. Did everyone bring their tents?" He looked around.

Gary raised his hand. "I brought my two-man tent."

Billy's hand popped up excitedly. "I did! I brought my six-man tent."

"Good, Billy."

Peter raised his hand, as well. Peter and Billy hung out a lot together, and I didn't see them much unless we were at Scouts.

"Sorry, we didn't bring ours," Matt spoke for both of us.

"No problem. You two help Billy out with his monster tent."

We commenced building our tents, and I shifted from helping Matt and Billy to helping Gary. After I explained to Gary how my day with Matt had all transpired, he was cool with it.

After the tents were constructed, we played a game of tag. Todd and his wife played with us, along with their three little ones, and then she made us root beer floats.

Afterward, Gary walked home with Matt and me, until we separated to our homes. I grabbed my stuff and headed back to Matt's for our sleepover. I brought my sleeping bag and pillow, along with a bag of licorice for snacks. We made homemade popcorn, which he poured into a brown paper bag with butter and salt then shook it up. I'd never done popcorn like that before. My mom always popped popcorn in an air popper, put it in a large bowl, and slowly drizzled butter over it, but I liked Matt's method.

We took the brown bag, which was now splotched with butter grease, and sat down to watch *Nightmare Theater* on TV. His parents had gone to bed. Otherwise, they never would have allowed Matt and me to watch *Nightmare Theater*. It was too violent, too scary.

The program came on every Friday night. It was hosted by a man dressed as a vampire. He would rise from his coffin and introduce the low-budget horror flick they were about to play.

Most of the kids in the neighborhood weren't allowed to watch the show, but that only drew us to the program more. The only way to catch it was to stay up really late, because it didn't air until around one or two in the morning. That made it easier to sneak into the living room while everyone was asleep.

I was glued to the show that night. The story followed a teenage boy who was bullied at school for being different, but he was brilliant at science. One night, he broke into the school lab and cooked up an experiment, which turned him into a raging monster. He made the bullies, and one innocent janitor, pay. They found the janitor's head bobbing in a vat of acid the next day. That bloody and horrific image of the eyes staring out of the slime stuck with me. Matt dozed off and slept through most of the movie. I had to wake him up to turn off the TV and go to bed.

The movie was my first real horror flick, and it had scared me, like the real-life ghost had. Maybe I found the movie so scary because I knew if ghosts could be real, then monsters in the movie *could* be real too.

We laid out our sleeping bags on his back porch, the same raised porch Matt and Wes watched us from. I looked beyond the field and saw the haunted house in the distance. Matt was right. He had a perfect view of it.

"You know the history of that house, don't ya?" Matt asked.

"Yes... sorta. Not really, I guess." I'd thought I knew, but instantly, I realized all I'd heard were rumors. I was eager to see if Matt knew the truth of the house.

He chawed on a stick of licorice as we stared at the dark house, and he told me the tale.

"A couple lived in that house a long time ago. They were nice folks at first, but something was off. They weren't like everybody else. They talked about children all the time, yet no one ever saw them with kids. It was just the two of them, or so people thought. It was like they had a secret. People started to disappear. One at a time. It wasn't very often at first, but it increased. People said they saw lights on in their home throughout the night, then you wouldn't see them in the day. They wouldn't come out until much later."

"Vampires?" I said, skeptical the story was leaning closer to the unrealistic ones I'd heard.

"No, not vampires. Something much worse. Monsters, vampires, or werewolves... Those things aren't scary... It's people that are scary. People like you and me, but do awful things."

Most stories told about the Crooked House involved ghosts or something supernatural, but his was grounded in something I could believe. He had me hooked.

"They had an axe. The man cut wood all the time in back of the house. He'd go out at night, and people could hear him chopping for hours, and there was always smoke coming from the chimney. A local boy came screaming home to his parents one day. Said he saw something in the basement window. Like another child. It'd screamed and pounded its hands on the glass, wild eyed and crazed. But that's not all he saw. He saw the bloody axe in the basement. Embedded in a log of wood, still dripping blood.

"It was enough to bring the police, and they searched the house inside and out. They arrested the couple. Put them in a squad car."

Matt stopped talking. Seconds rolled by, and I worried he wouldn't finish the story. The suspense was killing me.

"What?" I asked. "What was in the basement? What was that couple doing?"

"They were killing people. They'd lure people into their home. One at a time. They'd kill them, chop them up into pieces, and feed them to the children in the basement."

"Children!" I exclaimed. "So they had children?"

"Yeah, they had children all right. They kept them sheltered and locked in the basement and fed human remains to them. Like I said, it was so long ago. But on some nights, when it's real quiet, you can hear the children. They cry, beg, and scream for someone to help them. For someone to let them out."

We stared at the house in the distance. A sliver of moonlight outlined the south side of the home. It sat quietly. A cool breeze blew through my hair.

I turned to Matt, who sat in a stupor. Staring into the night, unblinking, he was in his own world. As if he'd locked gazes with something invisible, his eyes glazed over.

"Matt?" I called his name two more times, but he never answered.

Like he was in a trance, he lay down and pulled the bag up to his chin. As soon as his eyes closed, he was out, as if instructed to go to sleep by some unseen form. For several minutes, I wondered if he'd been talking in his sleep or if he was tricking me. I waited for him to roll over, laughing at his trick, but instead, he started to snore.

I sat awake, with nothing but me and the chilled breeze. I was too wound up to sleep. I wasn't sure whether I could believe Matt's story or not. I'd never heard anything like it before, yet on the other hand, it followed all the same scenarios of a campfire ghost story. He could've been pulling my leg. Either way, he was a good storyteller. If I'd heard the story a few weeks ago, real or not, I would *not* have stayed in that house.

I'd thought I would be up the whole night, but to my surprise, once I lay down, I fell asleep quickly.

A clang startled me awake. My eyes popped open into a wide-eyed stare. The wind had picked up through the night and become chillier. I realized it had blown something over beneath the porch.

I sat up and looked around for the source. All I could see of Matt was the tuft of his hair poking through the top of his sleeping bag. Another strong gust of wind blew past me, carrying the scent of lavender from nearby bushes.

I turned to the Crooked House, and my heart stopped. The upper-floor bedroom light was on, burning yellow in the darkness.

"Matt!" I whispered urgently and pushed his body with my hand. "Matt!"

"Whaaat?" He rolled over, groggy.

"There's someone in that house! Look! A light is on!"

A low snore rose from his sleeping bag. He was out again. I was on my own.

I stared at the house, looking for clues. There was a car parked in front of it, but I couldn't discern the make or model. A sillhouette crept through the light in the window. A person had walked into the house and turned on a light. *He must be insane!* The ghost was sure to appear and frighten the person.

I watched the house for the next hour, until the light turned off and there was no sign of activity. I stared at the stars for what seemed like hours, occasionally glancing at the house, but it remained dark. Eventually, I found my way back to sleep.

I woke up freezing in the morning. It was daylight, and dew was frozen on the grass and slick on my bag. Matt was still sleeping soundly. I looked at the house across the field and saw no movement, but the car was still there. It was black and looked like a Chrysler or Buick.

I put on my socks and shoes, rolled up my bag, and said goodbye to Matt, who mumbled something incoherent. I headed home to get ready for church, then I had to speak to Gary and Jax. There was a lot to go over with them, and we had spying to do.

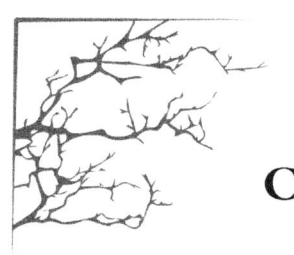

CHAPTER SIX
Lester

I immediately jumped in the shower and got ready for church. I was in a daze from lack of sleep and unsettled at the thought of someone staying in that house.

"Is it a bad thing?" I asked myself. "So what if somebody moves into the house of ghosts? No sweat off my back. Don't bother me, and I won't bother you."

But a feeling bubbled up from the deep, acidic pool in my belly and told me something wasn't right.

Before Sunday school class, I gathered Gary and Jax in the corner. "You'll never believe it, guys. I saw someone go into the house last night."

"What? Who would be crazy enough to go in there?" Jax asked. He knew exactly which house I'd meant. I didn't need to clarify.

Gary rolled his eyes. "You mean besides us?"

"This was an adult, and he spent the night. Maybe he bought the place and is moving in."

"Who is it?" Gary asked.

"I don't know. Matt and I were sleeping out on his porch, and I woke up in the middle of the night. I saw a light on over there and a car parked out front. I saw someone in the window too. It looked like a guy."

"Ooh." Gary shivered, no doubt revisiting the night we'd stayed. "With that ghost lady?"

"Not just her. There's more ghosts, for sure," Jax said anxiously. "I've had nightmares ever since, and I think there's more to that house than what we saw. I'm sure of it."

"Me too," Gary agreed. "Nightmares every night."

"Whoever he is, he won't last long in that house," Jax said.

"Maybe he'll get rid of the ghosts and clean the place up," I said. "I don't know about you guys, but I'm curious to know who this guy is. We should go check him out."

"Why?" Gary asked.

"I don't know. I just have a weird feeling."

"So you want to spy on him?" Jax said.

"I wouldn't say 'spy.'" I paused and thought about it. "Yes... yes—I *do* mean I want to spy on him."

"I can't. My parents won't let me play on Sunday," Gary said.

"Mine will, but I gotta go to my grandma's for dinner."

"I don't mean today," I said. "But first thing tomorrow."

"No, Ret, I'm not going back there," Gary said quietly. "I just... I can't."

I saw in Gary's eyes how much trauma that night had left behind.

Our teacher walked in and asked everyone to settle down as he set his books on the table and prepared to give the lesson.

"We don't have to go to the house," I whispered. "We'll watch from a distance. Completely safe. You can do that, right?"

Gary nodded reluctantly, and Jax gave a firm nod.

LESTER KILBORN WAS close to six feet tall and on the heavy side. His tiny eyes were like black pinheads stuck into his pudgy face. He had a full head of dark hair, and his bangs fell down over his face. He swiped them back constantly, but they never stayed. He dressed casually: simple striped T-shirts and blue jeans. He drove a black Chrysler and appeared to live alone.

My friends and I had been spying on Lester, and we weren't the only ones who had noticed him. As it turned out, Lester had become the talk of the neighborhood. Riding past Mrs. Crawford's house one day, I overheard her and Mrs. Anderson gossiping up a storm.

"I don't know who in their right minds would want to move into that house." Mrs. Anderson shook her head in disgust, and I slowed down, pretending to check something on my bike tire. "It's so old and falling apart. I don't even think it has running water or heat. It should be condemned."

I parked my bike, got off, and bent to check my chain while continuing to listen in. I thought they might be suspicious of me, but they were too involved in conversation.

"Well, if you ask me, it's not the house I'm worried about." Mrs. Crawford rolled her eyes, shaking a warning finger in the direction of the house. "It's that man who moved in there. I heard he's a pedophile."

Mrs. Anderson gasped.

I didn't know what a "pedophile" was, and I didn't bother to find out.

Later that night, my mom was talking a hundred miles an hour on the phone to a friend when I heard Lester's name come up in the conversation. Apparently, Lester had inherited the Crooked House from a grandfather he hadn't known—some rich guy named Charles Blackmore, who owned a bunch of property throughout the country. When he died, he left part of his estate to a daughter he'd fathered with his mistress—Lester Kilborn's mother, who had already passed away. When Charles's other heirs found out they were sharing their inheritance with Lester, they were furious. They found a way to give Lester only scraps from the table—and the Crooked House certainly qualified as scraps.

My friends and I snuck onto the property and hid behind a berm thirty yards away next to a tree and watched the house. It was our second day of spying, and four nights had passed since I'd first seen Lester in the house.

We'd been sitting behind that berm, watching the house, for two hours, and nothing had happened.

"What is he doing?" Gary asked.

Lester moved back and forth behind his windows. We couldn't imagine what he was doing. There was no moving van or trucks, and at no point had anyone seen him move a lick of furniture inside.

"Maybe he's just using the furniture that's in there," Jax said.

"Would you use the furniture in that house?" Gary asked.

"No, but this guy's creepy. He's a weirdo."

"You have a point," I said. "Come on. Nothing's going on. We've watched it all day yesterday, two hours today, and all he's done is go buy groceries."

"I'm glad you said it. I'm done with this." Jax let out a sigh.

"Hold on. Look." Gary pointed at the upper-right window.

Lester grabbed a lamp, threw it at the wall, then kicked the bedpost. Eyes closed and mouth open wide, he yelled in rage. His voice was so loud that despite our distance, we could hear him.

Then Lester entangled his fingers in his hair and pulled as if he meant to yank it all out. He yelled words, but they were unintelligible, then he stormed out of the bedroom. A few seconds later, he burst through the front door and marched to the front yard, where he turned and faced the house. He stood glaring at it for several minutes.

We sat, transfixed and quiet. My heart thumped like a rabbit's.

"Leave me alone!" he screamed.

We turned to each other, perplexed.

"I told you I would," he continued. "I've done a lot for you already. Now stay the hell out of my head!" He snapped his head in our direction and glared.

We ducked under the berm and held our breath. I thought for sure he'd seen us, but after a few minutes of nothing happening, I popped my head above the berm and saw Lester stomp to his car and drive away.

"Wow!" I exclaimed, and the others nodded agreement.

"That guy's crazier than I thought," Jax said, twirling a finger next to his head.

"Who was he talking to?" Gary shrugged and scrunched his face.

"No one," I said.

"Maybe it was the ghost lady," Gary said, his eyes filled with fear.

"Maybe. But I didn't see her."

"I saw this movie once," Jax said, "where this crazy guy had a bunch of voices in his head. They made him do things, made him kill people, and he argued with himself out loud. That's what's going on with Lester. This guy is nuts."

"Come on, guys. Let's get outta here." I motioned for them to follow me.

We ended up at Jax's house and lost ourselves in a long game of Monopoly, but I couldn't get Lester out of my head all day. When I left Jax's house, I couldn't help but replay the image of Lester throwing the lamp and arguing with himself. *He had so much anger.*

After dinner, while I was washing the dishes, he snuck into the back of my head and posed all sorts of questions I couldn't answer. Who had he *really* been talking to? What was his purpose in that house? Why wasn't he moving in furniture?

At night, I found myself awake in bed. All my thoughts revolved around Lester Kilborn and the creepy house. Everyone in my house was asleep. I got up and slipped on my shorts and a shirt, then without bothering to put on shoes and socks, I crept outside into my backyard. My bare feet were cold on the concrete pad of our patio, and I shivered in the cool breeze.

Across the field beyond my backyard was the house. My house wasn't as close as Matt's, but I had my brother's binoculars. There were lights on at the house, at least three. I put the binoculars to my eyes and trailed the sights up and down the house.

Lester's silhouette shuffled things back and forth across his windows downstairs. Then something moved in the upstairs bedroom! I caught it out of the corner of my eye: the blur of a body running. I questioned whether I'd really seen it. *That's impossible...*

Lester was definitely still downstairs. I could see the shadow of his bulky body. But I saw another shadow cross the light in the upstairs bedroom, the same bedroom we'd been in.

Someone else was in the house with Lester. More movement came from below, and I saw two bodies. There was a lot of activity, but I couldn't make out what was going on.

I turned my vision to the window of the room we had stayed in. I hadn't seen any activity in that room until now. There she stood, in the window, her white face aglow, eyes locked on me!

I stumbled and nearly dropped the binoculars. I trembled. Tears filled my eyes. I would have been happy spending the rest of my life never seeing that ghost lady again, but there she was, clutching my pillow.

I was done. Terrified, I went back inside and lay in my bed, as stiff as a stick. Clutching my sheets, I slept in fitful increments of fifteen or twenty minutes the rest of the night.

MY DAD MENTIONED LESTER during conversation at our dinner table the next day. Every so often he'd puncuate his words by stabbing his fork down at his plate. "Brother Anderson and I went over to invite our new neighbor to church on Sunday. We got assigned with that lucky task. Seemed like a strange guy. Didn't say much. Just squinted at us the whole time with a scowl. The strange thing is he's been in there nearly a week now, and I don't think he's cleaned one thing. Dust on all the furniture. Broken glass and things on the floor." His eyes widened, and he let out a sigh. "It looks the same as it has for years." He shook his head and took a gulp of his drink. "Exactly the same."

That he hadn't cleaned anything was weird enough, but the bigger question was what *had* he been doing all week? With all the activity I'd seen, I'd assumed he was moving furniture or cleaning, and he had several people in there to help him—including the ghost lady.

"He did mumble a few times, but it seemed like he wasn't actually talking to me. Yet, nobody was there!"

"Sounds like a real wacko," Tadd blurted out then chuckled.

We all laughed, but inside, I was sick, because nothing about the situation was actually funny.

"Nice enough fella, but definitely odd."

"Maybe he escaped the nut house!" Scott exclaimed.

"Honey," my mom said, "we shouldn't talk about people like that." She stabbed my dad with a glare. "We don't know the man, and we don't want to be the people who start bad rumors."

He nodded agreement, and my mom switched gears.

"So, Jeff, I talked to Suzy over at Sharp Stables. She said they could use someone three days a week to help feed the horses and clean the stables."

"Cool. Steve already works there and says they pay three-fifty an hour. I definitely want to do that."

The discussion went on as Scott blurted out how he wanted to work too, but Mom told him he was too young. I stayed silent as my thoughts continued to drift back to Lester and that house.

CHAPTER SEVEN
Mr. Beaumont

The next day started off boring. Two of my brothers were gone, doing something with their friends. Tadd was sprawled out on the couch, watching a daytime TV program. The minute I stepped out from the hall, he sensed my presence and started in barking orders.

"Get me a drink. One of those Shastas."

I rolled my eyes and got him the can of soda. My body language was so loud that it must have been hard not to notice how irritated I was. He ignored me, though. I decided to get out of there before he demanded anything else.

I ate my cereal, showered, dressed, and took off. As I was on my way out, he asked where I was going—technically, he was my babysitter—and I answered, "Jax's house."

"Just be home by twelve for lunch. Mom will kill me if I don't make sure you eat something."

When I got to Jax's house, he wasn't home. I went to Gary's next and found it just as empty. Then I remembered they'd both told me about family vacations coming up. I remembered being upset because they would both be gone at the same time. I hadn't paid attention to the dates, but clearly it was that week.

The new girl was with Morgan again. They were sitting on Morgan's front steps, looking my way. I moved my eyes in the opposite direction. A small voice crept up and dared me to walk over there and talk to her. *Maybe I could pass the time with them?*

I immediately shot down that idea. I wasn't brave enough yet. I was still too nervous to talk to girls.

I did have some loose change in my pocket, enough to buy a couple of treats at Pederson's—at least a few Zotz and some root beer barrels. Those were my favorite hard candy. If anything, the trip to the store would kill the time, which was crawling by like a snail, and the air conditioning inside would help me cool off from the immense heat.

The air conditioning hit my hot face the moment I stepped into the pharmacy, and I pictured steam rising from my body. The store was bustling with patrons, mostly women with their small children, pushing carts up and down the aisles. I hit the magazine rack before the candy aisle. I flipped through the latest *MAD Magazine*, which was always good for sarcastic humor and parodies of the latest films. Then I thumbed through the paperback books. I loved reading, and Louis L'Amour westerns were my favorite. My grandpa's favorite too. He had stacks of them in his basement, and he would lend them to me a couple at a time.

"Ret?" said a deep voice filled with kindness.

I turned around to face Mr. Beaumont. He was extremely tall, always in a suit, and in his late seventies. He placed a gentle hand on my shoulder, and his large fingers covered it completely. He bent down to my eye level. His dark eyes sparkled with the same joy reflected in his smile, something he always had when he talked to me. I knew him from church. Mr. Beaumont and his wife had taught my Sunday school class for a couple of years, and they were always friendly and kind.

"Nice to see you, son."

"Nice to see you too, Mr. Beaumont."

"How's the family? You always look so sharp in church. You do a good job passing the sacrament."

I nodded. "We're good. Thanks."

"That is good. I'm glad to hear it." He looked at me with admiration. "How's your dad?"

"Good." I nodded.

"He still cuttin' meat? He butchered a deer for me a couple of years ago. Best butcherin' I ever got."

I wanted to roll my eyes. Every time I talked to Mr. Beaumont, which was usually at church, he always brought up my dad and how he'd cut up that deer of his.

"I think so. He works two jobs right now. One at Happy Service Groceries and one for the state. I don't see him a whole lot."

"No, I bet you don't. I'm sure neither of ya like that. Where's your friends?" He checked up and down the aisle. "You here alone?"

"Yeah. They're gone on vacation. I'm just bored, trying to find somethin' to do."

"Summers are like that, aren't they?" He rubbed his chin with his forefinger, wheels turned in his head, and he looked down at me. "You know, I could use some help out at the mortuary from time to time. Tidying up stuff. You know, dusting and vacuuming, and cleanin' the restrooms. That sort of thing. Couldn't take more'n a couple hours a day."

Great! Work detail. Charity work, I thought with dread.

"I'd pay you five bucks each time. Maybe more, if it takes longer."

My eyes widened, and my heart beat faster. I thought of all the things my money could buy—more *Star Wars* figures, cool accessories for my bike, and firecrackers when the Fourth of July rolled around.

"Yeah, that, uh, yes. I'd like to." The mortuary didn't sound like an ideal summer job, but if there was money to be had, I could overlook the circumstances.

"Good." He chuckled. "I'm getting too old. It's harder for me to do everything, so I could use the help. Just be sure you ask your parents. Get their permission, and I'll see you at nine in the morning tomorrow. Sound good?"

"Sounds great!"

We shook hands and said goodbye, then he walked to the checkout stands to pay for the few items he was holding.

Wow! A job! Working for Mr. Beaumont would be better than the occasional babysitting detail, which I'd done for the Reynolds kids. They paid me five bucks, but I had to stay there for four hours and deal with rug rats. The mortuary would be much better, maybe even better than Jeff's job at the stables. Not to mention it would keep me busy while my friends were out of town.

I went to the candy aisle to get my goods, but I couldn't think of anything else but the job. As I searched for Zotz, I heard Mr. Beaumont's deep voice as he spoke to the clerk at the register.

"Looks like I'm getting all sorts of new help today," he said. "I hired a new assistant."

I lit up because I thought he was referring to me, but then he continued, "Comes from Wichita, Kansas. Lester Kilborn. He moved into that old house on Beck Street."

A shiver went through my spine, and hairs rose on my arms and neck. I couldn't quite hear the clerk's response—his voice wasn't as loud as Mr. Beaumont's, so I crept closer to the cash register to hear the conversation better.

"Who would move into that creepy old place?" the clerk asked.

"Good people see beyond the face of things. Lester's good people, and he sees something in that house. Even said it feels like home."

"Does he plan on fixin' it up, I hope?" the clerk said.

"I reckon. Needs a good amount a work. Lester's young, and he can do it if anyone can. Came highly recommended from the mortuary he worked at in Kansas."

"What brought him out here?" I asked, interrupting their conversation.

Mr. Beaumont turned to respond. "Well, said his grandpa passed and left that house to him in a will." He shrugged. "Might have family out here too, I suppose. Anyway, you'll meet him tomorrow. You'll be workin' together." His smile spread from ear to ear, creating waves of wrinkles.

THE NEXT DAY CAME FAST. My parents were okay with my new job. In fact, they were more excited for it than I was. My excitement had been short-lived. Once I'd found out who my workmate was, I couldn't stop stressing about it, and I wished my friends were around to blab to.

My mom also said it was okay to ride my bike to work since it was farther than Pederson's, as long as I promised to be safe and stay off the road. Of course I'd agreed.

I leaned my bike against the brick wall of the building and stepped inside. The mortuary was old. It'd been there since the early sixties, and the furniture and décor looked like they hadn't changed much since then. Heavy gold drapes hung over the windows, yellow shag carpet covered the floor from wall to wall, and the furniture was boxy and stiff. The air was thick and warm. No one was around. It took nearly five minutes for someone to show, and thankfully, it was Mr. Beaumont.

He trotted to me in a hurry, with his hand held out. I took his hand in mine and nearly pulled it back. His hand was ice-cold.

"Sorry for my cold hand. I've been in the basement."

Basement? What goes on in the basement? I didn't want to know.

"You're right on time. That's good. You McCoy boys are always sharp." He smiled.

Another figure approached behind Mr. Beaumont, and he turned to introduce us.

"Mr. Kilborn!" Beaumont called out, waving him over.

Lester was almost a whole head shorter than Mr. Beaumont, but he was still tall compared to most men. His body was shaped like a pear, with a wide belly and hips, then his legs narrowed to thin ankles. His eyes weren't as beady as I'd thought, though. They were round, but he always kept them half closed, like he was tired and ready to fall asleep.

"This is Mr. McCoy!" Beaumont motioned for me to come closer.

Mr. Kilborn pushed the bangs out of his eyes and shot his hand out. I shook it. His hand wasn't as cold as Beaumont's, but his shake was limp, and his palm was wet.

"Call me Lester."

"Call me Ret."

"Great! We're goin' to make a great team, fellas!"

I didn't see Lester the rest of the day, and I was glad. Mr. Beaumont showed me where the cleaning supplies were in the basement then gave me a brief rundown of my tasks, and I went at it.

I ran a vacuum across all the carpeted floors, including the viewing room, where a coffin sat with a dead body inside. Beaumont was preparing for a service later that day.

I'd only seen one dead body—my great-grandmother. She'd looked peaceful, but different than she had when she was alive. It hadn't been as creepy as I'd thought, but I tried not to look at the body in the casket.

As I vacuumed the room, curiosity finally got the best of me, and I peeked over the edge of the coffin twice. The man was lying in a suit, hands crossed over his chest and eyes closed. His skin was painted with more makeup and rouge than any living man would wear.

I continued to peek over my shoulder to be sure the corpse didn't exit his coffin and stumble after me. He didn't. I survived.

I vaccumed and dusted each room, including the chapel and foyers, and cleaned the men's and women's restrooms. It took me two and a half hours, and Mr. Beaumont was better than his word and gave me seven dollars. I was elated.

He asked me to come back the next day to polish the furniture and some more detailed work, then he handed me a key to the facility. I couldn't believe it. He trusted me with a key!

"I trust you more than I'd trust anybody." He smiled, his hand on my shoulder.

I thanked him a hundred times, said goodbye, and left. I bought a cheeseburger and fries from the burger joint across the street then rode home with a full belly, satisfied about putting in a good day's worth of work. I slumped on our couch and watched useless TV the rest of the day. Suddenly, I realized why my parents liked doing the same when they got home. *One has to decompress.*

CHAPTER EIGHT
Missing

I was eager to get back to work the next day. I felt important. Having a job was a fulfillment I hadn't realized I'd needed. The wind blew in my face as I pumped the pedals on my bike. Riding along Redwood Road, I looked at the rumbling sky. Boiling dark clouds crept across the sky and hid the sun. The air was dense with humidity. The storm was about to burst.

I parked my bike and walked in through the open back door. I stopped halfway down the back hall when I heard voices in the foyer. It was Lester, talking to a lady, who sounded older.

I moved closer and saw Mrs. Beaumont, looking frantic as her hands animated her tone. She was short, and the sweater and long skirt she was wearing seemed to swallow her up.

"He comes in early a lot. Are you sure you haven't seen him?" she asked.

"No, I haven't seen him at all today." Lester's voice carried no sympathy for her situation. In fact, he sounded bothered.

"Not even in the basement? He's probably down there."

"Nope. The doors were locked when I got here, and no lights were on. I opened the place and checked everywhere. No one's here."

Her hands went to her mouth. They were shaking, and her eyes were teary. "I can't imagine where he'd be. He didn't come home at all last night. When did he leave here?"

"I-I don't know. I left before he did. 'Bout five."

"He didn't mention anything to you before you left? An errand to run or something?" She was confused and nervous, and her eyes darted back and forth as if her mind were sifting through possible scenarios.

"Nope."

I felt it in my stomach. A darkness like a warning bubbled up from the depths of my gut, making my senses tingle. The situation didn't set right.

"He never does this, you see. He always comes home on time. I just don't understand."

I backed up before either of them saw me there. I headed to the basement to get the cleaning supplies and to get a look for myself. Maybe he was farther in the back, where the furnace and pipes were. Lester didn't have a shred of care to look for Mr. Beaumont, so I doubted he'd checked the furnace room.

The supply closet was on the left at the bottom of the stairs, but I walked right by it and headed for the furnace room. I passed the large entrance to the back parking lot, where double doors opened to a ramp leading to the basement. That was where they brought the bodies in. It was dark in the short hall. No one was there.

"Mr. Beaumont?" I called out with a soft voice.

I hadn't turned on any lights, so the rest of the hall was dark. The door up ahead was open. That was the room I was afraid of. Mr. Beaumont had been in there just before meeting me with an ice-cold handshake—I was sure of it. The cold room where they prepared the bodies was filled with hard tile, glimmering silver tools, medical devices, large sinks, and a freezer for the corpses. Like everything else in the basement, the room was dark, but some light from the upstairs leaked down the hall and cracked the blackness.

I edged around the door and peered in. Small bits of light reflected off silver cabinets, revealing a body lying on a thin metal table. The body was clothed. I could see only a pair of men's slacks and dress shoes. The legs crossed each other in an awkward, uncomfortable manner. The man looked tall, but I couldn't see his face or hands. Liquid dripped from the table and splattered into a dark pool beneath the foot of the table. The body was leaking blood!

Slam! The door shut fast, nearly clipping my fingers off, and the sound startled me into a nervous disaster. His hand against the door, Lester looked down at me in disdain. I hadn't heard him come down the stairs.

"What're you doing here?" he asked. When I stumbled over an attempt to answer, he persisted, "I asked you, what are you doing?"

"Just-just came to work. Mr. Beaumont wanted me to—"

"Mr. Beaumont's not here. You're not needed today. I got a service to prepare for, so you need to leave."

Who was I to argue or ask questions? Terrified, I just nodded and walked away, still shaking. When my heart settled down, I realized how suspicious Lester had been to run down the stairs and shut the door on me. What did he have to hide? Who was on the table? Was it Mr. Beaumont? *That's absurd... isn't it?*

I stumbled outside, and a few drops of rain hit my face. My mind swam. I was in shock.

Mrs. Beaumont's car was still in the back parking lot. The engine wasn't running, but she sat in the driver's seat, sobbing. She was in shock too, confused and uncertain where to turn. Butterflies swirled in my stomach. *What if the body downstairs was Mr. Beaumont? What if he's hurt and needs help? What should I do?*

I felt the need to approach Mrs. Beaumont, but I was frozen. Then she turned and locked eyes with me. They were filled with such despair, I knew I had to.

She rolled her window down as I walked toward her.

"Ret McCoy?"

"Yes." I nodded.

A small smile cracked her frown. "Gerald told me he hired you. Did you come to work?"

"Yes." I nodded again. "I guess they don't need me today."

"Oh." Her eyes filled with immense concern and fear. "Have you seen my husband?"

"No, I haven't, ma'am. Not since yesterday."

Her eyes dropped to the ground. "This is not like him. It just isn't."

"Have you told Sheriff Packard?" I asked.

"No." A small amount of hope returned to her demeanor. "Do you think I should? I probably should, shouldn't I?"

"Yes. He can help. Ask him to check here first. He can look in the basement. Make sure he's not somewhere we haven't checked."

I wanted Packard there right away. I wanted him to check on the body in the basement.

"Yes, you're right. I'm sure Mr. Kilborn hasn't looked everywhere. You know Gerald. He's always so quiet, tinkering with things. He gets on a project and forgets the time."

"I'm sure of it, Mrs. Beaumont. Maybe he's in the furnace room or something."

"Yes, the furnace room..." More hope bloomed in her eyes, and I hoped it wasn't a setup for more pain. If it was Mr. Beaumont on that table in the basement, he was probably already dead.

"Do you want me to go with you?" I offered.

"No, thank you, sweetie. You've been a big help." She smiled and started her car.

"Okay. Goodbye then." I walked to my bike and watched her drive out of the parking lot.

The sheriff's office was a little farther down the road. I rode slowly and stopped at its entrance. Through the window, I saw Mrs. Beaumont talking to Sheriff Packard, hands motioning again. Packard stood, put his coat on, and marched to the door.

Yes! I thought, certain he was going to inspect the mortuary.

I didn't want to leave the area, so I drove down a side street and back up, hoping I wouldn't seem nosey. That was where I saw the black hearse. Lester was driving down Redwood Road in the hearse at a good rate of speed.

"In a hurry?" I said under my breath.

About fifty feet down the street, I hid behind a large cottonwood tree that shadowed Redwood Road. I peered around the trunk and watched the sheriff's car leave the parking lot, followed by Mrs. Beaumont, and head to the mortuary. I followed but hung back, keeping a slow pace.

When I got to the mortuary, Packard was pulling on the front doors, which were locked. Mrs. Beaumont stood behind him, shaking her head in confusion.

I parked my bike and approached them. "Do you need to get in? I have a key."

Relief blossomed on both of their faces. I quickly opened the doors, feeling like a hero, and Packard trotted in. I wanted to tell him to check the basement first, but I didn't have to.

"Sheriff, can you check the basement first?" Mrs. Beaumont said, giving me a thankful smile. "I really think he's down there. In the furnace room, maybe."

Packard nodded and descended the back stairs.

Mrs. Beaumont reached down and grasped my hand for strength. I wanted to cry for her. Together, we walked down the stairs. My heart leapt into my throat. *The body! He'll find the body! What if it is Mr. Beaumont?*

When Mrs. Beaumont and I got to the bottom of the stairs, Packward exited the room where the body had been. I tensed, awaiting his word.

He looked at us. "Nobody in there. Furnace room, did you say?"

Mrs. Beaumont nodded.

What? Is the body not in there anymore? I couldn't believe it. I let go of Mr. Beaumont's hand and jogged to the doorway of the cold room. I peered inside. The light was on.

It was empty. No body on the table, floor, or anywhere I could see, and the puddle of blood was gone too... as if it had never been there. I turned to the freezer door, which was shut.

Packard came around the corner. "No one back there, either," he said.

"How about in there?" I motioned to the freezer door. I wasn't going to open it. I would let him.

Absent of the same fear I had, he opened the door and stepped in. A moment later, he exited with the same shake of the head. "Nothing in there."

"Lester said he was preparing for a service today," I said.

"Well, if he is, there's not a body anywhere that I can see."

Lester. He'd driven past me in the hearse like a bat out of hell. *Did he take the body with him and clean up the blood?*

"I saw Lester leave," I said. "He drove the hearse down Redwood."

"North or south?"

"North, going really fast," I said.

"Okay, we'll take it from here." He turned back to Mrs. Beaumont. "You'll want to go back to my office. Have Deputy James fill out a report for you. Meanwhile, I'll keep looking, and I'll check up on Lester. I won't leave any stone unturned. I promise." He reassured us with a confident nod. I believed him. I knew he was good to his word.

With nothing left for us to do, Mrs. Beaumont and I left. I rode my bike home. So many thoughts bolted in and out of my head, I was surprised I'd paid enough attention to make it home in one piece.

I was scared for both Mr. and Mrs. Beaumont. He was such a good man, and I didn't want to see any harm come to him. But my gut told me something already had. Beaumont was in peril of the worst kind. I wandered around the rest of the day, trying to keep myself occupied with TV or a book, but I couldn't keep myself still, especially my mind.

Just before bed, tears came to my eyes, and my jaw trembled. An overwhelming sadness shrouded me, and I knelt next to my bed and prayed for the safety of Mr. Beaumont with all of my heart.

CHAPTER NINE
Strange Happenings

The storm came in that night like the rage of God for what had happened to Mr. Beaumont. Howling winds assaulted Riverton while rain hit the panes of my bedroom window, sounding like pellets against the glass. Deep bellows of thunder filled the air, and flashes of lightning stabbed the earth. It was the start of something chilling and dark. I didn't fear the old ghost lady would come sneak a peek at me through my cracked door. Instead, it would be Lester Kilborn... or something worse.

I didn't get much sleep, but when I woke up, the last drizzle of rain had stopped, and the clouds were moving on. The sun peeked through the last remaining clouds and sent its rays of heat out to warm the earth, and the moisture rose from the ground like spirits from their graves, only to evaporate into the sky.

Around seven thirty in the morning, I dragged my bones to the kitchen. I rarely woke up that early during the summer, and normally, I woke up starving. But I didn't feel like eating anything that morning. Instead, I washed the cobwebs and dust from my throat with a glass of orange juice.

Something told me to step outside—into the backyard, to be precise. And there would be only one reason to go out there. I grabbed my brother's binoculars and stepped onto our steaming porch.

The hearse was there, as I'd expected, and two men were standing next to it, both wearing dark clothes. One was taller than the other, and the shorter man was wider. The second man was definitely Lester.

The tall man was older and stood with an erect stature, his shoulders straight, chest out, and chin up. His walk was precise as if a decision preceded every step, and he gave Lester a condescending look.

All of those mannerisms were in direct contradiction to Mr. Beaumont. He was tall, but because of his age and health, he hunched over slightly. He never stood his full height, and his walk had a hobble to it, as if the bones in his legs were constantly in immense pain.

The man couldn't have been Gerald Beaumont... but it was. I couldn't make out distinct details with the binoculars, but I could discern enough to identify my employer, and friend, Mr. Beaumont.

I wanted to scream with excitement and relief. He was alive after all! But I couldn't. Something was wrong with Mr. Beaumont. He was not himself.

Beaumont and Lester entered the hearse and drove away.

I questioned whether I should go into work or not, but quickly realized I must. My last conversation with Mr. Beaumont was a promise to come in the next day to work. Plus, I needed more physical reassurance that he was indeed alive. I threw some clothes on, jumped on my bike, and rode to work.

When I stepped in through the back door and marched up the hall, I heard Beaumont speaking to Lester. The tone of his voice was lower than usual and monotone. The underlying resonance in his voice chilled my bones.

"Mr. Beaumont!" I exclaimed and approached with a smile.

Lester stood next to him, scowling. Moving only his head, as if it were somehow detached from his body, he turned to look down at me. Not even the skin around his face moved to form a smile. He was a statue, cold and refined.

"It's so good to see you! You're okay?"

Saying nothing, he looked right through me.

"We were worried about you."

He scowled. "We?"

"Yeah, myself, Mrs. Beaumont, Sheriff Packard… even Lester, I think."

"What are you doing here, boy? Did someone die?"

"Die?" I was taken aback.

"Yes. Die. This is a mortuary, and most people come here because someone has died. I assume you're here on business matters."

"No. No one has died. I don't think."

"Then scoot along. We're very busy here and don't have time for silly games."

I was still trying to wrap my brain around what he'd said to me. *Does he even remember who I am?* Both of them stared at me, unmoving. My mouth was open, and one eyebrow was raised in question. "What about my job?"

"What job?"

"You're not needed anymore," Lester jumped in. He turned to Beaumont. "Mr. Beaumont, you gave him a job. To clean things for an hour or two."

"I did?" He turned back to me. "Are they clean?"

"Well… yes, but you needed other things…"

"What other things?"

"You said you had a lot of services this week and needed some deep cleaning."

He stared at me again in silence, and I stared back.

The eyes were the windows to the soul, or so people always said. When I looked into Mr. Beaumont's eyes, though, there was no soul. I saw a cold, hollowed-out shell. I was looking into the eyes of a stranger, not Mr. Beaumont. He had changed.

"Fine. You can finish your deep cleaning. When you're done, no more."

"Okay." I nodded.

I couldn't believe I was brave enough to fight for my job. The funeral home was suddenly a place I wanted to be far away from, but I had to stay. I had a responsibility to both Mr. and Mrs. Beaumont to stay, and maybe I could find out what really happened.

When I was nearly finished with my chores, I witnessed the saddest thing in my life, and it frightened me. Mrs. Beaumont entered through the front doors. By the look on her face, she still believed her husband was gone. She didn't know he'd been found.

Mr. Beaumont was in his office at the time, so she didn't see him. Lester stepped out and greeted her.

"Mr. Kilborn"—her voice cracked with despair—"please tell me you've seen my husband. Forgive me for bothering you, but I just don't know where else to go. My daughter lives out of state, and she'll arrive later today, but until then, I just... I just..."

Mr. Beaumont stepped into the foyer, straightening his suit jacket. Nose high in the air, he stopped fifteen feet from her.

"Gerald? My goodness, *Gerald*!" Excitement and shock beamed from her face, and even though every ounce of energy was depleted in her body, she quick stepped toward him, arms outstretched.

He backed away and held up his hands. In a cold voice, he said, "Excuse me."

She froze, clearly confused.

"I'm working right now. Very busy. You know I don't like to be bothered at work."

Words caught in her throat, and mouth gaping, she furrowed her brow as she stared at him. I too was surprised that Mr. Beaumont would be so dismissive with his wife.

"Where have you been, Gerry? You haven't been home in two nights. You didn't call. No one knew where you were..."

"I don't need to explain myself. You know how busy I am. Three services this week. The bodies rolled in last night. I've got a lot of work to do."

Mrs. Beaumont was crushed, and her body sank as if she'd deflated.

"*Gerry,*" she pleaded, attempting once more to approach with a hug, but he stepped back, with palms out, again.

Tears ran down her cheeks. *How could someone be so cold? This is not Mr. Beaumont.*

They exchanged a few more words, but Gerald cut her off cold at each turn then told her she had to leave. She asked him when he would be home for dinner.

"It'll be too late, so don't bother with dinner."

Mrs. Beaumont blinked, as if she'd been physically smacked. She was so confused that she almost went through the chapel doors to leave before she stopped and changed direction to exit through the front doors.

Beaumont caught me in the hall, holding a broom and doing nothing. He scowled. "I'm not paying you hourly, am I?"

"Sorry" was all I said. I turned and continued my work.

Once Mr. Beaumont and Lester were back in their offices, I stepped out into the parking lot. Like déjà vu, Mrs. Beaumont was sitting in her car, hunched over and sobbing.

I walked over and tapped on her window. She turned, red-faced, and mascara ran with her tears. Her eyes widened at the sight of me.

She rolled down her window. "Ret, how are you, my dear?"

I shrugged. "Not good. I'm sorry about..."

Sounding embarrassed, she said, "Did you see that in there? You shouldn't have to see such things. I'm sorry."

"Mrs. Beaumont? Can I ask you a strange question?"

"What could be stranger than what's just happened?"

"Well..." I didn't quite know how to say it. "Is that really Mr. Beaumont in there?"

She paused. "It appears so. He's never acted like this before. We've had our spats over the years, but nothing like this. I just don't understand." She said it not so much to me as to herself. For a moment, she stared silently off into nothing as the wheels turned in her head. Finally, she said, "I just want to know what happened. Is that too much to ask?"

"No, Mrs. Beaumont. Not at all."

We said our goodbyes and good luck to each other, and she drove away. I went back to my work inside a building electrified with tension, quietly kept to myself, and did my work.

I was nearly done mopping the women's restroom when I heard Sheriff Packard's voice, followed by muffled discussion, from the other room. I cracked open the door to listen.

"Gerald Beaumont?" Packard's voice boomed.

"Yes, Officer?"

"Officer? Since when did you stop calling me Orrin?" He chuckled.

"It's been a busy day. Is there something I can help you with?"

"Yes. You've been missing."

"You must be mistaken. I've always known where I was at."

"Your wife was frantic yesterday. You didn't come home at night, and you disappeared from work."

"Is that a crime?"

"You wasted a lot of city man-hours. Deputy James and I searched round the clock. Not to mention all your neighbors and friends who helped."

"I chose not to go home that night. I despise my wife, Mr. Packard. I always have. Fifty-five years with that hag, and I'd had enough. I don't live my life by when I should be home for dinner," he snapped.

I couldn't see Sheriff Packard from inside the bathroom, but in the moment of silence, I imagined his face in horrific shock.

"I did not intend for anyone to come looking for me," Mr. Beaumont continued, his voice smug and patronizing. "I can look after myself well enough. If I go missing again, I'll be the first to let you know."

"Where did you go?" Packard demanded.

"That is my own business."

"Were you hurt? In an accident? Did you fall down and lose consciousness?"

"It is really none of your concern. Now I must go. I have several services to prepare. Ironically, the dead do not wait."

"You've been unaccounted for nearly forty-eight hours. Let's at least have you come down to the hospital and have you checked out."

"Is that mandatory?"

Packard sighed. "No."

"I assure you I'm quite fine."

"No, you're not," Packard snapped. "This isn't you, Gerald. The Gerald I know wouldn't say such things, especially about his wife. Just last week, you told me how much you adore her." I could hear Packard's anger escalating.

"This is the real me. You may not have seen me before. I was living a life I wasn't happy with. I have finally awakened, Mr. Packard. This man you see before you *is* the real me. Like it or not.

"My only wish is that one day you too will open your eyes and look at your wife for who *she* really is, and who your *children* really are, and ask that dreadful question. 'Am I happy?' Because if you're honest with yourself, and let your secrets out, maybe you can finally live the life you deserve."

"You son of a bitch! Say one more thing about my wife or children again, and you *will* be missing."

"Is that a threat?" Beaumont chuckled.

"It's a promise."

"Mr. Kilborn? I take it you're witness to Sheriff Packard's threat?"

"I am," Lester answered.

There was silence again.

"Careful, Gerald. Make sure you treat your wife well. I don't want to see this happen again. I will have my eyes on you."

I heard the front door open and shut, then there was silence.

"Mr. Kilborn, is this going to continue happening?"

"No. I'm sure it won't. We'll be more careful."

I heard them shuffle back into their offices.

My body shook with fear and rage. I couldn't imagine how Packard felt.

I finished mopping, did a fast, sloppy job of putting everything away, and left. I didn't even ask Mr. Beaumont for my pay or say goodbye. I was too scared.

CHAPTER TEN
Fireworks

Over the next couple of days, I saw Mr. Beaumont around town several times, but never without Lester. They were like best friends, attached at the hip, never one without the other, and they spent quite a bit of time at Lester's haunted home.

Gary and Jax were still not back from their vacations. Matt was back to hanging out with his cohort, Wes. My brothers did their own things. The new girl roamed the neighborhood with Morgan, but I still hadn't worked up enough nerve to approach her. So I was left with myself and a nagging urge to find out more about the "new" Gerald Beaumont and Lester.

I rode my bike around the vicinity of the crooked dwelling and hid behind a nearby tree to look through the windows with my brother's binoculars. I never saw anything. No movement in the main level or upper floor. My conclusion was that they were in the basement—a horrible place I never wanted to venture into.

What could they be doing? Drumming up ghosts and having a tea party? They were so strange and creepy that the ghosts were probably too afraid to appear.

When Sunday came, Mrs. Beaumont was not at church, but her husband was. My family sat in the back of the chapel, and Mr. Beaumont was five pews from the front. He sat a head taller than everyone else, and throughout the whole meeting, he turned his head left and right, sweeping across the congregation. Occasionally, he would twist and scope the people behind him. He stared at people, then he would scribble notes on a pad.

As the meeting broke and everyone moved to their next class, I overheard several people asking Mr. Beaumont where his lovely wife was.

"Where's your better half?" they would ask.

"She's ill. Some sort of flu," he answered each time.

Mrs. Crawford scrunched her face in confusion. "She was supposed to speak in Primary today. Do you know if she got a replacement? She hasn't answered her phone."

The question seemed to catch him off guard. He paused, as if searching for words, and ended up using the same excuse. "She's sick."

He walked past Mrs. Crawford, leaving her standing there looking perplexed. I knew what Mrs. Crawford was thinking—the same thing I did. *This is not like Mrs. Beaumont.*

No one could remember the last time she'd missed a service, and she was not one to leave a commitment without finding a substitute.

THE NEXT DAY WAS GREAT. Gary and Jax were both back, and I was busting to spill my guts about everything that happened while they were away. As horrifying as it was, the mystery of it all was tantalizing. I expected them to feel the same way.

When I told them the story, even as my words came out of my mouth, they fell flat. The concern didn't register in their eyes the same way it had for me.

"So, you don't think Mr. Beaumont is Mr. Beaumont anymore?" Gary said with sarcastic disbelief. "Who is he then?"

"I don't know," I said.

"Maybe he's an alien." Oddly enough, I had missed Jax's nasally voice. "Like *Invasion of the Body Snatchers*."

"Really, guys? Come on. There's definitely something strange here. What about Mr. Beaumont spending all his time with Lester?"

"Yeah, but don't they work together?"

"Yes, but Lester is weird, and he lives in a haunted house. They spend all their time in the basement. And what happened to Mr. Beaumont's wife?"

"You said she was sick," Gary pointed out.

"No, I said *he* said she was sick. I don't think it's true. I'm afraid something bad has happened. And Beaumont is not the same person he was. Not by a long shot."

There was silence for a moment, but I felt like I still had to prove something to them.

"And what about Sheriff Packard? You should have heard the things Mr. Beaumont said to him."

"It's not like we don't believe you," Gary said. "But what are we supposed to do?"

"I don't know." I shook my head in surrender.

"I do." Jax's voice held excitement. "My mom gave me some money to buy fireworks. There's a Black Cat stand across from Pederson's."

Jax was right. That was exactly what I needed—a pleasant distraction. And I loved fireworks. Black Cat stands popped up a week before the Fourth of July every year, eliciting my excitement. I would stare at the array of products displayed on the shelves, wishing I had the money to buy it all.

When we got there, the Black Cat stand was crowded with kids. The skinny teenager behind the counter leaned over the countertop with as much enthusiasm as a dead snail. With his long hair hanging over his eyes, he asked me what I wanted.

I had some money from the mortuary job and bought snaps, sparklers, and black snakes. Gary and Jax had enough to buy a few boxes of snaps too. Nobody could walk away from a stand without buying those. We threw them at each other's feet all the way home, making each other jump at each pop.

ON JULY THE FOURTH, the skies were clear, and the temperature was forecasted to be into the high nineties. My parents complained about the temperature all day long. They nit-picked at each other from the start, until we got to the park, but that was normal, so it didn't discourage us from having a good time.

Jax and Gary were at Riverton Park with their families too. Almost everybody in Riverton was there, and the people who weren't were in their front yards, partying, barbecuing, drinking, and lighting fireworks. The Fourth of July was the one time of the year that I felt like the entire country celebrated together.

The best part of the park was the carnival. Each year, the city brought a full-blown carnival to the park with rides like the Zipper, Tilt-A-Whirl, and the Octopus. Those rides were always too expensive. That didn't matter, though, because I didn't care about riding the rides. I enjoyed the gears cranking, the smell of hot oil and gas, and the sounds of rides swooshing and brakes screeching. When the sun went down, their neon lights lit up the sky like it was Christmas.

It was fun to walk the carnival and listen to the hawkers calling out for people to play their games and check out the cool prizes. I played a couple of them but never won.

It was dusk, and I sipped on my third Ramblin' Root Beer for the day. My friends and I sauntered past the giant stone fireplace that had been there since the Mormon pioneers discovered Utah, and I saw Sheriff Packard sitting alone on top of a picnic table, finishing off food from a paper plate.

I didn't see his family with him, and I wondered where they were. His eyes wandered the crowd as he ate the last spoonful of baked beans. He looked like a kid sitting alone at lunch, looking around for a friend to sit by.

"Hey, guys, you go on. I'll catch up later," I said.

"No problem. I gotta run back to my family. We're supposed to be eating now," Gary said.

"Fine," Jax whined as he looked at his bag of fireworks. "I guess we can light these later."

I walked over to the pavilion Packard was sitting in, and he looked up at me.

"Well, the trouble starts now, doesn't it?" He smirked, and I smiled.

"Don't worry. I'm laying low. I've given up my life of crime."

"No more gang life, huh?"

"It's a dead-end road. Nothing but trouble and prison down that path."

"Sounds like you got it all figured out, kid." Packard stood up, threw away his empty plate, and adjusted his utility belt. "What can I help you with, Ret?"

"Mr. Beaumont."

"Mr. Beaumont? What's he done now?"

"Don't you think he's acting different?"

"Different how?"

"Just really strange. It's not him anymore. It's like he's someone else."

"Well, Ret, people change. Sometimes for the better, and sometimes for the worse."

"No." I shook my head. "Not overnight. He was the nicest man around, and now he's just plain mean. Something else is going on."

"I don't know where you're going with this." He looked at me quizzically.

"His wife is missing. I think he killed her." I couldn't believe the words that fell out of my mouth.

Packard's face went white, and his eyebrows rose. "What do you mean?" he asked skeptically.

"I mean she's nowhere to be seen. She's not coming to church, no one can get a hold of her, and she's not showing up when she's supposed to..."

"Hold on here." Packard let out a tense sigh. "Listen, son, he's gone strange—I'll give you that, but you're a mile away in a foot race from someone committing murder. I can't believe you'd even say that. Just because she's not been around, and Gerald suddenly has a stick up his a—I mean, he's ornery, but that doesn't mean he killed anybody, and certainly not his wife."

"You need to arrest him. Take him into custody and question him. Ask him where she's at. He'll probably still say she's sick."

"Well, she is at an age where she's going to get sick a lot. It's not uncommon. She could be in poor health, and I can't just run Beaumont in on no charges. There is no evidence. Hell, there's not even speculation!"

"Can't you go check in on her? See if she's okay?"

"I have absolutely no reason to. I haven't seen *your* mom in weeks. It doesn't mean I should run over to your house to see if she's okay. I have duties to perform. I can't run around and check in on everybody because they stopped going to church!"

I was exasperated, and he sensed my frustrations.

"I know how you feel." His voice became calmer. "It was pretty intense what you went through with the Beaumonts at the funeral home, and I appreciate your help. But everything's worked out now. Mr. Beaumont is found, and even though he's a bit weird, he's done nothing wrong, and Lester's done nothing wrong from what I can tell. You're letting paranoia get the best of you, and you're too good for that, Ret. You should be out enjoying your summer. Not worrying about these old folks."

"It's just… I just feel like something's wrong, and I can't get it out of my mind."

"How's everything at home?" he asked.

I started to feel defensive. My parents *did* fight a lot, but that didn't mean anything. Did he think I was acting out because things weren't good at home?

"Fine," I said aggressively.

"Okay." He nodded and looked around at the crowd. "I've got to make my rounds."

"How's everything at *your* home?" I asked back, and he stopped in his footsteps.

Without turning back to me, he stared at the ground.

"How are your wife and kids?"

"Fine," he said and walked away.

I walked back to our piece of turf amid the quilt of hundreds of other families who'd set down blankets and chairs for the fireworks show.

I felt deflated. I thought my night was going downhill until I saw my mom on a blanket, talking to another lady with her blanket camp next to ours. She looked familiar, and when I saw her daughter, I realized why. It was the new girl.

"Hey, honey." My mom turned to me as I approached. "Ret, I want you to meet our new neighbors. They live by the Andersons. This is Meg Williams and her daughter, Dawn. She's your age."

"Hi." Mrs. Williams shook my hand with a giant smile. "My husband, Jim, is around here somewhere with our two boys. They're five and seven."

I didn't care about the boys. I was only interested in her daughter. Dawn Williams, like the western singer Don Williams, but spelled differently, I hoped.

I kept my cool as I walked over to her. "Hi."

She looked up with a smile and a spry "Hello."

She was prettier up close. Her long strawberry-blond hair was pulled back in a ponytail, and she wore a peach-colored shirt, shorts, and open-toed sandals. She sat Indian style on the blanket close to the end and next to ours. I sat on the only spot open on our blanket, which was next to her.

She was reading a Ray Bradbury book, *Something Wicked This Way Comes*, and put it down to talk to me. "I've seen you around. With your friends?"

"Yes, Jax and Gary."

"Yeah, you guys like to ride your bikes a lot."

"My bike is my life. Without it, I'm a cowboy without a horse."

Her laughter excited me.

"You like Ray Bradbury?" I asked, motioning to her book.

"I love Ray Bradbury," she said with passion. "I read all his stuff."

"Me too," I lied. "His stuff is the best. Well, I guess I haven't read everything. I've read *Fahrenheit 451,* which was so good, and some short stories. I'm dying to read that one. It looks scary."

She nodded. "It's a bit creepy. Do you like scary things?"

I thought of the ghost in the Crooked House, Beaumont and Lester, the funeral home and the dead body, and tingles shot up my spine.

"Only in fiction." My joke came without missing a beat, and she laughed. "Scary things in real life... not so much."

"I admit I haven't read all of his stuff, either. He's got a lot, but I've probably read most of it. So, you like to read too?"

"Yes, I love to. I read mostly Louis L'Amour books. My grandpa has a stack of them, and I pick one up every time I visit. I like to write too. I wrote my first story a month ago."

It was true. The writing bug had bitten me at school back in April, when a teacher spotlighted my work to the whole class. I didn't have any friends in that class until she read my story out loud, then everyone wanted to work on the next project with me, and it made me feel special.

Her eyes lit up when I told her. "Really? What did you write?"

"A western, of course. It's about a showdown in the middle of Main Street at high noon. They have to walk ten steps away from each other and shoot. It's called 'The Ten Steps to Death.'"

Talking about my writing to anyone embarrassed me. I didn't know how it would be received, but Dawn seemed intrigued.

"Can I read it? You've got to let me read it. Is it finished?"

"Yeah, it's finished. You really want to read it?"

"Yes, of course I do."

"Okay. Yeah." I nodded. "I'll get it to you." My ego stroked, I felt proud.

We clicked together like the sprockets on the Zipper ride.

Boom!

It startled us both, and we looked up to see the first firework. Darkness had fallen, and I didn't realize how fast the time went.

More fireworks spread across the night sky in a colorful array, and the audience marveled over the display.

Dawn and I sat together for the rest of the show and commented on each firework.

"Oh, those are my favorite."

"Mine too," and so on.

WHEN WE GOT HOME, PUTTING things away was another chore, but it wasn't nearly as hectic as packing to leave had been. When we were done, I sank into the sofa in our front room and daydreamed of Dawn. Enough light came in from the kitchen to keep me from being blind in the dark.

My mom walked in and sat next to me. As if reading my thoughts, she said, "It looked like you got along with Dawn."

"Yes." I nodded. "She's real cool."

"You two talked the whole night. I think she's cute." Mom smiled.

Shyly, I said, "I think she is too."

"That's good you two are friends now. Her mom said she needs some new ones. The move has been rough on her."

Rough on her? I didn't know what that meant, and I hoped she was okay.

"Mom?" I didn't really quite know what to ask—or how—but I needed to. "I really like her."

My mom's eyes lit up with excitement.

"I kinda would like her to be my girlfriend."

"You do? That's great, honey."

"Well... I just don't know how to ask her. Or is that stupid?"

"No, not at all. You could always do what we did when I was your age."

"What's that?"

"Write her a letter. You're good at writing. You can ask her to be your girlfriend in the letter."

It was true. I *was* more comfortable with writing. "She also wants to read my story. I mean, she really wants to. That's how I know she's cool."

"She's going to love your story."

"You think so?"

"Who wouldn't? Now let's write that letter. I'll get a paper and pen."

The excitement in her eyes made her look like a schoolgirl again, asking boys for kisses and playing the flirting games.

CHAPTER ELEVEN
Rosco

A new family, the Tibbits, moved into Fernando's old house. I didn't know much about them, only that my mom had taken welcome-to-the-neighborhood cookies to their house. She said they were from Texas and had a daughter and two boys, one who was about a year older than me.

We were hanging out in front of my house under the shade of a tree when a tall, stocky boy ambled toward us. He had a confident, sly stride and a gleam in his eyes. His thick hair sat on his head like animal fur that had been combed to the side with a wire brush, and his giant smile slanted slightly to the right.

"Well, ain't you guys a sight for trouble with those shit-eatin' grins a' yers." He was Southern, and his accent was thick.

To say he took us by surprise would have been an understatement. I'd never witnessed anyone introduce himself to new kids like that, especially using a cuss word. That was when I understood he didn't care what anyone thought of him. He was who he was, like it or not, and no one was going to change him. I didn't know what to say, so I didn't say anything.

"Rosco Tibbits." He held out his hand, and we took turns shaking it. "Just moved in down the street."

"Hi, Rosco. I'm Ret, and this is Jax and Gary."

"Where are you from?" Jax asked.

"Texarkana. On the border of Texas and Arkansas. You ever been down that way?"

"No," I said, and Jax and Gary shook their heads.

"The best things come outta Texas. Like me." He laughed heartily at himself, and we laughed with him.

He snorted as if he had something in his nose to get out, then he turned and blew a glob of snot onto the sidewalk. He pinched the remaining strand from the end of his nose, flung it down, and wiped his fingers on his pants.

"I have some Kleenex in the house," I offered.

"No need. I got it."

Jax and Gary shared a disgusted look with me. He was gross, but I liked his confidence. I was drawn to him.

"What're y'all doin'? Mind if I hang out with ya?"

We all nodded.

"Great!" His grin spread and took up half his face. "What's there to do around here?"

"Well... we got a creek behind our house. We can catch water snakes. Or... do you have a bike?"

"Yeah, I got a bike." With his accent, it sounded like "back."

"We gotta show you the Moguls."

We followed him to his house, and it was strange to see someone else living in Fernando's home. I remembered his face in the crack of the open door and how withdrawn he seemed, and I felt sad.

Rosco opened his garage door and pulled his bike out from behind a stack of boxes and furniture I assumed were waiting to be unpacked and placed from their move. He pulled the door down and let it crash to the ground. Like mine, he had no electric garage opener.

"Let's go!" he called, and we rode to the Moguls. We rode up top to the biggest hill, the one we'd performed our terrible show on, and looked out across the long line of dirt hills and trails worn into the ground from long hours of riding.

"Bitchin'," he exclaimed.

"We do a lot of our bike shows on this mogul." Jax puffed his chest out to impress him.

"I don't know if I'd call them 'bike shows,'" Gary said in a low tone of honesty.

"You got people to come see yer shows?"

"We've had some neighborhood kids pay to see it," Jax said, and I wanted to roll my eyes and shake my head in embarrassment.

Rosco eyed the area slowly. Something was cooking in his head. "You guys do anythin' else out here?"

"Like what?" I asked.

"Like build a fort. That hill over there'd be perfect."

"What kind of fort?" Gary asked.

"A cave." A grin slid across Rosco's face. Then he bolted down the hill on his bike, jumped in the air off the second, smaller hill, lifted both hands into the air, and gripped the handlebars again in time to land.

"Whoo!" he called out and raced to the mogul he'd spotted.

"He'd be good in our show!" Jax said.

We tore off after him, each one of us taking the jump with more confidence than before, and rode up alongside Rosco, who was off his bike and scoping out the mogul for cave building.

"This'll be perfect! We can dig into the side here, and it'll be the entrance."

"It doesn't look like it will be tall enough," Gary said.

"That's why we gotta dig." Rosco turned to him, crazy excitement in his eyes. "We'll dig deep. I've built 'em before. It's like buildin' a mineshaft. We'll have to use support beams for the roof."

"Support beams?" I asked.

"Yeah. We'll get some two-by-fours and stick 'em in there to keep the roof from collapsing. Anybody got wood?"

"I do have a pile at my house," I said, thinking of the Millennium Falcon Jax and I had attempted to build.

We each went back to our houses to get tools. We all came back with shovels, except for Rosco. He brought a pick axe.

He stood in front of the hill, raised the pick axe high in the air, and drove it into the heart of the compacted dirt. He looked like a crazed hillbilly-murdering miner from *Nightmare Theater*.

We spent the rest of the day digging out our cave. I didn't know what to think at first. I wasn't much into it. But the farther we got, the more my excitement for the project grew. We got a lot of dirt out of that hill, enough that we could crawl into our small cave and start to picture the finished product.

"We gotta dig deeper," Rosco said. "So we can sit up in here."

The sun was going down on us, and I knew my parents would be anxious for me to return home, and the same went for my friends. We ended the day with a sense of accomplishment, excited for the next phase.

Arms shaky with exhaustion, I was hot and covered in sweat and dirt. As I lifted my bike to mount it, Morgan Anderson marched toward us. Her face was twisted in dismay and tight with fear, her eyes red and wet. Her body shook like a wet leaf, much more than my arms did.

"Hey, Morg," I called out.

"Have you guys seen my sister?" Her voice shook as badly as her body.

"Joanna?" Gary asked.

Joanna was much older. She was twenty and had moved out months prior to go to college, but word on the street was that college hadn't gone well and she'd moved back home.

"We haven't seen her," I said.

Tears that had been hanging on finally rolled down her cheeks and made me feel terrible for her. "She's been missing all day."

"Maybe she went somewhere and didn't tell anyone," Gary said.

She shook her head. "No. Her car is still at home. So is her wallet, and she doesn't go anywhere without those."

"Have you called the police?" I asked.

She nodded. "My mom did. They're at our house now. We're doing a search for her. Can you guys keep an eye out? Let me know if you hear or see anything."

"We will," I assured her.

She turned and walked away.

We were silent, but a thought kept racing through my mind: Lester and *that* house. *Could it be a coincidence that Mr. Beaumont went missing just a week ago? And Mrs. Beaumont...*

When I got home, all we talked about at dinner was Joanna. My dad wasn't home yet, but we held a family prayer without him and asked for Joanna's safe return.

My dad walked in on my way to bed, and I felt the tension heighten in the room as my mom's face hardened. She glared at him.

"Hello," he said sheepishly.

"Where've you been? I thought you were off at eight."

"I was at work. Randy called in sick, and we had a big order to prepare."

My mom pursed her lips and looked down, and I said goodnight to them both and hurried to my room. I heard their muffled argument through the walls for at least an hour.

I couldn't get any sleep, and not just because my parents were fighting. I couldn't stop thinking about Joanna's disappearance and the terrified look on Morgan's face. I had a sinking feeling that I knew what had happened to her—or at least who had taken her. Getting anyone to believe it would be impossible, though.

CHAPTER TWELVE
The Discovery

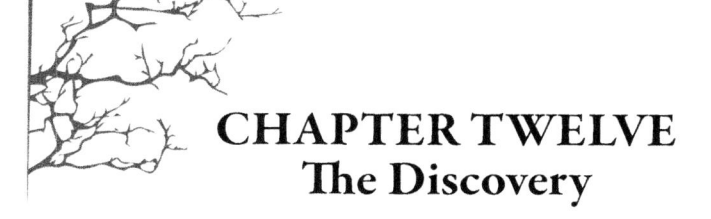

The sun was out and bright the next day, but I saw only gloom and darkness. An ominous feeling overwhelmed my soul, and I pictured myself as a cartoon with a black cloud over my head.

I didn't even step outside until eleven o'clock. Scott told me my friends had stopped by and asked for me while I was still in bed. It'd been a rough night. Between my parents fighting and my suspicions surrounding Lester Kilborn and Mr. Beaumont, so many thoughts had been shooting through my mind that I couldn't focus on anything, especially sleep.

I opened our garage door, dragged my bike out, and pulled myself up on it. I squinted from the bright sun, trying to acclimate to the day, then, absent of energy, I rode my bike down the driveway and into the street.

I headed for the Moguls, knowing my friends would be there working on our cave fort. I stopped at the fork in the road. Straight ahead were the Moguls. I saw my friends' bikes parked at the foot of the hills, but a house hid my view of the cave.

To my left, the road led to the Andersons' home and Dawn Williams's house. She hadn't left my mind, either. I saw activity in front of the Andersons' house, and I couldn't ignore it. I rode my bike toward their home and stopped about twenty feet short of it.

"I'm leaving!" Joanna, Morgan's sister, yelled as she stomped to the red Dodge Dart parked in the driveway. Her hair was a raggedy mess, and her clothes were wrinkled. It was Joanna, Morgan's missing sister.

"Joanna!" Her mother scrambled out the front door, face twisted with frustration, guilt, and grief. "I just want to talk to you for a minute."

Joanna snapped around, bloodshot eyes blazing with hatred and anger, lips tightened. "There's nothing to talk about!"

I couldn't describe her voice as anything other than pure evil. It was dark and deep, and it didn't sound right. Chills ran like ants up my arms. Morgan crept out the front door, watching in shock. She crumpled to her knees on the porch and sobbed.

"There's a lot to talk about, young lady!" Mrs. Anderson sounded stern. "Everyone spent the entire day and night searching for you, including the entire police force! We deserve an explanation!"

"The hell you do!"

Joanna opened her car door, and her mother grabbed the top edge of it to keep it from shutting. Standing in front of her daughter, Mrs. Anderson made it clear she wouldn't tolerate Joanna's behavior anymore.

"What has gotten into you? Did someone take you? Are you on drugs?"

Joanna looked dead into her mother's eyes, and I got a good look at her. Her skin was pasty, and dark rings circled her eyes. "Let me make this very clear to you. I am leaving. You will never see me again. In fact, I am no longer your daughter."

Mrs. Anderson might as well have been hit in the chest with a sledgehammer. She opened her mouth as if to speak, but the words caught in her throat.

"Let go of the door," Joanna demanded.

"Joanna... please. I love you."

"Back off." Joanna's words were like ice, and her arms shot out. Joanna pushed her mother so hard that Mrs. Anderson flew off her feet, and her body crashed to the ground with a thud. I couldn't believe what I'd seen.

Morgan ran to her mother's side as Joanna jumped into her car, slammed the door, and sped away with a screech. Mrs. Anderson stayed on the ground but placed a hand on Morgan's shoulder.

I rode my bike fast to their house to help. I ran to Morgan's side, and she lifted her leaky eyes to me, lips trembling.

Absent of better words, I said, "Mrs. Anderson, are you okay?"

"I'm fine." She groaned. "I just need to lay here a minute. Get my wits about me."

My immediate urge was to help her to her feet, so it was strange to sit idly by and stare at her lying on the ground. But just then, Mr. Anderson pulled his car into their driveway. In a flash, he jumped out and ran to her side. I stepped back as Morgan and her dad lifted Mrs. Anderson to her feet.

They thanked me, even though I'd done nothing but eavesdrop. They went back into their house, and through the screen door, I heard Mrs. Anderson say, "She just came home ten minutes ago... Didn't say a word. Went straight to her room..."

Morgan looked at me just before the door closed, her eyes filled with sadness and embarrassment.

Standing alone outside the Andersons' house, I didn't know what to do next. My friends waited for me at the Moguls, but I couldn't go there. Something tugged me in a different direction.

I'd seen in Joanna the same thing I'd seen in Mr. Beaumont the day he'd returned. She was someone or *something* else. Joanna was long gone, and no one knew where she was going. She had made that clear.

I couldn't follow Joanna, but maybe I could follow up on the Beaumonts. Where was Mrs. Beaumont? She was still absent to the world, and her husband continued to rattle off the same story about her illness.

I went home and pulled out our church directory, which listed all the members' names, phone numbers, and addresses. I found the Beaumonts' and headed for their house.

I didn't bother to tell my friends. The voice in the back of my head told me I was a crazy loon, and if my suspicion turned out to be a paranoid delusion, I didn't want to pull anyone into it with me.

I stopped my bike in front of the Beaumonts' home. It looked empty, deserted. No car was parked in the driveway, but that didn't mean there wasn't one in the garage. The lawn was unkempt, and weeds popped through the grass, which hadn't been mowed in weeks.

I walked up the steps and knocked on the front door. No sound or answer came back. I knocked harder then waited patiently. Nothing. I rang the bell, and still nothing. I pushed the doorbell several times rapidly then pounded on the door. Nothing.

I looked around the neighborhood. Not a person was in sight. I tried the door, but it was locked. I walked around to the back sliding-glass door. It was locked.

Silence surrounded me. The sun beat down. The dying lawn crunched under my feet.

I stepped back and looked at the house. *If Mrs. Beaumont was just sick, would she not be at home? If she's too ill to answer the door, shouldn't I still hear movement inside? A TV or radio?* I heard nothing, and my curiosity was not satisfied.

I crept to the back window and peered inside. It seemed to be the window to the master bedroom on the main level. I could see the top half of the room through a crack in the drapes, but not the bottom.

I found an empty milk crate beside the back door, set it on the ground below, and stood on top of it. My eyes barely cleared the lip of the window. The dirty window distorted my view, but I could see the whole room. The only sound was a dull buzzing inside. I saw a long dresser against the far wall, a mirror, and some pictures. A tall bed sat along the other wall. Its legs gave the bed nearly a two-foot clearance from the floor, and the mattress was thick. On top of it was a long gray object.

I thought it was a baseball bat at first. It had the same thickness, but it was longer and ended in a weird shape. As my focus improved, I saw it for what it was—a foot, attached to its leg, but it was *gray*. The toes were curled in like claws, and long purple veins snaked across the legs and ankles.

I followed the leg up the body, and I saw an arm. Hanging down off the side of the bed, it was also gray and veiny. Resting on the shoulder was Mrs. Beaumont's white-topped gray head. I could only see half of her face due to my angle. One eye open, glazed over like glass, stared at nothing. Her mouth hung open, and black dots flew all around her. I suddenly realized the source of the buzzing. Swarms of flies danced around the corpse in the bed.

Forgetting I was on top of a milk crate, I stumbled and fell to the ground. Small rocks and a thistle weed pricked the skin of my arm. I hopped to my feet and bolted to the front of the house. My heart in my throat, I tore out of the neighborhood on my bike, my stomach churning.

Instinctively, I rode to the sheriff's office. Houses and cars were a blur on either side of me as I pumped my legs up and down on those pedals and raced down the sidewalk along Redwood Road.

I stopped and waited for a light to change, and my focus and wits came back as I began to breathe regularly. I cleared the street and passed Pederson's. On my right was the back entrance to Beaumont's Funeral Home.

I glanced as I passed and caught the color of red. I skidded to a stop. A red Dodge Dart sat parked behind the mortuary. Joanna Anderson's red Dodge Dart. I didn't see Joanna, but I saw Mr. Beaumont. Wearing a black suit, he seemed freakishly tall and daunting, arms dangling like weights, and he turned his head to glare at me. His lip crept up into a slight grimace.

"Shit." I cursed at myself for not bringing my friends.

I sped ahead, one more block and across the road to the sheriff's office. I busted into the office like a tornado; the front door had lost its spring and flew all the way around to slam against the wall with a bang. The blinds on the door bounced and crinkled loudly.

Everyone in the office turned, on high alert.

Sweating and panting, I searched the room for Sheriff Packard. He stood in front of his deputy's desk, holding papers and talking. I ran to him.

"What in the Sam Hill?"

"Sheriff!" Without focus, my words tumbled out in no order: "Found Mrs. Beaumont. Dead. Joanna is in with Beaumont—over at mortuary. She's dead in her house—on her bed. Beaumont and Lester are stealing people—"

"Hold on, Ret, you're going to have a heart attack. Sit down. Take a deep breath." He turned to Deputy Gonzales. "Get the boy some water, will ya?"

I sat down in the closest chair, which was behind the desk Packard was standing next to.

He sat on the edge of the desk, folded his hands in his lap, and looked down at me with concern. "You look like you outran a ghost."

My face was cold and dripping with sweat. I couldn't wrap my brain around what I'd just seen. I had never witnessed anything as gruesome as someone's dead body not dressed in their best and lying in a casket for viewing. I thought of her sprawled awkwardly where she'd died, flies about her head, eyes open and gawking, skin gray and purple.

I wiped sweat from my forehead, attempted to get in control of my breathing, and sipped on the plastic cup of water Deputy Gonzales handed me.

"I know you're going to think I'm crazy," I said.

He looked at my hands, which were trembling badly enough to shake water out of the cup.

"I don't think you're crazy," he said with hesitation in his eyes. "Let's go talk in my office, shall we?"

I nodded and followed him in, and he closed the door. He sat across from me behind his desk and leaned forward. "What is this all about, Ret?"

"Well... you know Joanna Anderson was missing?"

"Yes."

"I was riding my bike past their house, and there she was. She'd been found—or returned."

"I just got off the phone with her dad. He told me all about it."

"Did he tell you how different she is? She's not the same. She swore at her mom and pushed her down. Really hard!"

"I know." He nodded.

"She said she wasn't her daughter anymore..." My voice shook. "And then she took off. She's never coming back!"

Anger flushed over me as I saw that none of this information was affecting Packard in the same way it had me. I'd expected some shock, a little surprise.

"Ret, I appreciate your concern. Sometimes people her age find themselves in a different world than they grew up in, or that we live in. They hang out with a different crowd. One that gets them involved in all sorts of trouble, like drugs, violence, stealing, and all manner of destructive behavior."

I scrunched my face in frustration.

"I shouldn't be telling you this because it's a private matter, but I see how much this has affected you. She stole money and other things from her parents before she went missing. Did they tell you that? They also found drugs in her possession. Drugs make people do funny things, act differently."

He went on for several minutes about drugs and how bad they were, saying it was more likely that Joanna was into drugs than anything else.

I couldn't believe the bullshit he was feeding me. I knew about drugs somewhat, but I knew what had happened to Joanna wasn't drugs. I just knew it. She'd told her mother, "I'm no longer your daughter." It'd sounded so definite. It was an admission she'd become someone else.

"The best thing you can do," Packard continued, "is to let the Andersons be. They have a long road ahead of them in dealing with Joanna, and it's not going to be easy for them. All you can do is continue to be their friend. Be a friend to Morgan."

I nodded and took another sip of water. He had a point. There really wasn't anything anyone could do at this point, and he was so good with his words that he'd almost convinced me Joanna had a drug problem, but it didn't add up. *But her car was parked at the mortuary! Right next to Mr. Beaumont! Why?*

"I have something else to tell you. It's worse than this."

"Okay." He settled back to listen.

I told him the story about Mrs. Beaumont, why I'd gone to the house, and what I'd found. For the first time, I saw my words sink in.

He sat back in his chair with a grim face. "You sure of what you saw?"

"Yes."

The look in his eyes could not be mistaken. He believed me. "I don't know quite what to think. You went to their house? Did you break in?"

"No. I told you, I just looked in through their back window, and there she was. She wasn't moving or breathing. She's dead all right, and she looks real bad. You have to go there and check it out."

He shook his head. "I don't like what you're doing, Ret. That's breaking the law. You can't go into someone's backyard and peek through their window. I don't condone it."

"I know, I know, and I'm sorry. I really am, and I won't do it again. But she is dead. And she has been dead for a long time."

Packard didn't say a word. He just stared into my eyes, and I stared back, waiting for his response.

The door opened, and Deputy Gonzales poked his head in. "Phone call for you, Sheriff. It's Gerald Beaumont."

My heart sank, and I felt chills. Packard gave me another grim look as he picked up the phone.

"Sheriff Packard," he answered.

I couldn't hear the other side of the conversation, only Packard's.

"Yes." He paused. "Yes, of course. I'm sorry to hear that." He paused again. "There is a process, Mr. Beaumont—you know that. I'll send a team right away. Don't move the body. We need a medical examiner."

He hung up the phone. I knew before he said anything what it was about. He looked at me as if I were a troubled, nosey kid.

"That was Mr. Beaumont. He called in to report that he found his wife deceased."

"Convenient. Good timing." I rolled my eyes.

"Ret! You are crossing into some dangerous territory. With what you told me at the fair, and now this... it's gotta stop. No more about the Beaumonts! You don't go to their house, you don't talk to him, and you leave them completely alone. Got it?"

"Sheriff, I passed by the funeral home to get here, and Joanna's car was parked there. Isn't that too much coincidence? Beaumont was there too, and he looked at me. He knew. I know he knew. I don't know how, but he did. That's why he called—"

"Ret!" He stood up. He'd lost his patience. "I don't want to have to talk to your parents about this, but I will if I have to. Leave it alone. You're not Sherlock. And even if you were"—his tone softened—"and even if everything crazy you just told me was true, this is dangerous. You can get hurt, and that would be on my conscience. Promise me, Ret, that you'll leave this alone."

He stuck his hand out to shake. I hesitated then shook it.

"Good." He nodded. "Do you need a ride home?"

"No. I got my bike."

Sheriff Packard left with two of his deputies. I said goodbye to Doreen, the woman who serviced the front desk, and she gave me a warm, sympathetic smile. I exited the department, feeling sheepish and deflated.

I didn't blame Packard for not believing me. I was just a kid. He'd said what he had to for my own protection. Even if he hadn't really believed me, I hoped I started the wheels turning in his head.

I rode my bike home and tried to sort things out. It would have been easier to believe Joanna was on drugs and Beaumont had just found his dead wife, but that wasn't the truth. There was still something at the bottom of my gut that didn't believe it, and I wasn't about to let it go.

Packard was right about one thing, though. The situation was dangerous, and I had to be more careful. I had to switch gears again for the moment. I decided to lie low, but I was going to keep my eye on everything. *I have to stay aware. This is far from over.*

CHAPTER THIRTEEN
The Funeral

I'd never been to a bleaker funeral than the one held for Mrs. Claire Beaumont. Not that funerals weren't bleak to begin with. There was just something different about her. An empty sadness overwhelmed the mourners.

Gerald Beaumont held the services at the funeral home, and waiting in line to view her, I heard the murmurs from people ahead. Mrs. Wilcox, a good friend of Mrs. Beaumont's who was around her same age, turned away from the casket with eyes wide. With a shaking hand, she brought her handkerchief up to cover her open mouth.

"It's a travesty," she whispered. She walked away with a group of other ladies, who put their arms around her and helped her walk. "She doesn't look right. She wouldn't want this."

My view of the casket was blocked by other mourners until I was right in front of it, and I immediately understood the mutters and comments. The casket was plain, a flat-board pine box and nothing else. It had no design cut into the wood and no brass. No frills at all. Inside, the casket's lining was simple, nothing fancy or comforting. Mr. Beaumont seemed to have picked out the least expensive, stripped-down casket in the store. But that wasn't all.

Mrs. Beaumont was on her back, hands crossed over her chest, and the color of her skin wasn't right. It was caked with makeup to cover the grayness. The effect hadn't worked out so well; the gray still peeked through the orange makeup. The rest of her face looked like a circus clown's. The red rouge was smeared onto her cheeks, not blended in. Bright-green eye shadow had been slapped on her eyelids, and her mouth, covered with dark-red lipstick, was slightly open. They hadn't even done that right.

She was a ghastly sight for someone so sweet. *She didn't deserve this.* Tears bubbled to the surface of my eyes, and my stomach churned. I remembered her in the car behind the mortuary, staring into open air, and the tremble of desperation in her voice as she asked me if I knew where her husband was. We'd made a connection as I'd helped lead her to Sheriff Packard and opened the mortuary doors for them.

"This doesn't look like her at all," Jeff said, and I agreed.

I couldn't help but flash back to the haunting memories of her bloated purple body surrounded by flies, head lolled on her shoulder and eyes wide open.

Numerous flower arrangements decorated the room and casket, and I read a few of the cards. None of them were from Mr. Beaumont. He'd bought no flowers from what I could tell.

He stood next to the casket to greet the mourners, only because it was customary. It was clear by the stoic look on his grim face and his constant yawning that he had no real interest in being there. It messed up his schedule.

He looked down at me as I approached, and I locked eyes with him. His long, lean, and lined face couldn't break a smile to anyone, least of all me. There were sparks in our stare. He would've had to be blind not to see my anger, and his condescending, irritated expression loomed over me. I was a pain in his ass. His face seemed to say, *I wouldn't have had to provide this useless funeral if it hadn't been for you. You just had to find her and run to the cops, didn't you?*

The funeral home was filled to capacity and then some. Many people loved Claire Beaumont, and we all craved the comforting words the service promised. There was only one speaker: the bishop of our church. I suspect Mr. Beaumont wouldn't have allowed anyone to speak if our bishop hadn't insisted.

The pianist played "Amazing Grace" and "How Great Thou Art" before Bishop Hammond spoke. Fortunately, he had great things to say about Claire Beaumont. He talked about her history, her upbringing, and all the charitable things she'd done with the Relief Society and our church. He shared examples of her bright personality and unwavering faith in Jesus Christ, and how she'd passed through the veil into a happier, peaceful place with loved ones and the Savior.

Gerald Beaumont's gaze never even wandered toward the bishop, and a dark frown painted his face. He looked disgusted. But then again, so would the devil while a man of God was speaking.

To say Bishop Hammond saved the day was an understatement. Before he stepped up to speak, the tension in the room had felt like the precursor to a riot, but the words Bishop Hammond chose were inspired and reminded us of the beautiful spirit of Claire Beaumont.

I left feeling satisfied that she would be remembered well. There wasn't a graveside service because Gerald had chosen to cremate her. The decision had caused upset among the congregation—especially her surviving sister, who swore it was against Claire's wishes.

Everyone headed to our church after the services, where the Relief Society held a buffet in the cultural hall. Consisting of ham, rolls, Jell-O, and lots of funeral potatoes, the food was standard funeral fare, but it tasted good. We needed something to fill our empty stomachs—and hearts.

I saw Sheriff Packard across the room. He loaded up his plate and sat down among a group of people. Later, I noticed him look off in a daze, troubled and grim. He turned and caught my gaze. I half smiled, gave a nod, and turned away.

The look in his eyes told me we were on the same team, although I doubted he was ready to admit it yet. He clearly didn't trust Beaumont, either, and he knew something was up. He just didn't know what. I was sure Packard had evidence pointing to an unnatural cause of death, but not enough to convict anyone. I knew who had caused her death, just like I knew who had caused Joanna's disappearance and her transformation. I just didn't know *why* or *how*.

Many pieces of the puzzle were missing, and the answers waited inside the Crooked House.

Later that night, I dreamed of the ghost lady who haunted the Crooked House. I hadn't thought of her in a while. I turned in my bed, and she stood in my doorway, in the crack between the door and jamb, clutching my pillow. With eyes like boiled eggs, she stared at me, mouth unmoving.

My entire body tingled with fear. My mouth went dry, and my heart leapt into my throat. Between sleeping and waking, I wasn't sure if I was in a dream or if it was real. I was so mentally exhausted that I fell right back to sleep.

I woke up the next morning staring at the underside of the bunk bed above me. My thoughts drifted, then I remembered the strange dream. *How could I forget that?*

I rolled onto my side. The door was cracked open, just like in my dream. On the floor in front of it lay my pillow—the one I'd left in the Crooked House. It was gray, dirty, and flat. I wanted to scream.

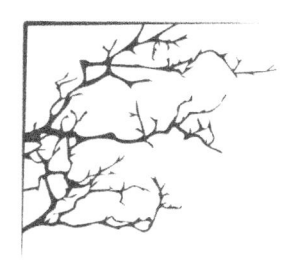

CHAPTER FOURTEEN
History 101

After I recovered from the mental breakdown caused by my ghostly visit, I realized it was time to take action. I needed to find out the true history of that house and find out who the ghost lady was. She was frightening and crazy, but... she hadn't killed me. *Was she trying to help me? She* did *bring my pillow back.*

There was only one place to go. The city library.

I planted myself in front of a microfiche reader for hours and scrolled through years of microfilm copies of newspapers. I had learned how to use one in school and was familiar with how it worked. I kept my search to the local newspapers but didn't find anything in my first hour.

"Findin' what ya need, Ret?" Mr. Dunlap, the librarian, stepped up to my side and put a friendly hand on my shoulder. He was a wiry man in his early eighties, and he wore the waist of his pants up a bit too high for my comfort.

He was a gentle soul. His eyes were dark and glossy with a warm sparkle, angled and squinted as if they belonged to a cowboy who'd stayed out on the prairie in the blazing sun for too long.

"I'm good," I mumbled, but he didn't hear me. Out of the corner of my eye, I saw him turn up his hearing aid.

"What was that?" he asked.

"Sorry." I spoke louder. "I'm doing just fine."

He patted my shoulder with a smile. "Just let me know if you need anything."

He meandered back to the front, where a lady immediately attacked him with questions.

A few minutes later, I found an article that tickled my spine. "Three Women Found Dead in Abandoned Home."

An eyewitness account from Sarah Wilkes states she was coaxed into going with a man she met in a bar. He then took her to an abandoned home in Riverton, where he attacked her. She was able to escape and run to the authorities.

The police later found Conner Robinson, 29, kneeling and sobbing in the basement next to three deceased women. It is believed that Robinson lured the women to the abandoned home and murdered them.

I continued to read the article for more clues about the house. I hoped to find an address or description, and although I didn't find one, I knew which house the article referred to. The date was April 6, 1967.

That was only fourteen years ago. To my parents and the older generation, the story was as fresh as yesterday. It was clear where the rumors of the house came from. Parents didn't tell their kids, but children had caught enough bits and pieces of conversations to come up with their own stories, and as those stories were passed on, they had become stranger and wilder, including things about a child killer who lived there and collected dead babies or the devil himself residing inside. All of the stories were fabrications and myths, but even myths consisted of partial truth.

I searched for more articles, but after half an hour, I still hadn't found anything else related to the house or the creepy pioneer ghost lady.

I sat in silence for a moment, flipping back and forth over several articles, and stopped again on the article about the three dead women and re-read it. I sensed someone behind me, turned, and saw Mr. Dunlap standing three feet away, his eyes fixed on my screen. His face looked whiter than before, and his eyes were glassy.

"Mr. Dunlap?"

His body jolted when I broke his stupor, and he turned his gaze to me. "You finding everything okay?" His voice was shaky.

"Yes, but I wonder if you can help me with something?"

Mr. Dunlap, who had a fascination with history and literature, was always eager to share his enthusiasm and knowledge with people. This time, he hesitated, though. His eyes shifted to the article then back to me. "Sure. Anything."

"I'm trying to find out more about the abandoned house. You know the one on Beck Street?"

He pursed his lips and shook his head. "Why would you want to know anything about that place? Ain't nothin' good ever came outta there... I see you found the article."

"I did, sir, thank you. I'm..." I hurried to come up with a lie. "I'm writing a new story. It's a western, and I want to have it take place here in Riverton. As far as I can tell, that's one of the oldest houses in Riverton. Maybe a historical home? It'd make a great place for my hero."

He nodded and sat down next to me. "Yes, yes, it is. I didn't know you write books." He lit up. "That's exciting. Anything published?"

"No, not yet. Hope to be one day. That's why this book has to be my best, so I thought if I wrote more history into it, you know, it would help make it authentic. More real."

"Yes, of course. I'd love to read it when you're through."

"You'll be the first I give it to. I promise. So, can you tell me more about this house? Who first lived in it or when it was built?"

"Well, let's see..." His eyes wandered into the past. "Archibald Gardner was the first to settle this area for farming land in the 1850s. It was first called Gardnersville. He was the largest landowner. He began to sell off pieces of land to other farmers, and they irrigated their farms from the Jordan River.

"By 1899, Riverton was a full-fledged town. Many people were drawn here for agriculture purposes. There was a meeting house, a church, and some stores. Henry Stockholm came from back East, I believe. Brought his family out here. A good churchgoing man. He bought a piece of land, built his home, and started farming. Built that home you're talking about in 1902. Yes, it is a historical home.

"My parents moved out here in 1919, and I've been here ever since. I know just about all there is to know about Riverton and who lived here and what's transpired."

"Can you tell me more about Henry Stockholm? And his family?" I asked.

"Well, he struggled out here. Planted his crops, but nothing would grow. Unfortunately, there was too much water. He'd built his home too close to wetlands, and over the next couple of years, the foundation started to sink. That's why it's tilted so, and where it gets its name. Water came up right through the basement, and he tried to contain it. He built bricks around it, and it looked kind of like a well. Nothing but bad luck followed him and his wife."

"Like what, sir?"

He opened his mouth to speak but held back. "I really shouldn't be telling you this."

"It's okay, Mr. Dunlap. After reading what's in this article, nothing more could shock me." I nodded, trying to assure him.

"I suppose..." He still didn't seem convinced.

"So, what happened with the Stockholms?"

Mr. Dunlap was a storyteller, and he couldn't resist spilling everything even if the better part of him warned him not to. "It was just sad what happened to that family. Henry Stockholm had put every last dollar he had into building his house and farm. He expected, like every farmer does, to grow crops and make a decent living for his family.

"Nothing would grow. He had two cows, and they never produced much milk and soon got sick and died. The bank pressured him for payment on the house and threatened to foreclose. He struggled to put food on the table. His daughter was six years old. Sweet little thing. His wife, Mathilda, people say she was cold, not friendly, withdrawn. It turned out she suffered from what we call today severe depression."

Mathilda! I thought to myself. She was the ghost lady I'd seen. I was sure of it.

Mr. Dunlap's eyes glazed over and stared sadly back into history. "She lost it one day. Drowned her child. Couple days later, she couldn't live with herself anymore and took her own life. It wasn't much longer after when Henry moved away. People were concerned for him. He was just as much drowned in depression and suffering as anyone could be. Moved back East with family, I heard. I don't know what became of him." His brow furrowed, and he rubbed his bottom lip with one finger. "'Course that house hasn't been lived in since. Not just because it was sinking in swamp land and no crops could grow, but a woman and child died in there. A thing like that leaves a mark that never goes away." He turned to me, his eyes wide, and shook his head with a scowl. "Tough to sell a home like that. People always wonder why it hasn't been torn down. There are those who want to preserve history, and that house is history. Unfortunately, it's not a good history. But then again, history is always marbled with blood and bad things.

"There's always been rumors of ghosts. People say they've seen Mathilda staring out from the second-floor window, waiting for her husband to return. But they're just ghost stories, and nothing happened in that house until then." He pointed at the article on my screen.

"That there was just awful. When it happened, there was an uproar. People wanted to see that house gone, said an abandoned home was dangerous to have around. People go there to do things. Bad things. Vagrants take up space there sometimes and have to be driven out. Then someone like that fella kills three women in there."

His eyes were intense, drilling into mine, and his lips quivered. "It draws people to it. Not so much the house as it is the ground it sits on. I believe it is evil. It attracts bad people to it, people who do bad things."

I remembered what Matt had said. "Monsters, vampires, or werewolves... those things aren't scary... It's people that are scary. People like you and me, but do awful things."

"Like Lester? The man who lives there now?"

Mr. Dunlap snapped back in his chair as if I'd hit him, and he nearly fell out of his chair. "Goodness gracious, boy, I don't know. Too early to tell." He rubbed his upper lip with a finger and looked away. When he turned back to me, he said, "He may not be a bad man. But I fear if he stays there too long, it might get into his head. But then again, I'm an old fool." He shook his head.

"What might get into his head?"

"The evil in that bad place. It's seductive. It tells you what you want to hear. It draws people to it. Makes one do things they otherwise wouldn't."

Draws people to it? I repeated in my head. *How does he know that?* It told me he was hiding something—an experience of his own, perhaps—and he was afraid to divulge.

"Like I said, people wanted to see that house gone. A group of them went out there one night. Like the mob who chased down Frankenstein to the windmill, they surrounded the house. They had gas cans and torches. They doused the house in gasoline and lit it. It burned all right. The flames lit up the sky. That house was built mostly of wood. It should have burned right to the ground just like any house would. But it's not just any house. The next morning after the flames died down, the house remained standing, and crooked. Black and burnt on the outside, collapsed in areas, but still intact. That's when I knew, and everyone else knew, that house sits on evil ground."

He took a deep breath and shook the memories from his head. "I said too much. Damn my mouth. Marge always says I run my mouth when I get to talkin' about history and things. You're too young to know those things. Just take my warning. Please hear me when I tell you to stay away from it. I know young kids want to mess around in that house. Go out there and dare to see ghosts, break a few windows, look at dirty magazines and such, but please, I beg you to leave it alone. Ain't nothin' good has ever come from that house, and nothin' ever will."

I nodded. "Okay." What else could I say?

Someone from behind me called out to Mr. Dunlap for help finding a book.

"I gotta go, son. Good luck writing your book." He winked. "And heed what I said." He stood up, patted me on the shoulder, and went to attend to the customer.

I was on information overload. My mind bounced from image to image of what I'd learned, trying to sort them out and file them in the right spots in my brain. If Mr. Dunlap was right—and I had no reason to doubt him—then Lester and Beaumont were drawn to that house to do evil things. I wasn't quite sure what they were up to, but I was determined to find out.

I turned off the machine, stood up, and marched toward the front doors. Out of the corner of my eye, I saw Dawn. She was sitting at a table, looking as beautiful as the sun, reading a book. It wasn't another Ray Bradbury like I'd expected, but a Louis L'Amour novel.

Was she reading it because of *me*? *Too good to be true.*

She turned and saw me. "Ret!" her delicate voice called out to me.

I turned with my best surprised face and waved. "Oh, hey, Dawn!"

"What're you doing? Come over here," she said, motioning.

Why can't I be more like her? Bold, direct, and inviting. I walked over to her and pointed at her Louis L'Amour book. "The Sacketts! You're actually reading L'Amour!"

"Yeah." She nodded. "I thought I'd take your advice."

"Well, that's a great one to start with. He wrote several novels about the Sackett family, and not only are they the most famous of his books, but they're the best characters."

"I know. I love them. They're tough, mean, and bullheaded, but always on the good side."

I nodded and found myself in an awkward fugue of not knowing what to say next. I loved hearing her talk. Her words were beyond her age.

"What are you doing here?"

"I-I'm just doing some research for a new book I'm writing." *Oh my gosh, now I'm lying to her too.*

"Wow. What's this one about?"

"A... a western ghost story."

"Really? That sounds so cool. Of course, I'm still waiting to read your other story. 'Ten Steps to Death,' right? I can compare westerns to westerns."

"I'm no Louis L'Amour, but yeah. Of course. I could bring it over tonight."

"You should."

"You here alone?" I asked. "No Morgan?"

"No." She shook her head sadly. "She hasn't been the same since her sister... you know."

"Yeah, that's pretty crazy what happened."

"I heard what you did. It was really sweet." She looked up and gave me a warm smile.

"Oh, I didn't do anything. I was just passing by." I waved it off.

"But you were there. I know Morgan appreciated it. If anything, it means you care."

"I guess. I just wish I could do more." I shrugged.

"Me too." She nodded agreement.

"So, tell me more about this western ghost story. What kind of history were you researching?"

Since she was pressing me for more information about my phantom story, I knew I couldn't lie to her anymore. I sat down and let out a breath. I could tell by the way her eyes creased that my demeanor had changed. Everything about Beaumont, Lester, and the Crooked House had my stomach tied up in knots, and I needed to tell someone.

"What's wrong?"

"I'm really not researching history for a story I'm writing."

She scrunched up her face. "What are you doing then?"

"Do you know about the Crooked House on Beck Street?"

"The abandoned one? Morgan mentioned something about it. She said it was haunted." Dawn shrugged. "Not sure about that."

"Well, I didn't think so either until a few weeks ago."

I started with the night my friends and I spent in the house. I told her about the ghost and how she'd visited my home and returned my pillow. I told her about Lester, Beaumont, finding Mrs. Beaumont dead in her house, and my suspicions surrounding Joanna. I told her every detail.

She sat back like the wind was knocked out of her. "What do you think happened to Beaumont then? And Joanna?"

"I don't know, but whatever it is, it's identical. They were one person one day, and someone completely different the next."

"And poor Mrs. Beaumont. Do you really think he killed her?" She leaned in to me and whispered as if afraid to say those words aloud.

"I don't know for sure, but the way he talked to her when he returned, and when he told Sheriff Packard how much he hated her, too many things add up. So I came here to find out more about that house and who lived there. Everything weird that's going on surrounds that place. I thought I might find some answers."

"Did you?"

I shivered at the thought of what I'd found. The killer who'd murdered women in that house and what Mathilda had done to her daughter churned my stomach.

"Sort of."

"So what do we do now?"

We? Was I taking on a new ally? "I don't know."

"We've got to find out more about them and what they're doing." Her voice rose with excitement and determination.

"I have an idea."

CHAPTER FIFTEEN
Spy Games

Dawn and I hid behind the berm my friends and I used to spy on Lester. We crouched down and peeked at the house. There were no cars, no one was outside, and no one moved inside.

"It looks like they're not home," I said.

"Are you sure?"

"No. I guess we just take our chances."

"And you think this is going to work?"

We had left the library together and stopped at my house to pick up my walkie-talkies and duct tape.

"I'm positive. While the Talk button is pushed in, we can hear them, but they can't hear us. I taped it so it will stay pushed in the whole time."

"Until the battery dies."

I shrugged. "Yes."

"You're brilliant." She grinned.

"But we have to get it inside somehow."

"We can do it." She stood up. "Come on."

Her bravery was inspiring, and I followed her.

"A little breaking and entering never hurt anyone. As long as it's for a good cause, right?"

"Yes."

We walked across the rocky, uneven ground of the field through tall brush and weeds to the house; nerves shook my body.

Dawn led us up to the front door. "I'm going to knock first. If no one answers, no one's home."

She pounded her fist against the front door, and I wondered if she was as nervous as I was. She didn't look it. I checked behind us to be sure no one was coming. The field and road were barren and quiet. Not even the air moved. She knocked again, and we waited, but no sound came from within. The door never opened.

"Coast is clear," she said, twisting the doorknob. "And it's unlocked."

She pushed open the door and stepped inside, and I followed hesitantly.

Dawn stood in the entry with her hands on her hips. Looking around, she nodded. "Yep. It looks like a haunted house, all right."

"Let's hurry and hide this thing before that ghost comes."

"Mathilda?"

"Yes," I whispered, motioning for her to soften her voice. "I don't want to wake her if she's sleeping."

"Gotcha." She nodded.

We walked down the hall to the kitchen. Sunlight beamed in all around, lighting the house and illuminating floating dust particles.

"I think the kitchen would be the best place to hide this," I said. "Most people hang around in their kitchens. What do you think?"

"Sounds good."

We tiptoed around the kitchen, with the floor creaking under our weight. Dawn eyed the countertops, which were filled with kitchen items such as tin boxes for flour and sugar. All of it was covered with cobwebs and dust. Her eyes stopped on the breadbox.

"Perfect." Dawn pulled the breadbox away from the wall, breaking apart a cobweb. She held out her hand for my walkie-talkie. "Here. We'll place it behind here."

I handed her the walkie-talkie, and she set it on the counter then pressed the breadbox into place. It couldn't quite fit flat against the wall anymore, but one would have to investigate closely to be able to tell. It looked good to me.

"Step outside," she said. "We'll try it out."

I trotted to the front porch and turned on the other walkie-talkie. Static screeched from the receiver, and I waited.

"Hello, hello. Testing one, two, three... can you hear me?"

Her voice came through the static sound. I turned to the open front door and saw Dawn at the end of the hall, waiting to hear my response. I gave her a thumbs-up.

We ran back to our hiding spot behind the berm and sat with our backs against the mound. When I started to feel like I was baking in the hot sun, I suggested moving beneath the shade of a nearby tree, and she agreed.

"How far is the range on that thing?" she asked, holding up the walkie-talkie.

"I'm not sure. I think it'll work from this distance. Last time I used it, Jax was at his house, and I was at mine. That was farther than this is."

"The true test is when they come home."

"Yeah. It could be a while, though. They're at work."

"Well, what do we do now to kill the time?"

I shrugged.

"What do you guys usually do around here?"

"We ride our bikes a lot. See over there?" I pointed across the field. "That's Dead Man's Hill. We ride our bikes down it, and there's a jump at the bottom. It's scary but fun."

"Have you lived here your whole life?" she asked.

"In Riverton? No. I've been here probably about three years now. I've always lived in Utah, but we move around a lot."

"Us too," she grumbled. "I mean, we move around a lot. Too much. Because of my dad's work."

"Hey, that's the same as us. My dad is always changing jobs, and we move practically every year. Until here. This is the longest place we've stayed in years."

"We've moved eight times since I was born. It's crazy."

"Really? What places have you lived?"

"I was born in Maine, way at the other side of the country."

"Holy cow."

"I don't remember it at all. We moved before I even turned one."

I recalled my mom telling me that Dawn could use some good friends because the move had been hard on her. If anybody could understand that, I could. "It's hard to move so much, isn't it?"

She nodded. "This last time, I had to move away from my best friend, Sadie. We lived there for two years."

"Have you seen her much since you moved?"

"Just once. It's kinda tough because she lives in Bountiful. It's sorta far from here."

"North, I think. That's one town we haven't hit yet," I joked, and she chuckled. "But give us some time, and we'll get there."

She leaned back and stared up at the branches of the tree, and I did the same.

"Why do you think that is?" she asked.

"What?"

"Why our families move so much. I don't understand my dad's job and why he can't keep it."

"Or if he has to change it, why can't he get a job in the same town?"

"Right."

"Well, hopefully, this will be your last."

"I hope so. They promised it would be. Riverton seems like a nice place."

"It is. I like it. There's good people here. It's a bit far from the city. When you want to see a movie or go to the mall, you have to travel.

There is a pool not too far from here, though. We sometimes catch the bus and ride up to it."

"That sounds fun. We should do that sometime."

"Yeah. We should."

We sat under that tree for at least two hours and talked about all sorts of things: our families, schools, teachers, and friends. We took a break and went to my house to pick up some Popsicles to cool us off. When we returned, there was still no sign of Beaumont or Lester. Soon after that, we called it a day.

We ambled down the street toward my house, and as we approached my stop, I started thinking about the next day and how I wanted to spend it with her again. She was so easy to talk to, and I'd never met another person I had as much in common with.

"Well, this is my house."

We stopped in front of it. She nodded with a sarcastic grin, but all she said was "Yeah."

"Thanks for helping me. You know, solve the mystery."

"We haven't uncovered one clue yet, silly. But I can't wait to get back at it tomorrow."

"Me too. Do you wanna meet again about nine? We'll go back and check the house. See if we get anything on the walkie-talkie?"

"Make it eight. Maybe we can catch them before they go to work." Her eyes widened with eager fire.

"Yes, great idea."

"Hey, how about that story of yours?" She jabbed my chest with her finger, and I caught a hint of disappointment in her voice that I hadn't given her the book to read sooner.

"Oh yeah. Let me run and get it."

I raced to my bedroom and pulled the pages from my dresser door. I saw the letter I'd written to her on the night of the fireworks. It sat on top of my story. I'd asked her to be my girlfriend in it, but I still didn't have the nerve to deliver it. Somehow, it didn't feel right. So I tucked it back into the drawer and jogged back to Dawn. "Here you go. I hope you like it."

"I'm sure I will." She ran her eyes over the first page, smiling. "I can't wait. I'll read it tonight." She looked up at me and said, "I'll see you tomorrow."

She turned to walk away, and I called out, "Hey, I'm glad you're in Riverton now."

"Me too." She smiled.

"See you." I turned and walked into my house.

I COULD HARDLY SLEEP that night out of anticipation for the next day. *What was she going to think of my story?* That was the biggest question on my mind, and of course I was looking forward to spending another day of spying with her. Hopefully, we would get some success.

I was waiting outside as she approached my house just before eight, and she held my manuscript in her right hand.

Oh boy. My first real critique.

"Hey, Dawn." I waved.

"Hey, Ret." Holding up my pages, she said, "I finished it."

"You did?"

"Mm-hmm. Do you wanna know the truth?"

"Only if it's good. If it's bad, just lie to me."

She chuckled. "Ret, it's not bad. I loved it."

"You did? Really?"

"Yes, you have a real talent. I could picture everything. The dusty town, Clancy the gunfighter, and the whole battle. It was exciting."

"Wow." I blushed, but inside I was on top of the world. "Thank you for reading it."

"You need to write more. I think you could give Louis L'Amour a run for his money."

"Yeah, right."

We both chuckled.

I put my pages away in my room, then we hurried to the berm to start our day of spying.

"He's here," I said, excited to see Lester's car parked out front.

"Turn it on." She pointed at the walkie-talkie.

I clicked it on. At first, all we heard was static, then there were muffled thumps.

"I think the battery's still alive, and I hear something."

"I do too. I think they're footsteps."

For another twenty minutes, the walkie-talkie picked up only silence, with occasional sounds, but no talking.

"Come on, guys. Let's hear some conversation."

Then we heard rhythmic steps that I guessed were from someone walking down the stairs.

"Lester," a voice said. Though it was difficult to discern through the static, I was sure it was Beaumont's voice.

I held the walkie-talkie between us, and Dawn and I both pressed an ear as close as we could. Some words were hard to make out, but I could piece it together enough to know what they were saying. As long as the outside around us stayed quiet, I could hear.

"Are you ready to go?" Beaumont asked.

"Yes," Lester answered. "Once I finish my cereal. Although, I don't know why we should go to work. There isn't anything going on."

"It's been days since we've had a body come through. We need one. You need to do more."

"I'm doing the best I can. I could do better if I could get some sleep. I still hear *voices*. Every night! They give me a headache."

"They are the cries of my people," Beaumont said. "They continue to suffer until we're reunited, and time is running out."

"Ever since I moved into this house, I've been bombarded by their voices. I've done everything they asked me to do. Everything *you've* asked me to. Can't you shut them up?"

Quick steps were followed by gurgling sounds.

Dawn and I shared a confused look. I didn't understand what was going on.

"They wouldn't have to suffer so long and wail in your head all night if you provided what was promised," Beaumont growled. "We haven't much time. We need to find someone else. A live one. We can't continue to rely on your failing business."

I heard a clatter, more thumps, and gasping for air, as if Beaumont had run to Lester, choked him, then when he was done, pushed him down. There was a long silent pause.

"What the hell is this?" Beaumont asked Lester.

"I-I don't know. It looks like a walkie-talkie."

"Who is this?" Beaumont's voice was sharper than before.

Dawn and I looked at each other in shock. *He's talking to us!*

"Whoever this is, you are going to regret the day you put this device in my house. I better not hear you or see you, and you better pray I don't!"

A cracking sound boomed from our walkie-talkie, so loudly that it pierced my ears. Then even the static was gone.

We scrambled to peer over the berm. The front door of Lester's house opened, and Beaumont stormed out. He stopped halfway to the car and turned, casting a baleful glare in our direction as if he *knew* we were there and *knew* it was us who had planted the walkie-talkie. He held the broken pieces of the device in his hand and threw it into the field.

Then he turned back to the house and yelled, "Are you coming?"

He stood for a few more seconds, staring at the open door, before Lester stumbled out, rubbing his throat. He raised his eyes and scowled at Beaumont. We watched as they entered the car and drove away.

"Good hell," I said. "Do you think he knew it was us?"

"No. There's no way."

"That was intense."

"What do you think they're talking about? Getting another body? Getting a live one?"

"I don't know." And I feared finding out. "We may be in over our heads on this one."

"Lester said he was hearing voices."

"That explains a lot. We spied on Lester when he first moved in, and we saw him arguing to himself and throwing things around like a crazy person. It must be the voices in his head."

"Do you think we should go to the police?"

"And tell them what? I've tried talking to Sheriff Packard about them before, and he dismisses it all like I'm just a paranoid kid. He even said *I* had broken the law when I found Mrs. Beaumont. And we still don't know what it is they're doing."

"We need to find out more." She turned and looked at the house. "We should go back in there and search the place. Maybe we can find something."

"Like Nancy Drew and the Hardy Boys?"

"Yeah! That's what they'd do."

I was nervous about going back into that house. My skin crawled every time I entered it, but here was this cute girl I really liked, who was braver than anyone I knew, and I couldn't chicken out.

"I suppose."

I turned off my walkie-talkie, and we approached the house cautiously. I looked around for anyone who might be watching. I saw no one.

We walked up the front steps and stood on the slanted porch. Dawn's hand was on the doorknob, and I suddenly felt the urge to pee. My nerves were wound up tight.

Then I heard a car pull up behind us. "Hey!"

I thought we were done for. I was afraid Beaumont had caught us. I was so keyed up that I assumed it was *him*. After a terrifying heartbeat, I recognized the voice, and I turned to see Packard in his police vehicle, his head out the open window.

"What's going on, Ret?" he said with suspicion in his voice.

"Hi!" Dawn stepped up. "I'm Dawn Williams. I'm going door-to-door, getting sponsors for the March of Dimes."

"The March of Dimes?" His eyes went back to me, and I felt them bore into me, searching me for the truth.

"Yes, it helps children with birth defects," she pointed out, flashing him a cheery smile.

"I'm aware of the foundation."

Dawn stepped toward his car emphatically. "Can I put you down as a sponsor, Sheriff?"

Her forwardness caught him by surprise, and he stuttered, "Uh—no, not right now. Maybe check back with me at my office." He eyed us again. "You sure that's all you're doing?"

"Of course. What else would it be?" Dawn beamed.

"Well, it looks like no one's home at this house."

"That's how it looks," Dawn said. "We'll be moving on to the next house."

"Good. You two be careful." He nodded then slowly backed out of the drive.

Once the sheriff was out of sight, I approached Dawn. "You are a genius."

"I *was* pretty good, huh?"

"Hell, yes. I thought he had us there for a moment. He's already warned me several times to leave this Beaumont and Lester business alone."

"That's why we can't stop. Sometimes adults only see what they want to see. Someone has to uncover what they're doing before more people get hurt."

We couldn't risk entering the house anymore. Our plan had been thwarted, so we decided to walk to Morgan's house to see how she was doing. She was elated to see us, and we played a few board games before I went home for the day, but we said nothing about our adventures or speculations to Morgan. We didn't want to upset her.

After dinner that evening, my mom asked me what I'd done that day, and I told her how I'd spent the last couple of days with Dawn.

"So you really do like her, huh?"

"I just... yeah, I really do. She's cool and easy to talk to. Like talking to Gary."

"Where *is* Gary? I haven't seen your friends around much lately."

"They came over today, asking for you," Scott chimed in from across the room. "I just said you were out with that new girl. I couldn't remember her name."

I nodded and looked at the floor. "Yeah, I feel bad. I need to hang out with them more."

"You should have a sleepover. Have Gary and Jax spend the night. I'm going to rent a VCR and a couple of movies tomorrow. We'll pop popcorn. I'll let you butter it because you are the best at that, and I'll get some treats. You can have them over then."

I agreed, and it sounded fun. I needed to be with my friends, and I couldn't wait to tell them all about everything Dawn and I had discovered, and suddenly that moment couldn't come soon enough.

CHAPTER SIXTEEN
A Good Friend

The next day, I had Scouts again, and as usual, we met at Todd Harrison's home. Then, our stomachs full of Mrs. Harrison's chocolate chip cookies, we rode our bikes home.

Jax was going out to a movie with his family, so he'd shot off right after the meeting, but Gary and I rode side by side.

"You're still sleeping over, right?" I asked Gary.

"Yeah. My mom said I could." He pushed his large glasses up to the bridge of his nose where they belonged and flashed me his usual sly grin. "I'll just grab some things from home and be right over."

"Cool. My mom rented some movies and a VCR. She let me pick one out. I got *Clash of the Titans*!"

I loved *Clash of the Titans*. Of course, I loved anything fantasy with swords, sorcery, and monsters. My mom let us watch it alone because she didn't care for that kind of stuff, and I was glad for that because a couple of parts showed a woman's bare top, and watching those scenes with my mom was uncomfortable. But wouldn't you know it, she stuck her head in the room to ask us if we needed any more drinks during the only six seconds of bare boobs in the whole two-hour movie!

After the movie, Gary and I sat up, halfway out of our sleeping bags on the floor of the living room, all the lights out except for a dim table lamp, and we shuffled through each other's stacks of Star Wars trading cards.

"I have a duplicate of Chewbacca wearing the gas mask and holding his crossbow," I said.

"The one when they're inside that creature's stomach!"

"Yeah, it's pretty sweet. Probably my favorite of Chewy."

"Cool. Thanks."

I handed it over to him and tugged a piece of licorice off with my teeth.

"So where have you been lately?" Gary asked.

My smile dropped, and my eyes turned to the ground. I was nervous to tell him. I thought he would be mad at me either for sneaking around on Beaumont and Lester without him or for hanging out with Dawn. Either way, I couldn't win. "Nowhere really. Just doing stuff."

"Doing stuff?" He called me out.

I nodded, keeping silent.

"We could use your help with the fort. Rosco really knows what he's doing, and we're almost finished."

"That's cool. I'll have to come see it."

"See it?" He gave me a sideways look, like he couldn't believe what I'd just said.

"I'll come help you guys. Sorry I haven't been there, man."

He shrugged. "It's okay, I guess."

"I, um, I've been hanging out with Dawn."

"Really? Is she your girlfriend now?"

"No. We're just good friends. I ran into her at the library, and we just started hanging out."

"We came by yesterday and the day before, but you weren't there. I just wondered what you were doing, if you were hanging out with Matt again or you didn't like us anymore or something."

"No, of course I still like you guys. We're best pals. It's just... I don't know. I was with Dawn and got caught up in doing stuff."

"What stuff? And what were you doing at the library?"

I saw myself in the reflection of his glasses. My face had gone dark and sullen again. He knew something was up. I had to confess.

"I've been doing some research."

"What kind?"

"The Crooked House kind."

His face went white like he'd seen the ghost again. He trembled, and genuine fear crossed his eyes. "Why can't you leave that place alone?"

Because the ghost lady came to my house and returned my pillow. I think she wants me to help. But I couldn't tell him that. "I don't know. I feel a responsibility. Mr. Beaumont and Lester are up to something. I don't know what it is, but people are dying and going missing. Like Joanna, and I know Beaumont killed his wife. Plus, Dawn and I heard them talking like they might hurt more people, and Lester admitted he hears voices in his head."

"Creepy. You've got to tell the police—or your parents!"

"I told Sheriff Packard everything already. I think he believes me even though he won't admit it. He says there's no evidence to go on."

"What is it you think you can do?"

"I just have to find out what they're doing, what their plan is for this town before it's too late. Parents aren't going to believe me, and the cops aren't going to do anything. It's all up to me."

We stared at each other in silence for a moment in the dim light. Nothing made a sound but the ticking of the clock in the kitchen. No doubt sensing my desperation and passion, he gave me a firm nod.

"Then I'm with you," he said firmly.

I hadn't realized I needed his support until he said that. My shoulders relaxed, like he'd lifted a weight off them. I needed my friends. "You are?"

"Yes. That's how this works. We're the Black Widows, for hell's sakes."

I laughed out loud, and so did he. It set off a chain reaction of giggles that we couldn't stop.

"Boys!" my dad called from the back room. "Time to go to sleep. It's late."

It didn't stop our laughter, but we covered our mouths to quiet the chuckles.

Gary was utterly terrified of *that* house. I could tell from his reaction every time someone brought it up. He was scared of the ghost who haunted it. The shock of seeing a ghost had already taken a piece of who he was, and he would never get that back. Still, without any hesitation, he was willing to stand beside me and face the horror together.

"Thanks," I said with sincerity, and he nodded.

I turned out the light, and we lay down. We fell asleep within the next twenty minutes, and I slept soundly for the first time in a while.

CHAPTER SEVENTEEN
The Death of Todd Harrison

They said it was an accident. His car had gone off the highway, and he was rushed to the hospital and died soon after, from trauma to the brain.

These were the only pieces of information my mind could process while my mom and dad sat me down and told me Todd Harrison was dead. I felt numb, and my head was cloudy. I'd just seen my Scout leader the other night. *And now he's gone?*

His body was prepared at the mortuary, then Beaumont and Lester brought him to the church for the viewing and the services. I was relieved, as I think the rest of the people were, that we didn't have to go through another cold, heartless service at Beaumont's mortuary. Beaumont and Lester kept a low profile and didn't interact with anyone.

I still couldn't believe Todd was gone, and I continued to not believe it until I witnessed his body lying in the casket. Right then, I realized why the viewing was so important—for closure. Seeing Todd Harrison was the moment the reality of mortality hit me.

Dressed in his Sunday best, he didn't quite look like himself. His skin was orange from the makeup, and his face lacked expression, which was in direct contrast to his animated expressions in life. His stone-cold look made him unrecognizable. Above his right eye was a six-inch scar that disappeared into his scalp.

I studied his face for a long moment, scared his eyes would flutter open suddenly and that he would grab me with his cold hands and say, "I'm not dead. They made a mistake." *Because how could he be gone?*

I turned to see some of my fellow Scouts gathered by the sofa in the foyer. Tears pooled in most of their red eyes, and Billy trembled, on the verge of weeping. Billy broke and ran into his mother's arms, sobbing uncontrollably. I couldn't blame him. I wanted to do the same. We'd all lost a good friend and mentor.

I wandered toward the entrance, where my family stood, and overheard a lady say, "This is just too much. Two funerals in under a month. And he was so young. Not to mention the Anderson daughter who went missing."

Another lady answered, "Poor Angie. She's left with three kids now to raise on her own. We brought dinner to them last night. She's holding strong, but you know she wants to fall apart."

Not wanting to look at anyone, I kept my eyes to the floor. A hand, a girl's hand, reached out low in front of me and took mine. I looked up and caught Dawn's eyes. They were sad and watery, not for the loss, but for me. Her mouth pulled up slightly at both ends in a solemn smile.

"Hi," I said.

"How are you?"

"Okay," I lied.

"I'm sorry," she said softly.

"Thanks."

She gave my hand a squeeze, released it, and walked back to her family.

Billy's sobs got louder, and his crying triggered mine. Tears filled my eyes and spilled over, my chest tightened and convulsed, and I hurried to my mom, who wrapped me in her arms. We left shortly after that. On the way home, my parents stopped at the store and ran in to buy a brownie mix and ice cream. My brothers and I stayed in the back of the station wagon. The slight breeze that blew in through the open windows wasn't enough to cool us from the heat. We tore off our ties and unbuttoned our shirts, flaring out our collars to release the trapped heat. Tadd pulled out his electronic handheld football game and was immediately lost in it. Scott tilted his head back and closed his eyes to catch a nap.

Jeff turned to me with genuine concern. "Are you okay?"

"Yeah." I nodded.

"It's pretty messed up what happened to Todd. He was a good guy."

"He was. I still can't believe what happened."

Jeff and I shared the middle place in our family. Tadd picked on Jeff, and Scott always pestered me. Because of that, we shared a sense of understanding. I found it easier to talk with Jeff about certain things.

"It's pretty shitty how someone ran him off the road."

I snapped around in shock as if a splash of cold water had hit my face.

"Ran him off the road? I hadn't heard that."

"It was a hit-and-run. That's what Larry said." Jeff's friend Larry was a reliable source as he was the son of the previous sheriff. "Larry said there were scrapes up and down the side of his car only another vehicle could have made. They left black marks from the paint of the other vehicle. Todd's car was bright red, so if you see a black car with red paint scratches on it"—he eyed me while nodding his head—"good chance that's the guy."

Once home, we all ran to our bedrooms to tear off our uncomfortable clothes and dress in our "comfies." Scott and I went into our room, and I slipped into shorts and a T-shirt and hung my dress clothes up in the closet. Scott threw his off and left them on the floor. The rest of the night was quiet. We ate our brownies and ice cream and watched a John Wayne movie on the TV, but I couldn't pay attention to it. My mind swam with the new possibility that Todd Harrison hadn't suffered from an accident, but was *murdered*.

CHAPTER EIGHTEEN
Another Vanishing

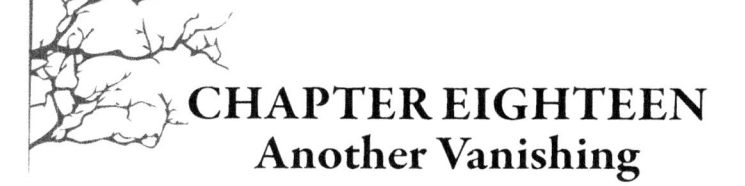

Todd's death continued to hang over me like a shroud of sadness, but finding out how he'd been killed started a fire of rage in my belly. I was bent on finding the black car with red paint scratches. I rode through our neighborhood, scouring vehicles for signs of the crash, but I came up empty. I went to Lester's house, but his car was gone. I was disappointed because his car *was* black. I rode to the mortuary with high hopes, but the parking lot was empty except for an old Ford truck.

I rode my bike slowly back to our neighborhood. I turned in the direction of the Moguls, where my friends were, and stopped at the head of Dawn's street. I looked at her house. No one was outside. I wanted to ask her—and Morgan—to join us, but I was afraid of upsetting my friends. I needed to make sure we were okay before I tried bringing the girls along, so I went to see my friends first. I continued to ride until the pavement gave way to a dirt road and opened up into the wide field of rolling dirt hills that stretched for two miles. My friends were at the tail end of a line of hills, which was next to the dirt road and the entrance to the neighborhood, working on our fort.

When I got there, Rosco, Gary, and Jax were already digging.

"Hey, Ret, come see what we've done!" Jax called out.

"We've got a bona fide fort right here." Rosco's smile spread up to his ears.

"Wow!" I said, genuinely impressed. The entrance was double the size I remembered it being. I still had to duck my head to get in, but that wasn't bad. I sensed the excitement from the others as I crawled in.

"Look how deep it goes," Gary said.

"We done dug a bunch out since last time. Dug deeper into the ground too, so we can sit in here without bumpin' our heads," Rosco explained.

I sat down, and the ceiling was two or three inches above my head. They'd built two support beams with some old two-by-fours my dad had lying around. It looked solid, but probably wasn't up to the state's building code. The dirt was moist and cool to the touch, and the fort smelled of freshly dug earth. I was amazed.

"This is really awesome," I said.

"Dig any further, and we'll find gold or China!" Rosco laughed.

All four of us crawled into the cave and scooted into a crude circle.

"We can all fit in here!" Gary exclaimed.

"With room to spare," Rosco added.

"We're gonna get some dates and bring girls here," Jax stated with confidence.

"Speaking of girls," Gary said, eyeballing me. "How is Dawn?"

"Yeah, heard you got a girlfriend." Rosco elbowed my side, chuckling. "You kiss her yet?"

"No." I shook my head, and my face got hot. "Honestly, we're just friends."

"You gotta kiss her!" Rosco bellowed. "With tongue." He wiggled his tongue in a repulsive manner which caused us all to twist our faces in disgust.

"Gross," Gary said.

"I'm not going to do that," I stated.

"That's what she'd want," Rosco went on. "I had me a girlfriend back in Texas, and we went out behind her shed one day, and she grabbed my shirt and planted one right square on my lips! So I kissed her back, and then she stuck her tongue in my—"

"Okay, okay." I stopped him. "That's enough. I'm getting too many images in my head I can't erase."

We all had a good laugh, then I heard footsteps outside.

"Ret?" It was Dawn's voice, and my friends made funny faces at me.

I crawled out of the cave and stood up to see that Morgan was next to her. "Hey, Dawn. Hey, Morg. Whatcha guys doing?"

The rest of my friends shuffled out of the cave.

"You guys building a fort?" Dawn asked.

"Yeah," Rosco said.

"Looks more like a cave," Morgan snarked.

"It's our man cave," Jax said proudly.

"Looks more like a kiddie cave," Morgan remarked, and Jax frowned.

Dawn bent to her knees and crawled inside it, nodding. She gripped the support beams and gave them a firm shake. "You got good supports in here. Could use a couple more in the back before this roof caves in."

Rosco gave me a surprised look.

Dawn stood up, smacking the dirt off her hands. "If you guys would like some help, I have some more two-by-fours at my house."

"What do you know 'bout buildin'?" Rosco asked.

"My dad's an engineer. He's built a thing a two, and I've always helped him out."

Rosco was hesitant at first, then grinned widely. "All right then. Let's do it."

Dawn flashed me a smile. "Do you wanna help me get the wood?"

"Uh, yeah, of course."

I heard the boys oohing and ahhing under their breaths as I followed Dawn away from the cave.

Morgan stayed with the boys and the cave. As Dawn and I walked away, she asked them, "It's hot out here. How do you stand it?"

"It's cool here in the cave. At least by twenty degrees. Try it out," Jax said.

"I hope this is okay," Dawn said to me.

"Are you kidding? I'm glad you showed up. I want you to get to know my friends, and this will be fun."

Dawn and I collected the boards, and we all went to work. Both Dawn and Morgan helped dig, carry dirt, and plant the support beams, and we increased the size of the cave by at least two more feet, including a few more inches of head clearance.

Dawn and Morgan left for a few minutes and returned with cold Shastas, then we all sat inside our cave and drank our sodas.

"Well? What do you think?" Jax asked Morgan.

She nodded. "Okay, this is cool."

"So, is it still a man cave?" Dawn asked.

"I think we can rename it." I looked at the boys for agreement. Gary and Rosco nodded, and Jax shrugged.

"What should we call it?" Gary asked Morgan.

"How about Cueva?" Morgan's face lit up.

"Cueva? What in the hell is that?" Rosco asked.

"It's 'cave' in Spanish. My mom knows Spanish, and I've learned a little." Her tone lifted with pride.

"I like it," Jax said, and we all agreed the fort's new name was Cueva.

My hands were caked with dirt, soil lined my fingernails, and my whole body was pouring sweat. Dirt smeared Dawn's forehead where she'd wiped sweat away with her soiled hand.

"That about does it for today, boys," Rosco said as the sun dipped behind the mountains. "At least we got new support beams in thanks to Dawn."

As we crawled out of Cueva, Mr. Tally, whom I recognized from church, walked toward us from the dirt road. I didn't know his first name, but I thought he was in his late fifties. His eyes turned down in a sorrowful way, and his lips quivered when he talked.

"You kids know Andrea Johnson? She'd be not much older than you. Thirteen, I 'spect." He handed me a wallet-sized picture of her—a school headshot. Her long blond hair draped over her shoulders, and brown eyes sparkled over a radiant smile. She was wearing a peach dress, and I recognized her immediately. I knew of her, but not directly. She was in different classes.

The others nodded, and I answered, "Yes."

"She's gone missing—" He choked on his words. "Last seen with her mother at the gas station just across the street from our neighborhood. She went in to pay for gas, and when she come out, Andrea was gone. No one saw what happened. She been by here? She was wearin' a blue dress. Silk, I think, and black shiny shoes."

"No, we haven't seen her," Dawn responded.

All the color drained from Morgan's face.

"Best you boys and girls run on home to your families. There'll be a meetin' tonight at the church. We're putting together a search party."

"You don't know what happened?" Gary asked. "Who took her?"

"We don't know she's been taken," he answered quickly. "Just missin' at this point. I don't know what's goin' on, but light's about out, and you kids need to be at home with your families. Understand?"

We all nodded. I saw in his eyes the same question I had. *What is happening in this town?*

The mountains had completely doused the light of the sun by the time I arrived home. A rustling uneasiness was already spreading through the neighborhood; parents shuffled their children into their homes, sweeping a wary eye around. A few of those stares had been directed at me because it was dark, my features were hard to decipher, and people were on the lookout for not only Andrea, but anyone suspicious.

Once I got home, my parents gathered me and my brothers in the station wagon, and we drove to the church. The meeting was held in the gymnasium of the church, and just about everyone I knew was there. The feeling of kinship, loyalty, and love was strong as everyone rallied to help out one of our own. We began the meeting with a prayer, and our bishop finished the meeting with a prayer. Choked by emotion, he struggled halfway through the prayer, and several people cried and sniffled.

Feeling empowered by the bishop's prayer, I left the church. Nothing was going to stop me or anyone else from finding Andrea. Unfortunately, daylight was already gone, and we were urged to wait until first light to start the search, but several men, including my dad, gathered on their own with flashlights and started combing Riverton and all its fields.

The morning came, and looking out over the sea of volunteers gathered at the gas station where she'd last been seen, I couldn't imagine how we wouldn't be able to find her. It wasn't only in my heart. I saw it in others' eyes too: the fear of finding Andrea dead. I didn't want to think about it, though.

Jax's and Gary's families were there, along with Rosco's. Sheriff Packard split everyone in groups and designated areas for each group to search.

The entire search party started at the gas station and headed west past some houses, around Dead Man's Hill, and into the field behind my house.

Once in the field, we formed a front line like soldiers in the Civil War and walked slowly through the weeds and brush. Sheriff Packard stood north of us, talking to Farmer Joe, who carried his usual scowl and a shotgun. Farmer Joe was loud enough for everyone to hear him, and he was so resistant to the sheriff that I thought he was going to start trouble.

"I can't have you carrying a gun." Packard pointed to the shotgun in his hands.

"What?" Farmer Joe exclaimed, his eyes wide. "I'm not going to hurt no one. This is just filled with rock salt. That's all." He shook his head.

"We have women and children out here." He glanced at me then nodded to a family behind me who had two children around five and seven years old.

"I ain't goin' no further without it. I tell ya that much. I got a right, and you can pry it from my dead hands."

Packard sighed and rested his hand on the pistol on his hip and locked his jaw as he stared Joe down. "Don't start anything. I asked nicely, but I won't ask again. Take your weapon back to your house."

Realizing Packard was serious and not backing down, Farmer Joe huffed and marched back to his house, cursing under his breath.

Toward the end of my row, Dawn was walking next to her dad, looking fervently behind every bush and small hill.

I tried several times to catch her eye, and finally on the fifth time, she looked my way. A smile tugged at her mouth. It was grim due to the circumstances, and I returned the expression, nodding my reassurance that everything would be okay. She appeared to read my signal correctly and nodded back.

As we continued, we flushed out a few pheasants and rabbits, but nothing else.

The Crooked House loomed in the distance, watching us, laughing at us. It knew where Andrea was. It probably had Andrea. I couldn't help but think of the irony of all the volunteers searching behind every rock and in every crevice, while Andrea sat just inside that house—tied up and gagged, probably.

We finished combing the field and continued up the trail that led to the Crooked House. I turned to my dad. "Dad, we need to check that house."

His face scrunched with thought. "Well, it's not abandoned anymore. If it was, I'm sure it would be the first place to look, but someone lives there now."

"All the more reason to look. Obviously, the man who lives there isn't here helping us. He's practically the only one in Riverton who's not."

"There's a lot of people who aren't here. We can't just accuse someone of a crime because they didn't show up or they live in a creepy house."

"Dad, this is a search. We need to look everywhere, right?"

He nodded.

"It's just a knock on the door. We'll ask him if he's seen her or anything suspicious."

Nodding, he said, "You're right. We have to check houses too. I'll get Jerry and Ross to go with me. You stay here."

"Why?" I demanded.

"Just stay back."

My dad gathered a couple of guys, and two more volunteered, including Dawn's dad, then five men marched down the trail to the house.

It looked as abandoned as it had the day before Lester moved in. It held secrets and history within its foundation and wood, and I couldn't help but think of Mathilda Stockholm, her hair in a tight bun, wearing her stiff pioneer dress. An image of her drowning her six-year-old daughter sent more than chills through my system. I felt my stomach churn, and in my head, I saw her crazy white eyes shadowed by dark rings.

Why did *she return my pillow?* I had a feeling she was calling out to me for help. *Help? She's a murderer! She was evil. Right?*

The search party gathered on Beck Street, and people compared notes, coming up with ideas of where to search next.

I wandered over to Dawn, who stood alone and was staring at the Crooked House.

"Hi," I said.

"Hi." She turned to me. "It's just awful."

"I know. I can't believe it."

"Vanished. Like that. Her mother turned away for a few seconds, and poof, she was gone." She shook her head. "Do you think it was them?"

"I do. They took Joanna, and now Andrea. I just can't prove it."

"Maybe they'll find something out." She nodded to the group of men approaching the house.

"That would be such a relief," I said.

"You know..." She perked with confidence. "I think they will. My dad is with them, and your dad. They'll see how suspicious he is and how he's hiding something. Sheriff Packard is here too."

I looked at Packard, who watched the five men approach the house.

"Let's go talk to him." Dawn marched toward him.

I had no choice but to follow.

"Sheriff?" she asked.

Keeping an eye on the house, he barely turned. "Hi. Dawn, wasn't it? Still needing sponsors?"

"I put that on hold for now. More important things going on, wouldn't you think?"

"Yes." He nodded and looked at me. "Hey, Ret."

I waved.

We all turned our attention back to the house and the five men knocking at the door. Lester was in the entrance with the door half open and a hand ready to close it. He appeared agitated as they talked to him.

"I wonder what he's saying," she said.

"I don't know." I turned to Packard. "What do you think, Sheriff?"

"They just got there. Let's see what happens." He looked down at both of us. "I know you think Lester and Beaumont are up to something. You might even think they're responsible for Andrea's disappearance."

"You have to admit it's pretty strange that shortly after Lester moved in, Beaumont went missing, then Joanna, and now Andrea. Not to mention the suspicious activity around Mrs. Beaumont's murder."

"I didn't mention there were any suspicions around Mrs. Beaumont's mur—I mean death."

"Why don't you at least search their house? Then you can be sure."

"Police have to have reasonable cause or a search warrant to do that. I can't just walk into someone's house and search it because you or anybody else thinks they're weird. There are laws and rules we need to follow. In other words, leave it up to me and my deputies. We're doing everything we can, and the best thing you two can do is continue to search. Understand?"

We nodded agreement, and Packard left us. Dawn and I watched as he walked up to the five men leaving the house and talked to them. Without saying a word, Dawn and I went back to searching.

THAT NIGHT, MATHILDA visited my room again. I woke up to her throwing things around. She swept both arms across the top of my dresser and knocked over my piggy bank, cologne, a pinewood derby trophy, a couple of Star Wars figures, and some papers.

I sat up straight in bed. She turned and growled at me, teeth bared in all their griminess, eyes two times larger and whiter than before. She was an enraged poltergeist. She threw something down on the top of my dresser, and like a whiff of smoke, she was gone.

Shaking, I stood up and walked over to the dresser to look down at everything.

"What's going on?" Scott rolled over, blinking at me. "What are you doing?"

"I... I just was going to the bathroom. Bumped into the dresser."

He scowled. "The dresser's nowhere near the door."

"Sleepwalking, I guess?"

I turned to our dresser to look for the item she dropped. It was a small, torn piece of blue silk. *Like the dress Andrea was last seen in!*

Hearing footsteps in the hall, I snatched up the cloth, stuffed it into my sock drawer, and closed the drawer just as my mom opened the bedroom door.

"Ret? Is everything okay? What happened?"

Words caught in my throat.

"He was sleepwalking again," Scott answered. "Ran into the dresser." He chuckled.

I shrugged sheepishly.

"You okay?"

"Yes." I nodded. "I'm fine."

CHAPTER NINETEEN
The Black Widows Reunite

I spread the piece of torn cloth out on a wooden plank that sat in the middle of us. We were in our new cave, where it was dark, dank, and private. Rosco, Jax, Gary, Dawn, Morgan, and I sat in an awkward circle. We stared at the clue the ghost had given to me. At first, they didn't understand what it was, but a second later, recognition illuminated Jax's face.

"Holy shit!" Jax exclaimed.

Dawn gasped. "Andrea was wearing a blue silk dress when she disappeared."

"What the—" Gary started.

"Son of a bitch!" Rosco said, looking up at me. "Where'd you get this?"

"You don't want to know." I shook my head, and Rosco looked at me, dumbfounded.

"No, we do want to know," Gary insisted.

I looked down at the piece of dress, afraid to speak but knowing they would continue to hound me until I spilled the beans.

"The ghost lady."

Jax and Gary gasped.

"Her name's Mathilda. She visits me."

"She comes to your house!" Jax's voice went so high, it was nearly a shriek, and he scooted back as if I were poison.

"Who the hell's this ghost lady?" Rosco asked.

We told him a quick rundown of our Crooked House adventure, and I filled them in on what I had found out at the library as well as what Dawn and I had heard on the walkie-talkie. Gary already knew most of it, but now everyone was filled in.

"And she threw this down on my dresser." I gestured to the cloth.

The others were silent, then finally, Dawn said, "Don't you know what this means?"

"No." Rosco's Texan accent was strong. "I don't."

"She's telling us something," I said. "Andrea is in that house! They took her!"

"This Beaumont feller and Lester, is it?" Rosco asked.

"Yes."

"Sum… bitch."

"We gotta tell the police," Gary said, pointing to the cloth. "Go to them with this."

"No." I shook my head. "They won't believe me. All they'll do is go to the house, knock on the door, and talk to Beaumont or Lester. They'll lie and say they don't know anything, and the cops will leave. Same thing happened yesterday. My dad said Lester acted confused, like he didn't know what they were talking about, and said he hadn't seen the girl."

"The cops just need to bust in there and do a search! Not stand on the porch and ask questions! Those bastards took my sister too. I know it." Morgan was heated, and I couldn't blame her.

"Of course, but they won't. They can't. Sheriff Packard said it's illegal. The cops need a search warrant."

"How do you get one of those? This should be enough." Gary motioned to the piece of Andrea's dress again.

"And tell them what? A ghost from the Crooked House came to my room last night and gave it to me?"

"Yes." Jax sounded certain, but the others sided with me in how ridiculous it sounded.

"They won't believe him," Dawn said. "Instead, they might wonder how he really got this and start accusing him of something."

She'd read my thoughts.

"Hell, I'll go down there right now and bust open their door and kick their asses!" Rosco said. "Take that girl back myself."

"I'll go with you," Morgan said.

"Is that what you're suggesting?" Gary asked me in disbelief.

"Not exactly but close. We must get into that house and save Andrea. Try to do it without being seen. Then we'll take Andrea to the cops, and they'll have to listen. They'll have to go arrest them."

There was terror in Jax's and Gary's eyes, but Rosco had a smile and gleam in his. "Sounds cool. I'm ready."

"We're doing this now?" Gary asked.

"No, we can't. Not in daylight."

"Daylight's much better than the dark!" Jax hollered. "Why do we have to wait until night?"

"There's too many people right now still searching for Andrea. They'll see us break into the house, and we'll get caught before we can help Andrea. I'm sorry, but we have to do this at night. We need to plan a sleepover. We'll sleep at my house in the backyard. Then when everyone's asleep, say around two in the morning, we'll go."

Silence filled the cave as reality sank in. I felt it too. My stomach squirmed with adrenaline and fear, and my body trembled.

"I know this is a lot, but we have to think about Andrea. That poor, innocent girl and what they might be doing to her. She's probably tied up and gagged in there, sitting in that house with *them* and the ghosts who haunt it. We need to be brave for her."

My words reached their hearts, and they breathed in more confidence and courage.

"We'll have to be heroes for her. We have to be the Black Widows."

"Yes," Jax said, excited.

Gary grinned. "We're back!"

"Who's the Black Widows?" Rosco asked.

Dawn and Morgan gave me a strange look.

"We are," I said. "It's our gang name."

"We have T-shirts made and everything," Jax said.

"You know the male black widows are killed by the females once they mate, right?" Rosco said.

"Well, let's make sure not to mate with any females," Gary said, and we all laughed.

Disgusted, the girls shook their heads.

"It's just a cool name," Jax said.

"All right! I like it." Rosco smiled. "Black Widows unite!"

He put his hand out in front of him, and the rest of us placed our hands on his for the cheer.

"One, two, three... Black Widows!"

MY BODY WAS TENSE AND jittery the entire day. I couldn't think or act straight, and when people asked me questions, I couldn't focus. I didn't want the night to come, but I wanted it over, and like Robert Frost said in one of my favorite poems, "He says the best way out is always through." And I could see no way out but through.

We had a bit of a struggle getting our parents to agree to us sleeping outside. Since Andrea's disappearance was still fresh, and there was speculation that she was kidnapped, they were extremely apprehensive. But my backyard was fenced in, and we agreed to sleep in a tent.

Rosco brought his pellet gun, Gary brought a baseball bat, all Jax had was a pocketknife, and I borrowed a six-inch army knife from Jeff. The weapons made us feel more secure. I also brought a small flashlight.

I'd pulled my Black Widow T-shirt out of my bottom drawer, and Jax and Gary were wearing theirs. We helped Rosco make his before we pitched the tent.

Dressed in our Black Widow T-shirts and jeans, we stood next to our tent as the sun settled down and invited the night in. As an armed gang, we had the courage to face whatever horrors awaited us at that house.

We stared at the Crooked House for a long time. There were a couple of lights on, one upstairs and one down. Beaumont's hearse was parked in the driveway, and another car sat in front of it, but it was covered entirely by a gray tarp. It had to be Lester's car, and I was reminded of the person who'd run Todd Harrison off the road. *Is he hiding the damage?*

"It'd be sweet if they drove away tonight, left the house for some time," Gary said.

"I wouldn't get a chance to use this," Rosco said, sounding disappointed, as he held up his pellet rifle.

"All that gun's good for is to piss 'em off. It won't really hurt them. Not like this knife will." Jax held up his tiny pocketknife. "I can stab 'em with this."

"That might pinch them a little." Rosco chuckled. "But wait 'til I pump this twenty times. It'll do more'n bite 'em a little. It'll puncture skin."

"While you're doing that, I'll be busting their kneecaps with this." Gary swung his bat.

"All right, bad boys, we each have a dangerous weapon, but we can't be stupid about it. We don't *want* to run into them. We don't want to use these things. Just get the girl and get out. That's it."

They all nodded agreement.

"When are the girls comin'?" Rosco asked.

"They're sleeping over at Dawn's, and they'll meet us here at two."

"We'd better get some sleep before then," Gary said.

We clambered into the tent and crawled into our sleeping bags. Rosco was sawing logs minutes later, but the rest of us couldn't sleep. I couldn't stop the jitters or get my mind to shut up long enough to catch any z's.

I exited the tent around one fifteen and stood next to it, staring at the Crooked House. Only the upstairs light was on.

Gary came out and stood next to me. "We're really going to do this?"

"Yes," I said. "We have to. As scared as I am, I can't help but think how more scared she is. If she can go through unimaginable terror alone, then we can together."

We heard footsteps behind us and turned to see Dawn entering my yard, alone.

"Dawn?" I whispered and walked over to her. "Where's Morg?"

"Her mom wouldn't let her sleep over. I had to sneak out of the house after everyone went to sleep."

"Won't you get in trouble?" Gary asked.

"If I do, I do. This is too important."

I saw an aluminum bat dangling in her right hand. "I see you brought a weapon."

"Good choice," Gary remarked.

At one thirty, we caught the break of a lifetime. The last light went out, then Beaumont and Lester exited the house. They got into the hearse and drove away.

I ran into the tent and shook Rosco awake. "Come on!" I whispered as loudly as I dared to. "We gotta go! They just left the house!"

We marched our way to my back fence that bordered the field, weapons at hand. Rosco's hair stuck out in several different directions. We hopped the chain-link fence and stomped through the field of tall brush toward the house.

It waited for us, pretending to be asleep to lure us in. If a house could grin, the Crooked House would have. The moon was bright and helped illuminate the house and our path.

We stopped short of the porch, and everyone looked at me for a decision.

"Let's go around to the back door," I whispered, crouched low, and we scurried around the house.

I stopped at the car covered with the tarp first.

"What are you doing?" Gary whispered.

"Someone ran Todd Harrison off the road. *That's* how he was killed. Whoever did it owns a black car, and it should have damage."

Rosco set his gun down and helped me peel the tarp back over the hood.

"Holy shit." Rosco stared at the passenger-side fender, and I ran to look.

I crouched to inspect the line of scratches and dents that marked up the side of the car, and several of the lines were red.

"Todd Harrison's car was red." I tapped the red paint, and both Gary and Jax gasped; Dawn put a hand to her open mouth.

We quickly covered the car again and crept to the back door.

"Who wants to stay outside and keep watch?" I asked, and everyone turned to Dawn.

"Not me. I'm going in," she insisted, and no one argued.

"I'll stay," Gary said.

"Whistle if you see anyone coming."

"I can't whistle."

"How 'bout a bird sound?" Rosco offered.

"Hoot-hoot?"

"What the hell's that?" Jax exclaimed.

"It's an owl."

Jax rolled his eyes.

I hopped over the two steps to the back door and tried the knob as quietly and slowly as I could. It was unlocked, and I pushed open the door. Darkness and a breath of dank mustiness greeted me. I froze at the entrance.

"You ready?" Rosco whispered, wearing a huge mischievous grin. It gave me confidence.

Behind him, Dawn and Jax stood ready to go.

I stepped in. The floorboards creaked and echoed. I turned on my flashlight but kept the beam low to the floor. Nothing seemed out of the ordinary, which *was* extraordinary. It looked the same as it had before, and yet someone was *living* there. I expected some furniture, pictures on the walls, or something by now. There wasn't even a dining table.

I stepped into the kitchen on my left and finally found signs of a tenant. On the counter sat a bowl, with a spoon cradled in it, next to an opened box of Cap'n Crunch. On the floor was a Styrofoam cooler filled with half-melted ice, a carton of milk, and two cans of Coke.

The house was quiet. No movement but ours.

"Andrea," I called out in a loud whisper. Nothing. "Andrea!" It came out louder the next time. I just wanted to find the girl and get the hell out of there.

My flashlight beam landed on a door in the kitchen. "Where do you think that goes?"

"The basement. I'm not going down there," Jax said.

I thought of the newspaper clipping. The killer had kept his dead victims in the basement. It sent chills up my spine.

Dawn stepped next to me, and we moved on through the dining room, the front living room, and the parlor. There was nothing but the same old furniture, shrouded with years of dust and cobwebs. No sign of Andrea or the ghost.

My legs shook with every step, and I knew everyone else's did too. Each time I caught their eyes in the light, I saw nothing but terror.

She wasn't on the ground floor. *Basement* popped in my head, but like Jax, I was scared to go there.

"Let's check upstairs," Dawn said, and I was relieved to go up instead of down. The boards of the stairs felt ready to bust at any moment, and they creaked and whined under our weight.

"What if she's here?" Jax asked.

"She is here. We're trying to find her," I answered.

"No. I mean..."

"Mathilda?" I said. "The ghost?"

"Yes." His voice trembled.

"If she is, she won't hurt you... I think."

"You think?" Jax asked.

We crested the stairs and checked the room we'd slept in weeks ago. It was empty, just like we'd left it. We continued down the hall, and I couldn't help but notice the invisible ghosts that cloaked every wall, door, and piece of furniture. There was life in the house, a dark one that reflected the lives of everyone who had lived—and died—there. It was all there, seeping through the wood and plaster, begging us to unravel the mysteries.

At the end of the hall was the master bedroom. We found the first evidence of life since leaving the kitchen. The bed was undone, and clothes were strewn about among piles of garbage from take-out food. The clothes, in a variety of colors, stood out against the gray background of the house's dusty interior. They belonged to Lester Kilborn.

We checked the closets, bathrooms, and under beds. No sign of Andrea.

"Where do you think she'd be?" Rosco asked.

"She's not here." Jax turned to me. "Maybe you were wrong."

Dawn looked at me with the same bewilderment we all shared.

"Where would she be?" Dawn asked.

Basement.

"Could the ghost be trying to tell you something else? Maybe she really knows where Andrea is, but you got it wrong," Dawn suggested.

I was confused and frustrated. "She has to be here," I insisted.

"We didn't check the basement," Rosco said.

"You're right." I was hesitant to go, fearful the basement was the right place, scared of what I might find. I wasn't ready.

"We'll go together," Rosco said with a steel gaze and a firm nod.

Dawn put a reassuring hand on my shoulder.

"Yes, we'll go together," I agreed.

I led the others from the bedroom and froze. The others bumbled into me.

"What the..." Jax started, then he saw what I saw.

At the far end of the hall, on the other side of the stairway, stood the tall, dark shape of a man. The hall was too dark to make out his expression, but he was facing up, and there was no doubt he saw us. His arms were at his sides, hands curled into tight claws, and I heard his breathing. It was soft, rhythmic, and slow.

We didn't move, and neither did he.

Beaumont and Lester were gone, and this was not Andrea. I hadn't seen anyone else with them before. *Who is he?*

My stomach curdled, and the chills up my arms and spine told me he was an enemy. Mouth like cotton, I couldn't speak or move.

A light caught the corner of my eye. I turned slowly to look out the window above the front door, where a pair of headlights approached. *Beaumont and Lester.* The lights bounced once as the car dipped into a rut and came out.

"Hoot! Hoot!" Gary sounded desperate at the back door.

The headlights illuminated the dark man's right eye. It was wild and crazed, like a rabid dog's. He was about to pounce on us violently. I clutched the knife in one hand and flashlight in the other.

"I'm going to stall him... you guys run," I whispered to my friends.

They didn't have time to argue. I charged the dark form ahead of me with a loud war cry. "Ahhh!"

I ran into him like a rhino square into his stomach, with my fists outstretched, but knife pointed down. I wasn't prepared to strike with my knife unless I absolutely had to.

Breath escaped his mouth like air from a balloon. I'd caught him off guard, and he stumbled back. Luck was on my side. He tripped over something on the floor behind him, and arms flailing, he slammed to the floor.

My friends stormed down the stairs. My momentum almost toppled me, but I steadied myself, turned for the steps, and ran. I didn't look back or listen for him. It took him a few seconds to readjust before he charged after us.

I took the staircase in three strides, landed, turned, and tore off toward the kitchen. The dark man thumped down the stairs.

My friends ran out the back door. Dawn was the last. She turned to make sure I was all right.

"Go!" I yelled, and before Dawn exited, she saw me open the door to the basement and enter.

I shut the door behind me. In complete darkness, I heard Dawn's muffled cry, "Ret!"

"Just go, Dawn. Please go!" I mumbled, and she did.

The Dark Man's footsteps pounded on the floor on the other side of the basement door. They halted. I heard his heavy breathing. His feet shuffled then stopped. He waited by the door like a sentry. Moments later, the front door opened, and more footsteps creaked the floor then halted.

"Look, Lester, he's up. Moving around." Beaumont's voice sounded muffled through the door.

"Hmm, looks like shit." Lester chuckled. "Not used to the air yet?"

The men were silent.

I began to second-guess going into the basement when I had a clear escape available. I may have caused my own death by doing so, but I had a responsibility, and my conscience wouldn't have it any other way. My hand had reached out and opened the door, and I'd followed. I *had* to find Andrea.

I moved my right foot to the next step, and it let out a small squeak. I grimaced and froze. The air was too quiet. No one made a sound.

A second later, they began walking around, making creaking sounds of their own and talking. They hadn't heard me, and they were loud and moving around. I saw my chance to take the stairs without alerting them.

I tiptoed down the staircase. I tried to hear their conversation, but I only caught pieces.

"We better move quickly. Before she starts to decompose," Lester said, and the words didn't register in my mind right away. I was too busy sneaking down the stairs quickly and quietly, bent on finding Andrea. Cobwebs caught my face and arms, and like a madman swatting at invisible bees, I pulled as many off me as I could.

There was a soft glow around the corner of the stairwell. I approached the dancing blue light and found a large circle in the floor lined with bricks. Blue light emanated from the water inside the circle, though I saw no light bulb.

I recalled the well that Mr. Dunlap had told me about—Henry Stockholm had built a well to contain the water seeping into the basement. But instead of being far below, the surface of the water was more like a small pool in the floor, like the reflecting pools Egyptians decorated their temples with. The glowing blue light within danced eerily.

A rumpled form lay in front of the pool. I stepped closer, and the figure's blue dress caught the glow from the water. Lying on her side, with her back to me, she didn't move.

"Andrea," I said softly, my heart in my throat.

Her dress was torn, and I was sure that if I pulled out my piece of blue silk, it would fit perfectly into the empty spot.

"Andrea?" I said again, on the verge of tears. It was what I feared the most. She didn't move. I heard no breathing. I touched her arm, and it was ice-cold. I turned her slightly, not wanting to see her face, but knowing I had to.

Her eyes were closed, fortunately, and her face was a mottled mix of blue and white. Dark blood caked the side of her face from scalp to chin, long strings of hair were plastered across her cheeks, and her mouth hung open. The glow illuminated her. I knew I would never forget her face. It was imprinted in my memory during that horrible moment.

She was gone. Her shell was left behind. Sobs came; I couldn't control them. I'd known Andrea only in passing, but seeing another corpse—especially a kid, like me—was horrifying. As I looked at her body, a reoccurring feeling set in. One I'd felt at each funeral and viewing I'd attended. A person I knew was there no more. Her body was there, but Andrea was somewhere else. In a better place. One of comfort and love. She wasn't in pain or fear anymore, and that gave me peace.

Then the door at the top of the stairs squeaked, and a slice of light split the darkness. They were coming.

CHAPTER TWENTY
Fear from Beyond

Frantic, I searched for a hiding spot and found one across the room, behind a stack of boxes, an old tricycle, a playhouse, an ancient stroller, and some toys. I crouched behind them, clutching my knife, and watched as Beaumont and Lester ambled down the staircase.

They stopped at Andrea's body.

"She's so young," Lester said. "Is this going to work with her?"

I watched through slats between the playhouse and boxes. I didn't see the man I'd knocked over, and I wondered where he was. Then I heard several creaks above me and realized the Dark Man had stayed upstairs.

"I've never tried it with a child. Her frame may not be strong enough. I told you to get an older teenager or someone in their early twenties."

"I'm sorry. I thought she was sixteen or seventeen at least. She looked older."

Andrea was tall for her age, but judging by the expression on Beaumont's face, he didn't buy it.

"Come on. Help me with her," he commanded, and I watched them pick her up on opposite sides like a sack of flour, shuffle to the pool, and set her on top of the water.

I expected her to sink, assuming they were disposing of her body in the pool, but instead, her body lay still on top of the moving water as if the surface were made of concrete. Her lifeless arms and legs swayed up and down with the motion of the water. The blue glow of the pool illuminated Beaumont's and Lester's faces in a grisly manner. Eyes wide, they watched.

"Come forth, my friend," Beaumont spoke to the water. Then he began to speak in a strange tongue, and the tone of his voice was deep and unearthly.

I stared at Andrea's body with them. It remained still, shifting with the tiny waves. He chanted more, then her eyes flew open!

Every nerve in my body exploded, and I gasped for air, fighting back a panic attack. *If they hear me, I'm dead.*

"Rise, my friend." Beaumont smirked.

She coughed and gurgled, and her body sputtered. Gasping, she struggled to lift her head, then shook it violently back and forth.

"He's not used to our air. This body is new to him. Help him up," Beaumont said, and they both took an arm and helped her step out of the water.

I wondered why he'd referred to Andrea as "he" and how her body was new to "him." He'd brought Andrea's body back to life, but it *wasn't* Andrea.

Then it hit me. The same thing had happened with Beaumont. He'd gone missing for days then come back as someone completely different. I wondered if his tall, lanky body had once rested on that water and brought in a soul from another world.

They set Andrea's feet on the floor, but her legs were like cooked spaghetti. She wobbled, tripped, and fell. She still gasped for air, then seemed to find it, because once she did, she howled like a banshee. The shrill scream ripped up my spine with icy nails.

She flailed about like a rag doll with a ghastly face and panicked, wide eyes. She clawed the air aimlessly, gagged, and coughed out black sludge.

I could only stare in ultimate horror. She fell and crawled along the floor, moaning a deep, rattling, painful groan. Beaumont and Lester laughed at her as if she were a carnival freak.

"I told you her frame was too weak," Beaumont said.

"It's going to be a while before she finds her legs." Lester chuckled, and Beaumont scowled at him.

"It is not a she. *He* is one of my trusted friends. We escaped prison together. It's because of him I'm here. If this body fails, which I think it will, I'll send him back, and we'll find a new body for him. One closer to his age. A male would be more fitting."

Lester sighed, rolling his eyes, and his shoulders sank. "Do you know how hard it is to get a man? The last one was hell. I twisted my ankle, still have bruises, and I'm sure one of my ribs is broken."

Beaumont snapped around and clutched Lester's throat in his clawed hand. "Is that why you brought me this young girl? Because she's easy prey? This work is too important to be lazy. My friends are still back there, being hunted by the Tormentor. We need to get them through before it finds them. Before it finds *me*! Get off your lazy ass for once and bring me some real bodies. You can use my friend Kayle to help." He gestured toward the stairs. I assumed he meant the Dark Man. "It appears he's getting around well enough, and he's strong."

Beaumont pushed Lester, and he stumbled back against the staircase.

"My friends need energy too. They're not strong enough when they enter these bodies. They need to be fed." He turned and burned another glare at Kilborn. "We need a couple of live ones to feed them."

"Do they *eat* them?" Lester's eyes widened, and his mouth twisted as if he'd swallowed something horrible.

"No. It's their souls we feed on."

I tried to pay attention to their discussion, but I couldn't get my eyes off Andrea. She still moaned. She rolled on the floor, changed directions, and started to crawl toward me.

Her arms were limp as if no muscle hid beneath her pale skin. She dragged her useless feet behind her. Her sunken eyes were white with fear, and her mouth hung open, dripping black sludge. Her hair was splayed across half her face, and her eyes transfixed on me. I'd been found. Her eyes widened as she saw me.

Heart in my throat, I froze. She kept coming, groaning, and with her eyes targeting me, I knew I had to move. Finally, I found the nerve to shuffle my butt deeper into the shadows.

Her fingers scrabbled against the playhouse and boxes, and she pulled herself forward enough to press her face against the plastic house. I saw one of her eyes through the upstairs window of the dollhouse. We stared eye to eye, inches from each other.

Suddenly, she disappeared as Lester grabbed her ankle and dragged her back toward them. Then Beaumont raised a shovel high above his head.

I turned because I couldn't look, but I couldn't spare my ears from hearing the sickening thud. I cried so hard inside.

"We can't afford to lose more time. I need three more bodies fast, and no more children," Beaumont growled. "Unless the children are for the *feeding*."

I continued to stare at the floor, holding back sobs, as Lester scooped her body into his arms and followed Beaumont upstairs. The door shut, and I was alone again. The only sound that accompanied me was the screech of the floorboards above.

Tears streamed down my face, and my chest heaved in and out as I shook with sobs for a good five minutes—partly because of my sheer horror and partly out of grief for Andrea and her family. An emptiness filled me and expanded to every finger and toe. I'd let Andrea down. I'd failed her. I should have been stronger and forced the police or my parents to listen. If I'd done something sooner, then maybe, just maybe...

I felt warmth on my shoulder and turned. Andrea stood behind me—the real Andrea, not the monster. Her spirit. Her form was luminescent with a soft glow.

She smiled. She didn't speak a word. She didn't have to. The gratitude in her eyes told me not to worry. Warm feelings washed over me, and I felt a strong sense of love and joy emanating from her. The feelings hit me like an invisible wave. The overwhelming sensation was like nothing I'd ever experienced, and I felt tears run down my cheeks. I would have guessed there would be sadness or anger, but maybe those didn't exist in the afterlife.

She was only visible for a matter of seconds, then her image faded, leaving me alone again. She left me with a gift to pass on, one of hope and love, and my own realization that there was more to life than just being alive. What we did in it was what counted.

I stood up, feeling rejuvenated and stronger. I looked at the ceiling and listened for footsteps. I needed to get out of that house, but first, I needed them gone so I could make a break for it. A few moments later, I heard footsteps that sounded rhythmic, perhaps someone ascending the stairs.

Mathilda appeared at the top of the basement stairs, looking at me with wild anticipation. She motioned for me to follow. She was signaling that the coast was clear! I wondered for the briefest moment why Mathilda seemed different than Andrea, then I hurried up the steps, and she disappeared. I listened intently at the door. Nothing. I slowly opened the door and peeked out. No one was in sight. The back door was only feet away. I bolted for it.

I ran across the kitchen floor as quietly as possible, but I got ahead of myself, tripped over the cooler of ice, and thudded to the floor. The milk jug inside split open, spreading its white contents across the floor, along with skating ice cubes. There was no way they hadn't heard the noise.

I jumped up and threw open the door just as I heard the men charge down the stairs. I ran outside, where I panicked, trying to decide which way to go. Then Rosco popped up from behind a berm about twenty feet ahead and motioned for me. I'd been in that basement for a while, and I'd thought my friends would be long gone by then. I'd never been so happy to see him. I ran to him and leapt over the berm to find

Dawn and Gary were still with him. They grabbed me in a group hug, then we crouched out of sight behind the berm.

"They killed Andrea. She's inside," I whispered.

"Bastards," Rosco hissed.

"Where's Jax?" I asked.

"He went to call the cops. We didn't know what was going to happen to you," Dawn said.

"We gotta go," Gary said. His nose was practically pressed against the dirt ledge of the berm, watching the Crooked House. He shuddered, and I crept up beside him to peek over the edge. The Dark Man stood in the doorway, silhouetted by a light inside, and Beaumont's face scowled over his shoulder.

"Go," I heard Beaumont order the man.

I grabbed Dawn, and we all tore out of there faster than rabbits. We moved to run the way we came, but the Dark Man cut off our escape to the south. So we ran to the north, directly opposite, and the Dark Man followed.

We ran hard, jumped over bushes and rocks, twisted around blocked paths, and flew over small hills like deer. Dawn stayed next to me. We started to curve back east and eventually south toward home, but then I realized we'd gone so far north that we were on the other side of the field and had a long way to go. I felt the Dark Man gaining.

Ahead and a little to our left, I spotted the dark shape of Farmer Joe's barn. Lungs burning, I gasped and pointed at it. "We're not going to make it. Go in there. Hide."

Dawn nodded, and the others followed.

The door on the side was open, and we ran in. Bales of hay were stacked to the ceiling, and loose hay covered the ground. Dust and particles of grass filled the air, threatening my lungs. There were a ton of places to hide inside the maze of stacks, and we quickly dispersed and found clever hiding spots. I ran to the back of the barn and hid behind a stack of four bales, next to an open path. I waited, panting and sweating heavily. I thought Dawn was next to me, but when I turned, I didn't see her.

Where are the cops? I silently begged them to come.

Gary hid a few feet behind me. He climbed two bales of hay and found a good spot. Rosco's position didn't look so good. He was fifteen feet to the side of me behind one square of hay. He held his pellet gun out and started pumping it rapidly.

"What're you doing?" I asked.

"Just in case," he assured me, but I was worried he would shoot early and piss off the giant man. The Dark Man didn't appear to be vulnerable to pellets.

Where is Dawn?

"Dawn?" I called out quietly.

To my relief, her head popped out from a stack behind me, and she gave me a wink then disappeared again. I had a tiny view of the entrance and watched as the dark form stepped in. He stopped and stood still.

Rosco rested his rifle on the bale of hay and took aim. I clenched and prayed silently for him not to shoot.

I looked around for anything that could help us and saw a worktable against the wall not far from me. I crept low and scooted my way to it. Scattered across the table were tools and one long shotgun, probably the one with rock salt in the shells, but it would be a hell of a lot better than Rosco's pellet gun.

Dawn turned and watched me as I took the shotgun and moved back into my hiding spot. Gary looked down at me, wide-eyed.

I'd fired a shotgun a few times before with my brothers, cousins, and uncles when we went rabbit hunting, so I was familiar with it. I couldn't pump in a shell yet because the sound would alert him to where I was.

The Dark Man approached, walking slowly through the aisles created by the stacks of hay.

"Here, here, boys..." The tone of his voice sounded familiar, despite the sing-song words. "Come out, come out, wherever you are."

His footsteps crunched on brittle hay. I clutched my gun. Rosco and I shared a glance.

The Dark Man twisted fast and looked behind a stack. Finding nothing, he kept moving.

"I don't like playing games. But I am sure going to love snapping your necks in two. Slow. Between my hands. Or maybe I'll just stomp on your neck. Either way, I'm going to have fun."

He jumped into another spot and came up empty. He was on the path closest to me. He would soon be on me. I took deep breaths and waited.

I saw his foot first, and I tensed. Then his whole body stood in front of me. He turned, and I saw his face in the moonlight streaming from the upper windows.

Suddenly, I understood why the voice was familiar. Though the voice was absent of his Southern accent, it had belonged to Todd Harrison. He was the man Lester had whined about being tough to take down, and now I knew why Lester ran Todd off the road.

He looked at me. A sly grin crept on his face. I quickly pumped a shell into place. He growled. Hands outstretched, he came for me.

Pop, pop, pop! Rosco fired the first shot into the man's back, pumped quickly, and fired twice more. The Dark Man arched his back and yelped. It irritated him, but nothing more.

I squeezed the shotgun trigger, but the trigger didn't move. *Oh shit, the safety!*

I couldn't find it in the dark. The creature came after me again, and Rosco kept firing, to no avail. A beam came from above. Gary shot a beam from his flashlight into the Dark Man's eyes, blinding him.

The light was enough for me to find the safety. I clicked it off, aimed, and fired. The gun kicked against my shoulder. The spray of rock salt hit his chest in a puff of powder, and he stumbled.

I pumped another one in and shot again. It rocked him back even farther, and he hollered in pain. I saw blood, and vapors rose from his wounds. I heard sizzling like cooking bacon, and the creature cried in pain. It all seemed surreal.

Enraged, the Dark Man attempted to shake off the pain. He wailed, and I pumped another salt pellet into him. He stumbled but didn't fall.

Dawn pounced out of nowhere and charged him, swinging a bat like she was going to knock him out of the barn, and smacked it hard against his chest. The Dark Man fell to the ground. More smoke arose from Todd Harrison's body.

It must be the salt, I thought. *Maybe it hurts him like it does demons.*

Gary hopped down, and Rosco ran over and grabbed the shotgun from me. Before we bolted out of there, he blasted another one into Todd Harrison's body. "For Andrea, you bastard!"

Then we bolted, and the Dark Man didn't follow. He didn't get up as far as I knew.

We ran across the field in record time and were almost to the fence behind my house when I heard the sirens. Seeing the flashing lights approach the Crooked House across the field, I sighed with relief and stopped running. I turned to my friends, who slowed to a stop—except for Gary, who leapt on the fence to climb over it. He craned his head back to me with a questioning look as if I were crazy.

"What are you doing?" Gary cried.

"We gotta go back." I gestured to Lester's house.

"What the hell for?"

"Ret's right." Rosco stepped toward Gary. "Come on, buddy. We gotta set this wrong right."

"Are you sure that's a good idea?" Dawn asked, with a squeak of fear in her voice.

"Someone has to tell the cops what happened," I said, looking into her eyes, then turned back to Gary. "Jax called the police because I was trapped in the house, right? They'll be looking for me. Besides, I need to show them where Andrea is, or this was all for nothing."

Gary hopped off the fence and stomped through the brush to me, still panting from the run. "That *Todd* thing is going to come charging out of that barn any minute and tear us into pieces."

"We best hurry then." Rosco grinned with confidence and a fire in his eyes. "The cops will call our parents for us, and they'll sort this whole thing out."

"You okay?" I asked Dawn. She took a deep breath and nodded.

"Let's go," Rosco ordered, and Dawn and I trotted after him toward the Crooked House. Gary stayed back, contemplating with both hands on his hips. I was about to call after him when he began to run for us.

CHAPTER TWENTY-ONE
Out in the Open

The next couple of days was a surreal blur of policemen, news reporters, and curious neighbors. My body was numb, like I was in a tunnel, watching it all play out in a strange slow-motion reel.

The police dogs found Andrea's body in a shallow grave beneath the trees next to the creek. The grave wasn't any closer to the Crooked House than anyone else's house, and nothing found tied her to Beaumont, Lester, or the house—other than my own testimony. It was enough for Sheriff Packard to bring them in for questioning and for an army of men, including a special crime scene investigation unit, to scour the house.

My mother was the first person I saw after we left the barn and met up with the police. I didn't know how strong I'd stayed until I crumpled into her arms and sobbed. She held me tightly and caressed my hair.

I talked to Andrea's parents briefly. Her mother looked at me, her eyes bloodshot and face full of pain, as if her soul had been left with an empty hole she would never be able to fill again. I was nervous about what to say, but I felt Andrea with me. I opened my mouth, and I'm not sure where my words came from, but they came out with honesty and sincerity. I told them what I had seen, despite what the police had found. I also told them about Andrea's spirit and that she was around them to comfort them in their grief. I owed her that much. I wasn't sure if my words penetrated or helped at all.

Sheriff Packard allowed me to visit with my parents and Andrea's family for a short while, but he kept close, listening and watching. I knew what he wanted. He couldn't wait to question me.

He was the same with my friends. He allowed their families to comfort them, then his deputies took each of them separately for questioning. I caught Dawn's eyes as an officer led her to another area to talk to her. She looked concerned but strong.

Packard gripped my shoulder. "I need you for a moment."

I looked at my mom, who nodded, then followed him to his squad car. I sat in the front passenger seat while he took the driver's.

"How are you doing? Are you okay?"

I was wrapped in a gray blanket the officers had given me, and I drank from a Styrofoam cup of water. I needed them both. "Good. Still shaky. Did you find the man in the barn?" When we first came upon the police I told them someone chased us into the barn and was still there, and Rosco backed me up.

"I sent a couple of guys to check it out." Packard stared out the front window for a moment then turned to me. "What brought you here, Ret? Why did you and your friends come to Lester's house?"

"I just—we wanted to find Andrea. We were looking through the field and ended up here."

"At night? In the dark?"

"Yes. I know it sounds weird, but we didn't want to give up. We wanted to find her."

"Lester and Beaumont said you boys broke into his house. They came home and found you running from his kitchen."

"We did sneak into their house, but—"

"Why? Ret, why did you go into their house?"

I thought of the torn piece of Andrea's dress in my pocket. I was afraid to reveal it. How could I tell him? Had one of my friends already divulged that information? If I didn't, and they did, that would look bad for me.

"Those two were acting real suspicious. I just had a feeling."

Packard's stare drilled into me. There was no escaping his lie-detecting capabilities. "Don't feed me a line of bullshit, Ret. I wonder if I hadn't driven by Lester's house the other day if you and Dawn would have broken in then. This is serious stuff. We're through with lies and excuses. If all of this is true, and those two are behind Andrea's disappearance, I need every bit of information and evidence I can find. Do you understand? Let's start again from the beginning. You and your friends got together, and what did you say to each other?"

I closed my eyes and let out a deep breath. I had to tell him. "I found a piece of Andrea's dress."

I pulled it from my pocket and showed him. His eyes widened, and his mouth dropped open.

"Where did you get this?" He took the cloth, holding it between two fingertips. He took a small plastic baggie out of his shirt pocket, carefully placed the cloth inside, and sealed it.

"You're going to find this crazy, but there's a ghost who lives in that house. She brought it to me. After that, I had no doubt where Andrea was."

"A ghost?" Packard rolled his eyes. "Come on, Ret, let's keep this story in the real world."

"You wanted the truth. No bullshit, Sheriff. Look at my eyes. Tell me I'm lying." My assertiveness surprised even me. He studied me again.

"Weeks ago, my friends and I snuck into that house on a dare. Before Lester moved in. Halfway through the night, we ran into a ghost who scared the hell out of us, and we tore out of there. Her name is Mathilda Stockholm. She and her husband, Henry, moved into this house in 1902. They had a daughter. She drowned in that house, and Mathilda took her own life. She now haunts the place."

Dumbfounded, Packard remained silent as he sorted his thoughts. I hoped the facts about the Stockholms and the house gave my story credibility.

"Well, you know your history, but I still can't buy the ghost story. What happened next?"

I told him everything and pulled no punches.

When I finished, he nodded. "Okay, you've been through a lot. I'm going to have the medics check you out. It's standard procedure, and I want to be sure you're all right."

"Okay, but there's one more thing. The man we left back in the barn. It's Todd Harrison."

Packard stared at me expressionlessly, as if not knowing how to react. "Todd Harrison? We just buried his body. You must be mistaken. Trauma can cause that."

"You'll find out soon enough." I shrugged.

"You'll need to come into the station and fill out an official statement. I'll be in touch with your parents."

"Are you going to arrest Beaumont and Lester?"

"There's a lot we have to do. They'll be brought in, they'll be questioned, and God willing, we'll have enough evidence to make them fry. But I'm a steward of the law. I can't do anything without evidence."

"What about everything I just told you?"

"It does have merit. Believe me, it helps. I'd have nothing else to go on if I didn't have your testimony. But your word is not enough all by itself. Andrea is not inside that house. They deny any involvement. I'm going to do my best to get every piece of evidence I can find and present it to the district attorney. It's up to him to decide if there's enough to prosecute."

"How long is that going to take?" I asked.

"Let's just say we have a long road ahead of us. I'm going to hold them as long as I can. It's my job to protect this city." He turned and gave me an earnest look. "I need your help, Ret. You need to come to me before you do anything like this again. Is that understood?"

"Yes." I nodded.

"I'm serious. You are in no position to take this on. You just kicked a hornet's nest, and I need to keep you safe. You come to me next time. I am on your side." His eyes held sincerity and caring. I was no lie detector like him, but I could recognize the truth.

A photograph on his dashboard caught my eye. It was Packard and his family. His wife stood on one side, with two children—a boy and a girl—between them.

"Is that your family?" I pointed.

"Yes," he said hesitantly.

I looked at his hands. He was twisting his wedding ring back and forth between his forefinger and thumb nervously.

"You guys look happy together."

"We were." His eyes turned glassy. "We surprised our kids one day by taking them to the zoo. That picture was taken on that day. It was a good day."

"They look really nice. How come I haven't seen them?"

"My kids live with their mother. We divorced, and she moved back to Massachusetts and took my kids with her. I don't see them much." He forced a quick, brave smile and rubbed his eyes. I remembered our conversation at the park on the Fourth of July, when I'd asked him about his family. He said they were "fine" and walked off. I knew I'd struck a nerve then, and I suddenly understood why.

"My mom and dad fight a lot." I didn't know why I'd shared that. Perhaps I thought if I shared a similar pain in my life, he wouldn't feel alone. "They don't seem happy anymore."

He rested a hand on my knee and smiled. "It may not mean anything, and it may mean something. Whatever happens, just know your parents love you, and it's not you they fight about. Life happens, and it doesn't always go the way you want it to go. Bad things happen to good people, like Andrea and her family, and they don't make sense, but we go on because we have to. If something does happen with your parents and they separate, just know it's done because it's the best thing to do. Staying together hurts more than it helps. Life will change. Just embrace it the best you can and roll with the punches. Okay?"

I nodded. "Thanks."

He eyeballed my Black Widow shirt. "I thought the Black Widows retired."

"They came out of retirement for one last mission."

"Let's keep it their last."

"You got it."

"And for hell's sake, call me before you do anything stupid like this again. I couldn't stand it if something happened to you."

I felt a tingle of warmth in my chest.

"I'm getting kinda used to you being around." He grinned and gave me a friendly wink.

Once I left the sheriff's car, I headed through the crowd to my family. Officers were guiding Beaumont to a squad car, hands cuffed behind him, his head down. The crowd parted for a moment, and there was a clear line of sight between us. He was fifteen feet away.

Beaumont lifted his head, and his eyes burned a glare into me like sunlight through a magnifying glass. His lips peeled back from his teeth, and his face shook. If he could have willed harm to me with mere thought, I would've been dead on the spot.

My breath caught in my throat, and my heart skipped a beat. I'd never felt so much hatred from someone. I remembered what he'd said in the basement about the Tormentor—he was running out of time to save his friends he'd escaped from prison with. He needed more bodies to pull his friends into our world, and I had just thrown a wrench into his whole plan. It was no wonder he hated me.

The cops opened the back door to the squad car, pushed his head down, and directed him into the back seat. Once inside, he resumed his burning stare.

"Ret?" My mom approached me and wrapped an arm around my shoulders. "Ready to go home?"

I nodded and followed her to our car.

"GROUP OF LOCAL CHILDREN Claim to Have Found Missing Teen's Body in Neighbor's Home" was the headline next morning, and we were the top story on the local TV news. However, my parents didn't allow me to be interviewed on TV because they were concerned about the trauma I'd already been through.

I lay in bed most of the day, and at irregular intervals, my body trembled and convulsed in shock. I was silent, and my family left me alone, except for my mom, who brought me food, warmed up a blanket for my shivers, placed an extra pillow under my head, and treated me to a shake later.

We watched the local evening news together. It was all surreal, like a nightmare come true. My brothers asked me questions after it aired, and I told them how the news got some things wrong. Even though only Jax had gone to call the police, the reporter had said we'd all run from the house and gone straight to a neighbor to call the police. They didn't talk about the barn incident at all.

I filled in my family on all the actual details, including the grisly ones and supernatural elements. On each of their faces, I could see the inner debate as to whether to believe my story wholly or not. I felt my mom's stare, and I knew what questions were behind her eyes.

Later, my mom asked everyone to leave and get ready for bed, except for me. Scott said mockingly, "Oooh, Ret's in trouble."

"Scott!" Mom snapped at him, and he stopped then raced down the hall to his room. Mom stepped over to the couch and sat next to me. "Ret, I can't believe all of this has been going on. All this time?"

"I know." I looked at the floor.

"I'm just... in shock." She shook her head. "I didn't know you guys snuck into that house for a sleepover. On a dare? I have always warned you to stay away from there. It's dangerous. And all this Nancy Drew mystery act you've been doing, researching at the library, following and spying on Mr. Beaumont and Lester, finding Mrs. Beaumont's body! And then you break into his house! Did you really see Andrea in the basement?"

I nodded.

"That's awful. How could I not know all of this was going on?" Guilt filled her moist eyes. "I know it's been an adjustment since I started working full time during the days. I've had to in order to afford this house, but it's not worth it. Not if these things are happening to my kids."

"No, Mom. It wouldn't make a difference if you were here or not. This whole thing was my idea. I haven't told anyone. I didn't even tell my friends until the other day. There's not anything wrong with me. It's just that terrible things are happening to people in this town, and someone had to do something. I saw things while working for Beaumont and felt it was my responsibility to follow through."

"But I need to know about these things. You do understand that, don't you? I'm your mother, and it's my job to protect you. A big part of that is knowing what you're doing." She started to sob and rested her forehead in her hand. "I should be here."

I put my arms on her shoulders, and she cradled my head into her. "It's not your fault, Mom."

She wiped her nose with a Kleenex, hugged me, then pulled back to look at me again. "You could have been hurt—or even killed—last night, Ret. Did they really send a man after you? And he chased you into that barn?"

"Yes," I said.

"I talked to Sheriff Packard earlier, and they detained Mr. Beaumont and Lester for questioning, but he found no sign of the man in the barn. If it's true, then that man is still out there, and I'm scared."

"I know."

"I'm going to have to ground you."

"What? Why?"

"For your own protection. At least until this blows over. There are too many unanswered questions. Children are being stolen and killed. From now on, nothing outside this house."

"For how long?"

"At least a week. Let's see where things are at in a week." She took my face in her hands and looked at me. "Okay?" She gave me a warm smile and hugged me tightly. I knew she was thankful I was still alive.

I went to bed, and an hour later, my dad arrived home. I woke up to the front door slamming shut. Not long after that, I heard my parents arguing. I sandwiched my head in my pillow, attempting to muffle the sounds, and fell back to sleep twenty minutes later.

CHAPTER TWENTY-TWO
Public Enemy Number One

The next few days were hell. I was imprisoned in my own home, and it was driving me insane. They told my parents how Beaumont and Lester were released after questioning because there was no evidence to hold them. They were free to kill and steal bodies, and no one could do anything about it, least of all me.

Jeff came in to the front room, where I was spread out on the couch, reading Louis L'Amour's *Milo Talon*, and Tadd sat in a chair chatting on the phone to his latest girlfriend, curled cord stretched around the wall and into the kitchen to the wall jack.

"Ret, I think you might be right." Jeff swallowed hard, and I saw in his eyes he knew something.

"What is it?" I sat up and put the book down.

"News is all over the town. People have seen Todd Harrison walking around."

"You're shitting me." I perked up.

"I overheard Mrs. Crawford, over at the gas station, telling the attendant how her son saw Todd and another guy digging up bodies at the cemetery. The attendant asked her, 'Did they call the cops?' and she didn't know what to say." Jeff chuckled.

"What do you mean? Did the cops come or not?"

"No. You know her son, Chase. He's a pothead. He was at the graveyard, smokin' dope with his buddies. He's not going to call the cops.

She knows it too but doesn't want to tell the attendant that. She just said, 'No, they were too scared, so they ran.'" He rolled his eyes and waved it off with his hand.

"I didn't think much of it at first, until I went down to Pederson's with my friends, and there was Joey Rascone, talking to a whole bunch of people. You should have seen his face. If you did, you'd know he wasn't lyin.'"

"What did Joey see?"

"He said he woke up to girls screaming next door. You know he lives next door to the Harrisons, right?"

I nodded agreement.

"He grabbed his shotgun and ran outside, and that's when he saw Todd Harrison in the front yard, tugging on his daughter, trying to pull her out of Angie's arms. Joey cocked the shotgun, pointed it, and told him to stop. Fortunately, he did, and this is the creepiest part.

"Todd Harrison turned his head slowly and spread a crazy smile across his face, and he said, 'That's my girl!' He pointed at Cheyenne in her arms. Joey said his voice didn't sound right. Said it sounded like he had marbles in his mouth, and thick black liquid dripped from his lips. 'They got to come with me,' Todd said. 'No one's goin' with you, mister,' Joey told him, and threatened to call the cops. Then Todd started to laugh, and not in a funny way. Then he took off."

Jeff's hands were trembling. The fear was in his eyes too.

"That night you told us the whole story of what happened, I wasn't sure if I could believe it all. But now..."

"Geez," I exclaimed. "So, did Joey call the police?"

"Yes, and Sheriff Packard came. They told him everything. Of course, he thinks it was someone else who happened to look like Todd Harrison, and he said something like 'In light of his recent death and the traumatic grieving, it's not unusual to see a stranger look like your loved one.' Basically, he's chalking it up that they're crazy. But Angie was frantic and couldn't be consoled. She demanded they exhume her husband's body for proof."

"What does 'exhume' mean?" I asked.

"That's when they dig someone up from their grave."

"Really?" I gasped.

"Yes." He nodded. "She kept fighting Packard on it so much that they're exhuming the body later today."

"Wow," I exclaimed.

I got a twinge of excitement. Things were happening. More witnesses were popping up, and once they exhumed Todd's body and found out he was missing, Sheriff Packard would have to start believing me. *I can only hope.*

"Anyway." Jeff slapped my thigh. "Looks like you're not crazy." He grinned.

He stood up to walk away, and I stopped him.

"Did you think I was?"

He paused and turned his eyes to the ceiling as if in thought. "I didn't know what to think. I know you wouldn't lie or make up shit."

"Thanks."

"Just be careful. Don't do anything stupid like sneaking into that house again."

I agreed, and he walked into the kitchen to get a drink. I turned to look at Tadd, who was leaned far back in the recliner, flirting with a girl on the phone.

"Bring her with you, and I'll bring Steadman. We'll make it a double date." He grinned and glanced at me. I was staring at him and mouthing the words, "Are you finished yet?" He scowled and returned to his conversation. "Steadman's not a jerk, I promise. We'll both be on our best behavior." He paused as she talked. "Yes, tonight. We'll see you around seven. Okay, you bet. See you then." He pressed the button on the phone to hang up and glared at me.

"I just need it for a few seconds."

He held the phone out for me to grab it, but I gestured with a stop motion. "I'll take the phone in Mom and Dad's room."

"Whatever," he grumbled, and I walked into my parents' bedroom to use their phone in privacy. I had to call Gary.

"You're public enemy number one," Gary said to me over the phone. "My mom and dad grounded me from you forever."

"Not a surprise. I guess I'd do the same."

"You're not the enemy. I chose to go with you. You didn't force me. I think it's just easier for them to blame it all on you than to think I'd do anything wrong."

"So, are you grounded too?"

"No. Just from playing with you, and no more sleepovers this summer. Geeze!"

"I'm sorry I pulled you into this."

"You didn't pull me into this. You needed help, and I'm your friend. That's what friends do. I made the choice to go with you."

"Thanks." I was itching to share the news about the Harrisons with Gary, but I was hesitant it would force him to make another choice that could put him in hot water.

"So, what's up?" Gary asked, and I couldn't hold back.

"Did you hear about the Harrisons?"

"No. What about them?" His voice cracked anxiously.

"The police are digging up Todd Harrison's grave today. Apparently, he's been seen around town. Mrs. Harrison demanded they open his coffin for proof."

"Holy *shit*!" His voice was barely a whisper, and I heard a deep breath taken in and blown out.

I needed to see my friends. I was still grounded, but I had to find a way at any cost. "We gotta find out what's going on. Do you think you could break away? Meet me at the cave?"

"I can go out. I just can't go with you. If my parents catch me with you, I'm dead."

"It won't be for long. I've been cooped up in this house for three days, and I can't stand it anymore. I'm going to call Jax and Rosco too."

"I know Jax won't be able to. He's on a strict lockdown. His mother is home all day and watches everything. He's not going anywhere. I don't know about Rosco."

"I called Dawn," I said. "Her little brother answered. He said she's grounded from the phone and going outside at all."

"How are you getting out?"

"Tadd is supposed to watch me." I lowered my voice so no one outside the room could hear me. "He's busy talking to his girlfriends on the phone and watching TV. It was all I could do to pull the phone away from him for a few minutes to call you. He'll be easy. I'll sneak out the back while he's on the phone."

"I guess if I get caught, I'll say I just ran into you."

"That'll work. See you in about fifteen?"

"Yeah."

FOR OVER TWENTY MINUTES, I stood next to Cueva, watching and waiting for Gary to show. The sun was hot and baking my scalp. Sweat ran down my temples. Finally, a cloud crept in front of the sun and gave me some relief. I concluded Gary wasn't coming and that his parents had probably found out.

I rode my bike across the street and climbed atop one of the Moguls. Gary's house was at the far end of the Moguls, on Redwood Road, and it was visible in the distance.

Gary appeared on the south side of his house, riding his bike toward me. He stopped a few feet from the house. I vaguely heard a voice bellow to him. It sounded like his dad, but I couldn't make out the words.

Gary's head turned. He responded to the yelling. He sat for a good few minutes, and I could see the frustration as he shook his head and gestured with his arms. Finally, he turned the bike around, rode slowly toward home, and disappeared around the corner. I was alone, feeling guilty about the trouble I'd brought on my friends and that I'd been able to escape my house even though they couldn't.

I rode my bike back to our cave and parked it. As soon as I'd crawled inside, the shade was a relief from the sun and heat. I shuffled to the back of the cave and curled into a comfortable lying position. I looked at the structure and remarked on how well it was built. It was the best structure we'd ever created.

A shadow crossed the entrance, and I shot up in a sitting position. Two adult legs stood in front of the opening, and when the man bent down to peek inside, my heart nearly leapt out of my mouth.

"Hello, Ret." Lester's greasy smile spread across his face. "You in here all alone?" His beady eyes ran across the interior of the cave.

Body clenched, I sat still.

"Pretty nice place you boys have built here."

"What do you want?" I asked.

Lester bent his knees and crouched. "I want your head." He smirked. "To be completely honest, I want to pin your body to the ground with stakes in each arm and leg and scoop your eyeballs out with a spoon." He chuckled with a sick glee in his eyes.

"That's very detailed," I said.

"That's what I'd like to do… but it seems we're under a bit of scrutiny from the police. The cops and media won't leave us alone." He dug his forefinger into the dirt wall of the cave and dug out a small clod that crumbled to the floor.

"Maybe you should give yourselves up," I said.

"Well, you've put us in a desperate mode. I'll give you that. We have dire work to finish that can't wait. Thanks to you." He shook his head, and his face colored up. "You little shits should have left us alone!" Spittle flew from his lips as his anger erupted. "We're out of time now, and lives are at stake!"

"*Our* lives are at stake! You're stealing and killing our people! *Why*?"

"'Our people'?" He sneered. "Why should I care?"

"Why do you care about *them*?"

"Because they care about *me*! No one in this world cares for me! No one sees me." He pounded his chest with his hand. "But *they* care, and they have more to offer. A whole lot more."

"They're only using you. Why can't you see that?"

"No, they're not!" he snapped defensively. "People use me here all the time, but not these people. They *need* me. There's a difference."

"And what happens when they've made it through? Once Beaumont has all his prison buddies back? They'll throw you to the wolves, Lester."

There was a pause as he pondered, then he scoffed and chuckled again. "What the hell do you know? Just a punk kid? You got a lot more growin' up to do, and when you do, you'll see the world for what it really is. Like I do."

Lester wiped sweaty bangs from his forehead. "It's a dog-eat-dog world. An eye for an eye. You do someone wrong, well... they'll do something equally wrong back to you. You have to pay for the things you do to people. That's the way of this world, and you have to pay for what you did, Ret. You and your friends." He pounded the wall of our cave with a fist, and a crack appeared in the dirt.

"Just leave me alone, please. I won't break into your house. I won't involve the police. I'm finished doing anything. I'm not even supposed to be here. I'm grounded."

"It's too late for that, Ret. You cost us time and lives, and you have to pay for that." He hit the wall harder, and a large chunk of dirt fell.

He crawled deeper into the cave, and I scrunched my knees to my chest. His arm bumped one of the supports, nudging it slightly out of place. Small clumps of dirt rained down on his head and the back of his neck. Gritting his teeth, he glared at me and kept coming.

"What are you doing? Get out of here!" My leg shot out and kicked his head, and it really set him off.

He bolted forward faster than I'd imagined he could, then he grabbed the front of my shirt in both hands and pulled my face to his.

"We have her, Ret." He snarled then giggled. "We took your girlfriend. That's how it works. You mess with us, you call the cops, try to blame Andrea's death on us, and well... you only brought this on yourself."

"No," I said. "Please leave her out of this."

He pushed me, and I landed against the back of the cave. The wall cracked, and a ton of dirt fell on top of me.

"You want her? Come and replace her. Tonight, before we feed her to *them*. Or save yourself and don't come. Either way, I don't care. Just remember to come alone. No cops!"

He erased his smile. His face went dark and grim as he backed out of the cave. He swept two standing support beams out of place with his arms. They tumbled to the ground, and more dirt fell.

Once outside, he stood and began kicking at the sides of the entrance. I watched in horror as the roof crumbled and a cloud of dirt blocked out all sunlight coming through the entrance.

"No!" I cried. It was all I could say. "No!" I started to crawl to the entrance.

He went to the south side, and without the support beams, it only took two strong kicks before the entire fort caved in.

An immense weight hit my back, slamming my stomach against the ground. My knee scraped a rock, and pain screamed inside me. Dirt, clods, and rocks buried me, and panic set in. I heard his muffled laughter outside as he walked away.

I pushed against the weight on top of me, arching my back as dirt ran off and surrounded me. I still had a pocket of air in front of my face, but it was quickly filling up.

Come on, come on... I moved my legs and arms, pressing and crawling. I clawed at the dirt and shoved massive amounts to either side. Sunlight peeked in, and soon I broke the surface, pulled myself out, and fell onto my back, panting.

I stared at the sky until I heard footsteps approach.

Startled, I turned to see Tadd standing a few feet away from me, looking pissed off. I smiled with relief that it wasn't Lester.

"What are you smiling at?" he snapped.

CHAPTER TWENTY-THREE
Escape Plan

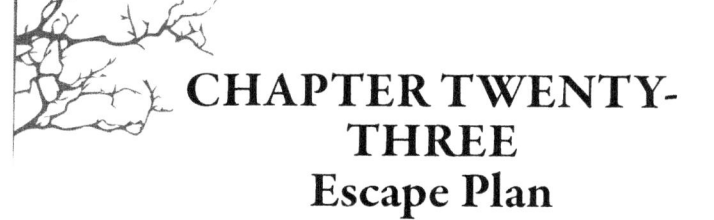

I winced as I put the cold rag to my bleeding, scraped-up knee and washed dirt from the wound. I sat on the toilet seat while Tadd, arms folded, leaned against the doorjamb and glared at me.

He walked over and slugged me in the arm. I think he put all his anger and energy into that punch, and he did it while wearing his bulky school ring. It felt like a bullet, and I knew the spot would swell into a large purple bruise.

"That's for sneaking out of the house. It's not going to happen again. When you're done putting Band-Aids on, get your ass to the living room."

When I got to the living room, he made me sit in a corner, away from the TV. "Don't move from that spot!"

"What if I need to pee?"

"I'll bring you a bucket."

I sighed and did my time. I sobbed on the inside, not wanting him to see, as I thought about Dawn and the trouble she was in. The whole town would be in an uproar looking for her. I only hoped they had the sense to go to the Crooked House first.

But there I sat, grounded to a corner—helpless. With nothing but my worry to keep me company, I wondered what Beaumont's plan was. It was crazy to think that while under so much scrutiny he would risk everything to continue to steal people, including *children*, and bring them to that house. But desperation made people do crazy things. Like

Lester had said, he couldn't wait any longer. The Tormentor was after them, and they planned to *feed* Dawn to them. *Does that mean what I think it means?* I couldn't let myself imagine it. One thing was certain: once they had everyone into this world, they would disappear. The next day, they would be long gone.

An hour into my sentence, I asked Tadd if I could use the restroom.

He rolled his eyes and sighed. "Fine. Make it quick."

I walked past the bathroom and into my parents' room.

"Hey! Bathroom's right there!" he yelled.

"I'm using Mom's bathroom."

"Fine! Go!"

In my parents' room, I plopped onto their bed, grabbed the phone off the nightstand, and called the police station.

"Riverton Police," Doreen answered on the third ring.

"Hey, Doreen, is Sheriff Packard there?"

"He's not here, Ret. He has a lot on his plate today. Anything I can help you with?"

I sank, defeated. The sheriff was my only chance. As my thoughts raced, I was silent.

"Ret? You still there?"

"Yes, sorry, Doreen. Will you please tell him I called? It's urgent. Just have him call me as soon as you can."

"Yes. I will."

The phone ripped out of my hands and shot backward as Tadd yanked on the cord. He was pissed. He slugged me again, and this time, he tied my arms up with rope and told me if I had to pee or shit, I would have to go in my own pants and sit in it until Mom got home. Things couldn't get worse.

CHAPTER TWENTY-FOUR
Alone

As Mom pulled into the driveway, Tadd raced to untie me. "You didn't run away, and I didn't tie you up and hit you. Understand?"

"Deal," I mumbled.

I had to come up with a plan to sneak out of the house that night. Dawn's life depended on it. I just hoped it wouldn't be too late. *What if they start the crossover of his demon friends before I arrive?*

I kept my deal with Tadd, and Mom wasn't any the wiser.

She started pulling ingredients from the cupboards to cook dinner, and I walked into the kitchen to help her. Tadd went to his room, got ready for his date, yelled goodbye to us, and tore out of the house. Mom made extra servings of spaghetti that night so she could take a meal over to Dawn's family. She shook the last bit of salt onto the browning meat and turned to me. "Ret, get more salt out of the cupboard, will you?"

I brought the container of Morton salt to her. There were only a few granules left. "Looks like we're out."

"Out? We can't be out. I just bought some last week. I need salt to season the meat!" She turned and called out, "Scott! Go across the street to the Crawfords' and borrow some salt."

He rolled his eyes dramatically and sauntered outside.

There was no salt left in the house because I'd used it all concocting a mixture of extremely salty water and filled up two of our water guns with it. I'd filled five sandwich bags full of the rest of the salt. They were my weapons for the night, and I hoped they worked.

When my dad came home, he told us that Sheriff Packard and the FBI had searched the Crooked House. "Half the town was at Lester's house, causing an uproar," my dad told us as he sat down at the dinner table. "I went over there earlier, and the Williamses were demanding to be let into that house and search for their daughter. Things got so out of hand it turned a bit physical."

"Physical?" My mom's eyes widened.

"Just some pushing and shoving." My dad began scooping noodles onto his plate from the bowl in the center of the table. Shaking his head, he said, "Someone pushed Lester down, and that's when Sheriff Packard showed up with his deputies."

"Do people really think Mr. Beaumont and Lester *took* Dawn?" She glanced at me as if to check if I was okay, knowing Dawn was my friend. "I don't know Lester, but I still can't believe Mr. Beaumont would do such a thing."

"It's always the last ones you'd suspect who turn out psycho."

Scott kept silent, looking at his plate and twirling spaghetti on his fork. Jeff finally walked into the kitchen and grabbed a plate.

"Did they find her?" I asked my dad.

He stopped chewing his food and looked at me. He shook his head solemnly. "No. I'm afraid not."

After dinner, I climbed our back fence to check on the police activity at Lester's house. Through the binoculars, I saw the FBI and CSI units, along with uniformed officers. A man I assumed was Beaumont's lawyer stood next to Beaumont, talking to the police. The last cop car left just before dark. From what I could see, they left empty-handed and disappointed.

No Dawn in sight. I watched as long as I could, hoping to catch them as they snuck her into the house after everyone was gone, but I saw no strange activity.

I knew they'd kept Andrea in that house. *Why couldn't they find any evidence of her being there?*

I'd seen enough police shows to know they always found a hair, footprints, or fingerprints, maybe even a piece of clothing. But nothing? *How could that be?*

The spirit inside Beaumont was from another world—a parallel universe or hell, or both. He did have powers to bring a spirit from his world into a dead body and give it life. Perhaps he had the power to make evidence disappear too.

"Ret!" My mom summoned from the back window. "Time to come in."

"Is everyone going to bed?" I asked my mom when I walked inside.

"Not yet. We're staying up to watch the news and Johnny Carson. You can stay up with us if you want."

I was anxious for everyone to get to bed so I could make my escape. Sheriff Packard hadn't called me back, and that bothered me. "I just think it's late, we've had a big day, and we should all get to bed."

Mom chuckled. "Big day? You can go to bed if you like. I need to wind down first."

Waiting for the world to fall asleep was painful. Minutes dragged on like dripping molasses. *Come on!*

Finally, Johnny Carson was over, credits rolled, and my mom and dad got into a long discussion about the guests on the show. I couldn't remember the last time my mom and dad had talked decently to each other and for twenty minutes. *Boy, did they find the wrong time to get along.*

Fortunately, Tadd and Jeff were both gone for the night, so all I had to deal with were Mom, Dad, and Scott, who would all go to bed at the same time.

The discussion finally wound down, and then Scott said, "Mom, can you look at this sliver in my hand? I can't get it out."

"For hell's sakes, Scott, can't it wait for the morning?" *Did I just say that out loud?*

My mom snapped her head to me, eyes wide and lips pursed. "Ret! What has gotten into you? You need to go to bed."

"I think we all do, don't we?"

"After we get this sliver out of Scott's hand, we will. But *you* will go to bed now."

I sighed, rolled my eyes, and meandered to my room.

IT WAS ONE O'CLOCK in the morning before I was relatively certain everyone was asleep. As stealthily as a cat, I snuck out of my house. Avoiding every creaky spot in the floor, I put my weapons in a satchel, hung it over my shoulder, and made my escape.

The chain-link fence was a bit noisy, but I couldn't avoid it. I landed in the field, crossed the creek, and headed for the house. It stood alone in the dark, waiting for me with its one eye lit. Beaumont and Kilborn were waiting for me too; I could feel it.

Please let her be alive, I prayed. I couldn't help but be reminded of Andrea. My guilt over not saving her weighed heavily on my soul. If they did to Dawn what I imagined they would do, I would be devastated.

The air was crisp, with a cool, quiet breeze. I crept to the side of the house, where a small window sat just above ground. It was the window to the basement. I wiped muck and film away from the glass with my sleeve, which didn't clean it much, but enough to get a blurry vision of the interior.

I saw the sparkling pool. Its blue radiance illuminated the room, and my goal was single-minded: finding Dawn. I saw her legs. She sat farther to the right of my point of view, so all I could see was her bottom half. She wore jeans and white tennis shoes. I was positive it was her.

For what seemed like a century, I waited for movement. Then her foot shuffled, and she bent forward enough for me to see her red hair. She was blindfolded with a wide strip of burlap, and I couldn't see her hands, which led me to believe they were tied behind her.

Relief coursed through me. *She's alive!*

A rank smell reached my senses first, a stench of rotted flesh mixed with formaldehyde. Then I heard grunts and raspy, quick breaths, followed by the sound of saliva being sucked in and out of someone's mouth, like a vacuum that didn't have enough power to extract water. The thing approached me, shuffling the weeds behind me.

I reached into my satchel, withdrew one water pistol, and spun around. The thing grabbed me by the throat, lifted me off my feet, and slammed my back against the side of the house before I could defend myself. It was a large man with grotesque pasty-blue skin. Fat and bald like the Dee Burger clown, he had dark rings around his eyes, and black sludge dripped from his mouth. Blue veins webbed his face, neck, and arms. The stench of death hit my face like a truck. He cocked his head as he looked at me quizzically. His eyes were bloodshot, and he coughed, flinging black droplets onto my face. He choked as he breathed in air.

Gun in hand, I twisted my wrist, aimed it down at his face, and squeezed the trigger. The salt water hit his eyes and face. His eyelids fluttered, and he paused then squealed in pain as the salt took effect.

He released me. I dropped to the ground, bounced up to my feet, and ran for the back of the house. I pulled out the second gun and double-fisted both of them.

A lady in a flowered dress, only one foot in a high-heeled shoe, came around the corner. Mud and scrapes covered her arms, legs, and face, and her curly hair looked like a matted wig. She hobbled on uneven legs, gasped, and clawed at the side of the house with one hand to help her balance. At her side was a tall man. He was thin and elderly, with a balding scalp. His crisp dark suit was too small. It was probably the one he'd been buried in. His eyes were wide and confused, his fingernails long and dirty. He was busy looking at his surroundings before he focused on me. Then his face scrunched into snarling rage, and he growled.

I was reminded of the time I'd snuck into the family room while my older brothers and their friends were watching *Night of the Living Dead*. Even in black and white, the movie had been nightmarish. This was much worse. I was in it.

I turned and ran blindly into the fat man, who was still squealing. I bounced off his chest and fell to the ground, landing hard on my tailbone. Pain flared through it. The odd couple lurched for me and grabbed at my collar and hair. My heart raced, and I twisted around, guns in hand, and sprayed them with rounds of salt water. They pulled at me, snarling through gray teeth, and finally, the salt absorbed into their bodies enough to cause them pain. Tiny wisps of smoke wafted from the spots the water hit. They shrieked, released their hold on me, and clawed madly at their wounds like they had an itch that couldn't be scratched.

The fat man dropped to the ground and crawled toward me. When he grabbed at my feet, I yelped and kicked his face several times before hopping to my feet.

I tore off in the opposite direction, careened around the front porch, and bolted in through the front door. The slanted floor of the Crooked House caught me off guard, and I nearly toppled. I ran for the kitchen, toward the basement door, in a last desperate effort to save Dawn.

Todd Harrison appeared in the kitchen doorway, wearing a devilish grin. I aimed both guns and fired. He jerked back from the burning liquid, and I heard the sizzle, but it wasn't enough to keep him from wreaking his vengeance upon me.

With one sweep of his arm, he knocked the pistols out of my hands, and the other fist hammered against my left cheek. Airborne, I twisted completely and plopped to the floor.

"Ouch." I heard Lester's voice as he entered. "That's gotta hurt." He laughed. "Boy brought his water pistols?"

I rolled and looked up at them both. Todd frowned, one eye solid red from the fiery salt. The left side of his face was peppered with red dots from where he'd been shot with the rock salt the other night. He was not happy. Todd kicked my forehead, and the back of my head slammed against the floor. Then my world went dark.

I WOKE UP LYING NEXT to Dawn, hands tied behind me with duct tape. Dawn was still blindfolded, but they hadn't bothered with me. I struggled to a sitting position and took in my surroundings as they came into focus. The basement was cold and damp, and the only light came from the magic pool and its blue aura.

All the living dead, including Harrison, were with us, standing against the opposite wall, watching and waiting. The lady in the dress continued to struggle; she bent over and gagged on black sludge.

I felt something bulky next to me, against my thigh. I looked down and saw my satchel. I was perplexed why they'd leave me my bag, but I don't think they knew it was a danger to them.

"Dawn?" I said. "It's me."

"Ret?" Dawn's voice shook. Tears streaked from underneath her blindfold, and her lips were wet with them. Dirt mixed with sweat smeared her forehead and cheeks.

"What are you doing here?" Her voice rose in panic.

"I came to save you. Some rescue, huh?"

She frowned and shook her head. "You shouldn't have. Nobody should. They'll end up like *them*."

She nodded to the living dead across the room. They continued to grunt, groan, and shuffle around awkwardly.

"The whole town is looking for you. So many people love you. My dad said the police came and searched this whole house. Why couldn't they find you?"

"Beaumont did something so they couldn't find me. I was right here the whole time. I heard them, they called out to me, and I called back. I screamed, I cried, but they couldn't hear me. They were right here! Right in front of me! I kicked and yelled and rolled my body around!" She gulped. "Something is evil here. Can you feel it?"

My body tingled. I knew what she was talking about. It weighed the air like an electric charge. "Yes."

"They dug up those bodies. Lester said they were the freshest ones he could find. I recognize Mrs. Jones from the grocery store."

I looked at the lady in the flower dress again. Dawn was right—she worked one of the registers, but she'd quit months ago because of cancer. She must have passed away, and the bastards dug her up then stuffed the soul of one of their friends into her body.

"Beaumont is really mad at Lester," Dawn whispered to me. "They had a big argument about the bodies and how they're not fresh enough. I think that's why they can't talk or walk very well. He also said they hadn't eaten in days."

With a shiver, I thought about Lester's threat to feed Dawn or me to them.

"When the police came, Lester blindfolded me and left me down here with these dead bodies, and Beaumont chanted some strange words. Like a spell or something. I think that's why the police couldn't see me or see them."

"I'm sorry." My head drooped.

"Me too."

We took a break from speaking for a moment, and then she leaned her head to me and rested it on my shoulder. I snuggled my head back into her. It felt warm and good.

The basement door opened, and a sliver of light sliced the darkness. Beaumont and Lester marched down the stairs and halted in front of the living dead. Mrs. Jones was curled on the floor, coughing and gagging uncontrollably.

Beaumont bent down and softly ran a hand along her cheek. She looked up at him, eyes horrified, chest heaving rapidly.

"*Chokanna*," he spoke in his tongue lovingly. "*Mo seeka, vi cobiki soka Asson. Mi mo vana.*"

Tears ran from her eyes. "*Ki! Ki jee!*" She choked words out passionately. "*Ki ki jee!*"

Beaumont closed his eyes, pursing his lips, and a tear ran from one eye. He kissed his fingers and placed them on her forehead. He turned and looked at Lester with disdain and hatred, then burned the same glare at me.

He stood up, crossed the room, and picked up a long-handled axe. Mrs. Jones's body shuffled on her back, and the others stepped out of the way. Her chest pumped up and down faster.

"*Mi mo vana, Chokanna!*" Beaumont said his last words to her then buried the axe in her head with a sickening *thuck*.

I turned away, and Dawn shuddered at the sound.

"What was that?" Dawn asked me.

"You don't want to know."

Confused, the others looked down at the lady on the floor. The water in the pool shimmered, and rings spread as if a rock had dropped into the middle of it. Beaumont looked at the pool as his friend's spirit raced home to the other world.

"You see now, Lester? Does it finally make sense to you?" He hammered his words into the shorter man. "I need fresh bodies. You gave me one plagued with sickness!"

"It's all I could find," he whined. "You don't give me enough time."

"We're out of time!" Beaumont threw the axe, and it clattered next to us.

"I'm sorry!" Lester yelled sheepishly. He looked around the room then pointed at us. "We still have them!"

His gaze burning into us, Beaumont pointed at us and said, "We were going to use their souls for food. We need energy." He stepped closer to us, looking us over. "They'll have to do. I'm out of choices. One can be my Chokanna, and one can be the food." He turned to Lester. "It better work this time."

"It will for now. Until we find another one. A better one."

"Shut up!" he snarled.

Sickness boiled in my stomach.

Beaumont crossed the room and tore off Dawn's blindfold. Her eyes fluttered and squinted, adjusting to the light.

"You said it'd be just one of us," I said. "Lester said if I came, I'd take her place and she could go."

Beaumont shrugged. "Things change. I'll still give you a choice, though. Do you want to be the food or the vessel? Either your soul will be torn to pieces and eaten, or it will be trapped in a dark void forever. You decide."

CHAPTER TWENTY-FIVE

The Tormentor

I didn't consider either of those much of a choice. No matter which I chose, we were both going to die. "I'll be the... food. Just let her go. Like Lester promised you would."

He grabbed the back of my collar, lifted me off the floor so that my face met his, and snarled, "I promised nothing."

"You son of a bitch!" I spat.

He gripped the back of my hair and shoved my face in the water. I held my breath and squirmed. I was helpless. Not having my hands free was a frightening feeling. I tried to pull my wrists apart, twist, and fight to break the duct tape, but I was at his mercy.

My face hit the water with a hard smack, and I felt my spirit rip away from my body, leaving me empty. My spirit self floated far below the surface of the water. I still felt my body outside the pool, but it was far away from me and struggling to breathe.

I am dead, I told myself. *This is it.* I gulped in fear. *You're not dead,* my other inner voice argued. *Just hold your breath.*

While immersed, I opened my eyes and saw a dark figure far below. It was a giant monster with hundreds of arms and jagged claws that reached up to the surface. After a second, I recognized the shape for what it really was: an immense tree several feet below—in *their* world. The arms and claws were branches. *No—not branches... tree roots.* It was an upside-down tree with its roots planted in our world, *feeding* from our world.

Entangled in the roots was a small, dark creature. Though humanoid, with arms and legs, its form was as black as the night and thin like a stick. Its face consisted of only a nose, no mouth or eyes. It sensed I was there and moved its head in my direction. It was his beloved Chokanna!

Beyond her, I saw their realm below. I was amazed at the clarity, as if the water had no effect on my vision, and I saw mountains in the distance—tall, narrow, and jagged monoliths of stone. Purple lightning shot out and electrified the tops of them, revealing a dark form of immense size approaching the tree. Then Beaumont suddenly jerked my head back.

As if pulled by a powerful force, my soul flew back into my body. Tingles of life returned to my fingers and toes, and I felt different, reborn somehow.

I gasped for air desperately once Beaumont pulled my head out of the water, and I burped from the water I'd swallowed.

Dawn was screaming my name. "Ret!"

Beaumont chuckled. "How should I murder you? Should I drown you?" He brought a knife to my throat and pressed the blade to my skin. "Slit your throat?"

"No! Please no!" Dawn pleaded. "You can't do this!"

"You could use a new grin." He chuckled. The muscles in his arms and hands tensed, and he made a hissing sound between his teeth. He was going to enjoy killing me. He raised the knife, and mere seconds of my life remained.

Mathilda popped up out of nowhere. The ghost of the Crooked House ran through me, and her face materialized in front of Beaumont's. Her face pressed against Beaumont's, and he stared back at her, stunned. She opened her mouth wide and loosed a wretched, high-pitched wail that shook the house.

The shock was enough to cause Beaumont to release me, and he stumbled back. I crumpled to the floor, gasping. I felt blood run down my throat. *The bastard cut me!* I didn't know how bad yet and hoped it wasn't fatal.

"Bitch!" he howled at the ghost in frustration.

Gunshots rang out, and Beaumont's body shuddered as two bullets pounded his chest. He looked down at his body. Blood blossomed through the torn holes in his white shirt and tie, but he had no reaction to the pain or damage.

He looked up at the assailant. I turned and saw Sheriff Packard halfway down the stairwell. He crouched and aimed his gun.

There was silence for a moment before Packard broke it, speaking slowly and forcefully. "Nobody move."

"You're not the threat you think you are," Beaumont said. "You kill this body, then I'll just take yours." He pointed then glanced at Todd Harrison and commanded him with a nod.

Packard turned to Todd, shock in his eyes to see Harrison alive.

Todd took five stairs in one massive leap, grabbed Packard's gun hand, smashed it against the wall, and swung his other fist down to hit him. Sheriff Packard blocked it with his other arm and was quickly engaged in a fight with a man nearly twice his size and powered by a demon inside. Mathilda continued to distract Beaumont with screams in his face, despite his attempts to move and run from her.

I saw the axe next to Dawn and rolled my body over to her. She turned herself so her tied hands could pick up the blade of the axe. I turned my back against it and, with my fingers, guided the blade of the axe toward the tape that bound me. It was slippery with blood. I sliced my finger, but after a few tries, the blade made contact with the tape. The axe cut through the tape like butter, and I yanked my hands apart.

I turned and quickly freed Dawn. We shared a glance, and my first panicked thought was to run, but I knew we wouldn't get far. The fat guy and the old man had been slow to react at first, but they charged us.

I grabbed my satchel, pulled out the baggies of salt, and handed two to Dawn.

"Wha—"

"Trust me. Open the top, then throw it at them. In the face would be best."

The fat man grabbed for her, and she did as I'd instructed her. The bag hit him square in the face. A cloud of salt covered his entire head, and he backed away, yelping like a hurt dog.

The old man grabbed my shoulders and pulled on me. I twisted and smashed a baggie against his face just as he sucked in air. He fell back, gasping and coughing. With sizzle and smoke, holes opened in his throat, and vapors escaped.

Lester cowered in the corner, staring in awe at the crumbling plan.

Packard snapped a foot into Todd's gut, doubled him over, and smashed two roundhouse punches to his face.

"Help him!" Beaumont shouted to Lester and pointed at Todd.

Finally ignoring Mathilda altogether, Beaumont marched toward us and the axe. He kicked Dawn in the ribs, and she fell. I withdrew my knife from the satchel and sliced it at him. It cut open his hand, but he still picked up the axe.

Packard had dropped his gun during the fray, but after managing to pick it up again, he aimed it at Todd, who twisted his body out of the line of fire just as Lester ran up the stairs to help him.

Bang! Bang! Bang! Bang! Four bloody wounds popped open in Lester's chest and stopped him cold. He shivered and gasped, eyes pleading for mercy, then he toppled. Packard's revolver was out of bullets, and he didn't have time to reload before Harrison lunged at him.

Packard stood and smacked the butt of his pistol against Todd's temple then brought it around again, crashing into his nose. Blood sprayed from Todd's nostrils as his head was knocked back. The sheriff shot a kick to Todd's chest and sent him flying. He dropped to the floor at the foot of the stairs.

With madness in his eyes and clenched teeth, Beaumont charged toward me, gripping the axe with both hands. I backpedaled and was stopped by the wall behind me. He raised the axe high above his head just before Dawn threw her second bag of salt into his face. He winced, trying to cover his eyes, and released the axe. He sucked in the cloud of salt and coughed, stumbling backward.

"Ret! Dawn! You two okay?" Packard ran over to us.

Reeling from how close I'd come to death, I needed a moment to respond. I took a deep breath as Dawn shuffled to my side, and I turned to Packard.

"You came?" I said to Packard.

"I got your message. I figured you'd be here." He smiled, and Dawn wrapped her arms around him in relief.

Harrison stood up and shook the cobwebs from his head.

"We gotta go," the sheriff said.

A deep, guttural growl from below us shook the floorboards and the walls. It was heavy and loud, like the horn of a locomotive, but with a low baritone. The sound reverberated throughout the cellar, toppling old jars and cans from shelves in the back corner. Cracks in the concrete floor spread like spiderwebs as if a colossal force were trying to enter from below.

Everyone froze.

I looked at Beaumont. His face shook with more terror than I had ever seen. All the blood drained from his face, his mouth dropped open, and his bloodshot eyes widened. A tear ran from his right eye. The others shared the same look.

The wailing growl came again, louder and more forcefully. The entire house shook. It threatened to crumble on us at any moment. The pool bubbled and splashed. Blue rays of light bounced off the walls and throughout the basement.

"It's coming." Beaumont whimpered and looked at his friends sorrowfully. "It found us!"

"What's going on?" Packard asked.

Beaumont started to run but grabbed his chest in pain. The gunshots were starting to take their toll on him.

I remembered the form I'd seen approaching the bottom of the pool in the other world, and I knew we had to make a run for it, but Harrison and the other two things were blocking the stairs. Beaumont was on the other side of the well, backing up.

"This thing is here for them. Let's stay out of his way, and maybe we'll be all right."

We backed up as far as we could to the opposite corner and crouched. A geyser shot from the well and sprayed all of us. Rising from the pool, so gigantic it filled the entire opening, was a beast so tall that it had to bend its head from the ceiling. It planted muscled arms flat on the floor on either side of the pool. Black claws six inches long curled from the tip of each finger and clacked against the cement floor. Its head was similar to a man's, but it had wide nostrils and a mouth full of sharp teeth. A thick vine covered with sharp three-inch thorns was wrapped around his face in an uneven fashion, pressed so tightly against its skin that flesh bulged and leaked blood. The thorny vine ran down its neck and continued around its torso and arms. Its black skin was coarse with scales, and long hair draped its shoulders.

Two thorns pressed into its eyes. Blinded, it used other senses to find its prey. The creature opened its maw filled with rows of razor teeth and howled so loudly that I thought my head would burst open like a melon.

Todd Harrison bolted for the stairs, and the recovered fat man and old guy followed him.

"*Cerran! Jubaia!*" Beaumont called to them in his native tongue. They glanced back but continued to run.

Beaumont finally found his feet and ran, but the creature was fast like a cat after its dinner. One clawed hand snatched him from the floor, tore through his body, withdrew the glowing soul from his corpse, and popped it into the gaping maw. The torn form of Mr. Beaumont splashed to the floor.

Trembling uncontrollably, the three of us clung to each other and watched in horror as it plucked the fat man and the old guy off the stairs before they reached the landing, tore through their bodies, and devoured their souls.

Harrison had made it through the basement door. I heard his footfalls as he ran to escape the house. The giant creature scrambled up the stairwell after him.

The creature was too large for the stairway, and it demolished the steps and part of the ceiling. The wooden floor joists above us snapped, raining dust, as the creature forced its upper body to the first level.

The Tormentor's torso stretched through the pool and seemed to go on forever. I never saw its legs or the rest of its body—if it had any, those parts remained below. The entire house tipped toward the beast because of its weight, and we began to slide across the floor. Harrison squealed, but the sound was cut short by a loud crunch.

The Tormentor lowered itself back into the basement, dragging broken floorboards and stirring up clouds of dust and debris. Torn clothes hung from the jagged teeth, and the beast munched on its dinner without much care. I watched with fearful anticipation of what it would do next.

It snorted, sniffed the air, and turned to us. Its blind gaze locked on us like targets. We stared at the beast, and it stared at us. No one moved.

As it started to open its mouth, Dawn grabbed the last two bags of salt from me and ran toward the beast.

"Dawn!" I yelled after her.

She dodged its massive claw, careening toward the pool. The Tormentor twisted her way. She slammed the last two bags into a small space between its body and the lip of the pool just as the creature swiped at her.

Her back arched, and she flew forward then disappeared into the cloud of salt, smoke, and sputtering water.

An explosion erupted from the pool, and the Tormentor wailed in pain. Water crackled, and it suddenly looked more like acid than water as the creature began to sink back into the pool.

Its claws scrabbled wildly at the cement floor, scraping and clicking against the cement, searching for the one who'd hurt it. The Tormentor bucked and twisted as the water boiled higher all around it. The pool sizzled and popped like cold water tossed into hot grease, and something pulled the creature down below the surface.

CHAPTER TWENTY-SIX
Aftermath

"Dawn!" I scrambled to my feet. Water continued to splash around me as I ran through the smoke in the direction of where I'd last seen her.

I found her lying still on the floor, dark, bloody lines across her back, clothing torn.

"Dawn?" I knelt next to her. Lump in my throat and tears running, I placed a gentle hand on her side.

The creature's nails had torn through the back of her shirt and ripped into her skin. It didn't look good. Her eyes were closed.

"Dawn," I pleaded, sobbing. "Please. You're okay. You're okay."

Packard walked over and stopped a few feet short. I brushed the hair back from her face. Her eyes fluttered open, her body trembled, and relief settled my fast-beating heart.

She opened her blue eyes, sat up, and fell against my chest to wrap her arms around me. I hugged her back, but she winced in pain, so I withdrew my hands.

"This was a strange first date," she said.

I chuckled with relief.

"Wait 'til we go on our second," I said.

Just then, someone called down from the upper floor, and I turned to see James and Gonzales gaping at us from the hole in the kitchen where the basement door used to be. The stairs had been demolished.

I helped Dawn to her feet, and my hand came back wet with blood. "We need to get Dawn help," I said to Packard. "She can't make it up there alone."

Nodding, Packard looked around the basement and locked eyes on an old desk. "Stay with her. I'll pull this desk over, and we can use that."

He pushed the desk across the floor and placed it underneath the hole. Packard stood on top of it and helped hoist Dawn up to his deputies. The two top stairs were still intact. She grabbed onto those, and the deputies grabbed her from there and pulled her up.

"You okay?" I called to her, and she stuck a thumb up in the air for me.

"Paramedics just showed up!" Deputy Gonzales hollered.

"Good." Packard nodded. "Get her to them fast. Make sure she's taken care of."

Packard turned and motioned for me to go next, but I wasn't ready. Mathilda's ghost sat in the corner, head down and eyes sullen.

"I'll catch up," I said, and I stopped Packard before he could disagree. "Really. There's someone I need to say goodbye to."

"Then I'm staying until you're done. But hurry." He stepped back and kept an eye on me.

I couldn't argue with that. I walked over to Mathilda, who looked like a sad child, and sat down in front of her. She raised her dark eyes to me. They were full of despair, regret, and pain. An image of her child came to mind, a daughter, barely six years old. I looked at the pool. Her child had drowned, and I understood how. Images appeared in my head, revealing truths I couldn't have known... and I realized I'd been given a gift.

When Beaumont pushed me into that pool, I'd felt my soul pull away from me, and for a moment, I'd hung between two worlds. Then my soul reunited with my body when I came back out of the water. I felt part of me still connected to the other side of elsewhere and part of me connected to the afterlife. I looked down at Mathilda as images and words filled my head, and I understood her story. She'd been a victim. The nightmares began the first night she moved into the house, then the voices came. Soft at first, they were persistent and coaxing. Her spirits were weak at the time. Moving halfway across the country away from her family had been hard, and it had filled her with anxiety and depression. The voices recognized her weakness and exploited it to their advantage.

They hadn't broken her overnight. It had taken a long time for them to seduce, maybe even brainwash, her. She'd become a walking zombie and followed instructions like a soldier.

They'd wanted her child—the tree beneath the pool *wanted* her. The voices convinced her to take her child to the feeding pool. The tree was the life source of the other world, and it needed to be fed. It suddenly became clear to me that it was fueled by our souls, our weaknesses, and our fears.

Tears streaked the ghost's face. She lived in constant torment in this house, reminded of the evil she'd committed, the worst sin that anyone could commit. The guilt kept her from moving on, and the Crooked House had become her hell.

I saw another image of her daughter. She was older than six, but still young, beautiful and glowing. Radiating warmth and forgiveness, she awaited her mother on the other side.

"She's waiting," I said. "On the other side. She needs her mother."

Mathilda shook her head, fearing she wasn't worthy of that role anymore.

"She'll understand now. You should go. There's nothing left for you here. I'm glad you were here because you saved my life. You saved Dawn's life. And I know you did everything you could to save Andrea. Your daughter will understand that too."

Her face shook with fear and tears.

"It's time. She's waiting. Pass through the light, and she'll be there. It's okay... really."

Her body unclenched, and her shoulders sank as a large weight was lifted. Mathilda broke and fell into my arms and sobbed. I didn't feel her, not physically. I wrapped my arms around her anyway, feeling the tingles of her energy.

A bright light illuminated us. It was warm, comforting, and inviting. She wiped her eyes and looked up. A shadow of a smile crept in the corner of her mouth, and she rose and disappeared into the light, and then the light was gone.

As I walked over to Packard, I had to step over Lester's body. I looked down at the dead man, the terror and pain frozen on his face.

I walked back to Packard, who was cautiously looking into the pool, perhaps afraid something else might jump out of it. He turned to me with a perplexed look on his face.

"I don't get it, Ret." He wiped sweat from his brow and scratched the back of his head while looking around the room. "I'm not sure what happened here, or who you were talking to over in the corner, or what the hell that thing was that came out of that well. I'm not sure I'll ever know."

I shrugged my shoulders. "I told you there was some crazy stuff going on."

"This is beyond crazy, and I don't know whether to thank you or kick your butt."

"Sheriff!" Deputy Gonzales called down. "You two need some help up?"

"Hold on a minute." Packard motioned for him to wait. He looked at me and said, "I need to fill out a report about all this."

"How are you going to explain all of it?"

"I'll need your help with that." He placed a hand on my shoulder, and a smile crept up his face. "You're something else, Ret. Take care of yourself."

I SAT IN THE BACK OF an ambulance as the paramedics finished bandaging the wound on my throat. Fortunately, it was a minor cut, which they smeared with ointment then taped a square piece of gauze over it. They also checked me for a concussion since I'd taken a big bang to the head, but I'd suffered nothing more than some aches and bruises. My parents came around the corner of the van, and my mom let out a breath of relief, putting a hand over her chest.

I glanced at the paramedic, who said, "You're good to go." He smiled and patted my back.

I jumped down and embraced my mom and dad. I wasted no time in convincing them to take me to the hospital to see Dawn right away. To my surprise, they hadn't even argued with me, and they let me buy a small flower arrangement in the gift shop.

Dawn was in a private room in the emergency room, and my parents helped me find it.

"We'll be in the waiting room when you're done. Don't be too long," my mom said before she and Dad walked away.

The door was open, and I lightly rapped on it with my knuckles. Dawn's mom turned with a welcoming smile and gestured me in. She glanced at my flowers, gave me a wink, and stepped back to let me by. Dawn was sitting up on the edge of the bed and talking to her dad while placing a hand on her side, and her face was wrinkled with discomfort.

"You're going to be in pain for a long while, and every time you take a breath, you'll feel it," her dad was saying with a comforting hand on her shoulder.

The expression of discomfort turned to a smile when she saw me. "Ret," she said with excitement, and I smiled back.

"Hey, Dawn. How are you doing?"

Jim, her dad, turned his eyes to the ground with a frown and stepped back.

"A little banged up, but not bad."

"She has two cracked ribs," her mom added. "And six-inch scratches on her back that will probably scar, and she has to take an antibiotic for the infection." She raised her brows to emphasize the situation was more dire than Dawn had let on.

"Right. Like I said, a little banged up is all." She grinned in spite of her mom.

"Wow, cracked ribs has to hurt," I exclaimed.

"Only when I laugh," she said.

"There go all my jokes." I shrugged, and she belted out a laugh that quickly turned into squinting her eyes in pain and gritting her teeth.

"Oh, I'm sorry." I winced then stretched out my flowers. "I brought these for you."

"That's very sweet." Her mom took them from me and handed them to Dawn.

"You shouldn't have." Dawn shook her head.

"Ret, I hate to break this up," Jim grumbled. "But we gotta get Dawn home. She needs to get some rest." He moved to usher me out.

"Yes, of course. Dawn, take care of yourself, okay?"

She nodded. "You too. Call me later, okay?"

"Will do."

I turned and walked out of the room, and Jim followed me into the hall. He stepped next to me and placed his arm around my shoulder, but not in a comforting way. "Ret, can I speak with you?"

I nodded.

"My daughter's been through a lot—more than many adults will ever have to—and she is my pride and joy. Understand?"

I nodded again.

"I'm not saying you're a bad kid. I barely know you. You may not be, but one thing's for certain. There's a lot of talk in the town, there's been a lot of trouble, and your name keeps popping up. I'm not one to believe in gossip, and I don't make my judgements until I have proof. But this is my daughter, and she was taken from me. She was nearly killed, and God knows what else. I believe they took her because of something you did."

I couldn't deny any of the things he'd said.

"I'm not going to allow that to ever happen again. Got it?"

I nodded, keeping silent.

"That means I can't have you seeing my daughter anymore. You can't come over, you can't hang around her, and you can't even speak to her." He let out a sigh and shook his head. "Now, Dawn is a stubborn girl, just like her mother. She's going to want to see you, God knows why. You can't allow it. You have to cut it off with her and ignore her. Is that clear?"

I didn't nod or speak.

"I asked you a question, son."

"I'm not your son. Your daughter can make her own choices, and I can make mine." After all I'd faced, Jim didn't scare me.

"I'm not asking, Ret. I'm telling you, and you will listen, or there will be hell to pay. Mark my words. I'll make sure of it, even if I have to ground Dawn until the day we move."

"Move?"

"Yes. In a little over a month, we're moving back to Portland."

My heart sank, and all the energy drained from my body. I was sad for Dawn and pissed at her dad for making them move again. I was most disappointed about losing a good friend—perhaps my best friend. I wasn't sure about romantic love. I didn't know what that meant, but I did know friendship. And losing that hurt like hell.

"You take care, Ret." He tightened his lips and walked back into Dawn's room.

Feeling empty, I walked out into the waiting room, where my dad was transfixed with a game show on the TV and my mom was thumbing through a magazine. We got into the car, and I fell asleep before we got home.

THE NEXT DAY, MY MOM and dad took me into the sheriff's office to fill out a formal report of what had happened, and Packard said he would have to do the same with Dawn. I told him the truth about everything, but he left out certain supernatural elements when he filled out the report. Afterward, he turned to my parents and said he was going to tell the reporters a different story—something about how he suspected a gas leak explosion was likely the cause of Lester and Beaumont's deaths, and upon his arrival, he'd found us miraculously alive but tied up, along with remains from the missing bodies from the cemetery. There were no reports of the dead walking around or anything to corroborate the several sightings of Todd Harrison's life after death, and Lester and Beaumont's motives were unknown, but rumors flew about them being a part of a cult.

I understood Packard's reason for omitting the supernatural elements. He was a man of the law, and not only would no one believe him, he'd be crucified for stating it. Secretly, he knew it was all real, and that was all I needed.

Revisiting all those events was traumatic, and I think my parents recognized the amount of energy it sucked out of me, but the process was also cathartic. I'd told my story, held nothing back, and left it all at the police station, where it could remain behind me. For the first time, I felt the evil that had plagued the town that summer was gone. Safety had returned to Riverton.

That night, as if I'd suffered a painful day at the doctor's office, my mom made sloppy joes and let me invite my friends over. She even convinced Gary's mom to let him come.

We sat in the living room and talked forever, then halfway through dinner, a knock came at my door. When I answered the door, I was as surprised as I was elated to see Dawn standing there. I stepped out onto the porch, closed the door behind me, and wrapped her in my arms. We hugged tightly for a long time before releasing.

"How are you feeling?" I asked.

"Much better. My wounds still sting, and we have to keep ointment on them. My ribs still hurt, but other than that, I'm fine."

I sighed relief. "Hey, the whole gang is here! You should join us. We're eating sloppy joes and—"

"I can't. I'm going to get in trouble as it is for sneaking out, but I had to."

"Yeah, your dad had a talk with me. He warned me to stay away, but we don't have to."

She shook her head in disgust. "I can't believe he did that. I was so upset when I heard. But it doesn't matter. We're moving. Again," she said with revulsion. "This time, it's so far away that I won't..." She choked on her words.

"Your best friend, Sadie," I said, knowing the pain of loss she was going through. I'd gone through it so many times myself.

She nodded, holding back sobs. "And you. And them." She pointed at my house, referring to our friends.

"There's something my old Scout leader taught me once. He said, 'Experiences, both bad and good, make us who we are.' And you're an amazing person, Dawn."

"You are too, Ret. I wasn't kidding about your writing. You really are talented. Don't give it up."

"I won't. I'll send you my first published copy and sign it 'Best wishes.'"

She laughed, then cringed, holding her ribs. I was saddened about her aches, but more so to know it was the last time I would hear her laugh.

We hugged again. She told me to say goodbye to the gang, and I told her I would, then she surprised me with a kiss. It was a quick peck on the lips, but it was warm and stayed with me for a long time.

I waved and watched as she hurried down the street to her house. With a lump in my throat, I stepped back into the house, and my friends turned to me.

"Was that Dawn?" Jax asked.

"Yes."

"Tell her to get her butt in here," Rosco said.

"Yeah, it wouldn't be the same without her," Gary chimed in.

"No, it wouldn't, but her parents won't allow it. She's going to be moving in a few days anyway, and she wanted to say goodbye."

There was silence for a moment.

"She's one of us," Rosco said. "So is Morgan."

"Always will be," Gary said.

"Damn right," Jax confirmed. "Black Widows forever."

I agreed. "I wouldn't be here without Dawn."

We talked for only a small moment about the events at the Crooked House, then we moved on as if it didn't deserve another moment of our time.

"We need to rebuild the fort," Rosco said.

"Damn straight!" Jax said, and I stabbed him with a glare.

"Don't swear. My mom can hear us," I whispered urgently.

"Bigger and better than the one b'fore," Rosco said. "I got it all laid out. Been scopin' out some of them new moguls on the other side and found a perfect one. My dad said he can get a lot of wood and two-by-fours we could use."

"Cool!" Gary exclaimed. "We should start working on it when we get back from camp."

"When's Scout camp again?" Jax asked.

Scout camp wouldn't be the same without Todd Harrison, but Rosco's dad was appointed the new Scout leader, and Gary's dad was his new assistant. Knowing the Scouts were in good hands helped to heal some.

"Next week. All week," I answered.

"Shit," Jax said.

"Jax!" I scolded.

"Sorry, man. I'm not even ready for camp. I gotta get a new mess kit and canteen. My little brother lost 'em."

"You going, Rosco?"

"Hell yes, I'm goin'!"

"Please, guys. Not in my mom's house," I pleaded, and we couldn't help but bust out in belly laughs. It wasn't even very funny, but our laughter was loud, and we held our bellies and laughed for a good five minutes. It was a release of all the tension and fear. The nightmare that had kept the town up at night and held us all hostage was lifted, and we finally felt free to laugh long and hard, and it felt good.

Gary wiped tears from his eyes. Curled up on the couch, Jax was caught in a silent laugh, mouth wide open, eyes squinted shut, holding his gut. We all stared at him, and finally as he took in a breath, the laughter burst and filled the room again. We were all caught up again in a chain of laughs.

It was the last night I ever saw or spoke to my friends.

EPILOGUE
An Abrupt Departure

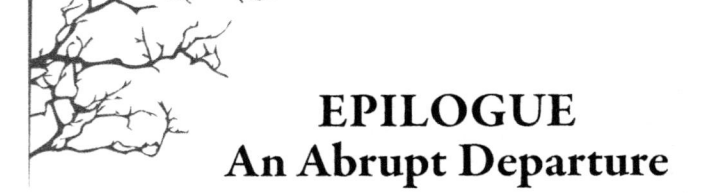

In the middle of the night, the night after the sleepover with my friends, my mom woke my brothers and me.

I peeled my eyes open and asked, "What's going on?"

"We're going to go on a little trip. Just for a couple of nights. At a hotel."

"Right now?" I asked.

"Yes. I need you guys to get dressed and help me pack whatever you need to take, and don't forget your swimsuit. The hotel has a pool." She attempted to elicit excitement from us, but I saw the tears in her eyes, and the anxiety.

"What's going on?" Scott sat up, eyes still closed and curly hair pushed in an awkward bunch on his head.

I didn't understand. Something was wrong. I realized I hadn't paid much attention to my mom that summer. I was busy in my own life and adventures. I knew she and Dad fought a lot, and I was sure what I'd put her through was stressful. But something had happened to make all of that worse.

I'd believed my mom when she said we were going to be at a hotel for just a couple of nights, but we never did return home. We went to stay at our grandparents' for a while, about thirty minutes north of Riverton. I asked my mom a lot of questions. She gave a lot of vague answers and always promised we were only staying with Grandma and Grandpa temporarily.

Scott and I slept on the couches in the basement, and one night, I heard my mom crying and went to check on her. I stopped midway when I heard my grandma consoling her. My mom told her Dad had an affair, and she just couldn't stay with him anymore, not after everything else.

I crept back to the basement and crawled under the covers on the couch, but I couldn't fall back to sleep. I was too angry with my dad over whatever it was he'd done to cause my mom so much pain.

Each morning, I would wake up, eat cereal, and watch Bob Barker on *The Price is Right*, followed by *Wheel of Fortune*. Summer was almost over, and we spent most of what remained indoors. My mom had brought our bikes, but I didn't feel like riding. We had some of our toys, but I didn't feel like playing.

"Why don't you call Gary or Jax?" Scott asked. He'd kept in touch with his friend Daryl and even arranged times to see him.

"No," I said, even though I didn't have a reason not to. My mom urged me to stay in touch with my friends, but I didn't.

Funny thing is, to this day I still don't have an answer. I have speculations. I may have felt too embarrassed to call them, to tell them we'd moved because my parents split. I'd harbored a hope that we would move back home before school started, then I could fit back in like nothing had ever happened.

The truth is I don't know what I was afraid of. I do know, however, that in the first ten years of my life, my family moved six times, and each year, I had to fit into a new neighborhood and make new friends. Keeping in touch with old friends was useless. Keeping in touch with the past was more painful than admitting it was useless because even then, I'd known, deep down, that it would never be the same.

I'd done it with every friendship I'd left behind until Riverton. We would arrange a sleepover or get together maybe twice or three times a year, but we never really called each other over the phone because boys don't do that. Before long, we drifted apart, farther and farther year after year, until eventually, they disappeared from my life for good. Why prolong the inevitable when I could make a clean break and avoid the stretch of pain?

My friends in Riverton were harder to leave behind because we'd lived there the longest. Three years had given me time to start planting my roots, and I'd deluded myself into thinking there would be no more moving. And then we'd experienced something not many people ever would in their lives—an eternal bond created by traumatic events.

I thought of Dawn. Only she could understand what I was going through. It gave me some solace to know I wasn't alone in that sense; she was experiencing the same thing at the same time. To my friends, I must have seemed like I didn't care, just disappearing without telling them where I went, without leaving a forwarding address or new phone number.

I'm forty-two now, and I still think of those friends today. I think of Dawn, who helped me realize the importance of friendship before love can truly exist. I met Haley many years later. She became my best friend, then we fell in love and were married.

I think of the lives taken that summer, of the lives changed forever by those incidents, and the town that will never be the same. I felt a responsibility for the knowledge I had of those creatures and the possibility of their return.

I also grieved for the loss of Sheriff Packard in my life. He'd been a father figure I looked up to during a period of time when my own father was absent. Packard helped fill that void for a time. I hoped he knew that. There were times when I saw someone in a crowd who looked a lot like Gary, who might have even been Gary, but I didn't have the nerve to ask.

Was it better to let things lie? I'd thought so then, but I wasn't so sure anymore. As an adult, I lived in forward motion, trying to stay ahead of the past that kept chasing me. Sometimes, it's managed to catch me, pulling me back with its icy claws, making me remember, and filling me with grief and regrets. That was why I finally wrote my tale—to spill my guts and leave my regrets behind for good.

Driving through Riverton decades after leaving, I found Gary's house hadn't changed. The house I used to live in was still there, but its yellow paint had been covered with a dark brown, which was faded. The yellowish grass was tall and full of weeds. Rusted auto parts filled the backyard. The tiny willow tree my dad had planted in the front yard had grown giant, overwhelming the yard with too many thick limbs that needed to be pruned.

Jax's, Rosco's, and Dawn's houses seemed the same but older, and Rosco's front yard had been completely transformed into xeriscape. A neighborhood had replaced the field behind my old house, and beyond the newly built church stood Dead Man's Hill. The hill was less intimidating, as if it had somehow shrunk. Buildings and homes had sprung up around it as the twenty-first century shut it out, like it had so many things, leaving me with only memories of what it had once been.

Homes had been built along Beck Street—developers had no doubt solved the problem of the swampy land that had caused the Crooked House to sink. I drove past those homes until I reached a dead end. Cement barricades prevented my vehicle from going farther, and two large maples planted behind them blocked my view of what I'd come to see.

I drove to the other end of the street and found a small space between two homes in a cul-de-sac. A dirt path, carved out by vehicles long ago, led behind the homes. It was overgrown with weeds and brush, but I drove my truck down the bumpy path and around the last home.

The Crooked House sat alone in the shrunken field at the far west end, more weathered and worn than before. Its bottom half was hidden by overgrown bushes and weeds, and I could barely see the top.

I parked my truck twenty feet away and walked to the house, pushing aside branches and weeds. I stepped onto the slanted and cracked porch. The front door was open just a crack. *Was it open before?* I couldn't be sure. *Did the house open its mouth to let me in?*

I stretched out my hand to push the door inward and stopped. A strong energy hit me, filling my body with immense heat. The invisible force was either pulling me in or pushing me away; I couldn't tell which.

Being pulled into *their* world through the pool had given me the gift of second sight, which allowed me to see things and communicate with the dead. But in turn, it gave me the gift of seeing *them* in *their* world, *their* dead, and *their* intentions. I didn't see them all the time, but it had become more frequent recently, with more clarity and intensity.

A recurring dream had been haunting me for the past week, and it wouldn't let go of me. A woman with long black hair, black pupils, and a grin full of sharp teeth was searching for *me*. Had we gotten them *all*? I thought of Joanna Anderson. During the summer of eighty-two, she'd disappeared and returned as someone—*something*—else, and she'd run away from her family. They never saw her again. She was still out there, and something told me she threatened our world.

I didn't know where to look for her. She was a grain of sand in the desert. To find her, I had to visit the pool. My hope was the pool would connect my telepathic energy to hers and lead me to her, and the closer to the pool I got, the impressions were stronger. My senses were about to explode, and I knew I was on the right path. My fear and anxiety threatened to overwhelm me, but I'd come too far. I had to go forward. I pushed the door and stepped inside.

About the Author

When Brett McKay isn't conjuring demons and bloodthirsty psychopaths to put on paper, he sells landscaping. He loves all types of music, but hard rock and heavy metal fuel him the most. He enjoys the outdoors, spending time with friends and family, and curling up in front of a good movie with his wife and a bucket of popcorn.

Brett lives in Utah with his wife and two sons. Fall is his favorite time of year because he gets to decorate his house for Halloween much too early for his neighbors.

Read more at https://www.brettmckaybooks.com/.

About the Publisher

Dear Reader,

We hope you enjoyed this book. Please consider leaving a review on your favorite book site.

Visit https://RedAdeptPublishing.com to see our entire catalogue.

Don't forget to subscribe to our monthly newsletter to be notified of future releases and special sales.

Printed in Great Britain
by Amazon